CHILLING ADVENTURES

SABRINA

Path of Night

BY SARAH REES BRENNAN

Scholastic Inc.

For Beth, my friend from work, with many thanks for inviting me into the witch's house

© 2020 Archie Comic Publications, Inc.

All rights reserved. Published by Scholastic Inc., *Publishers since 1920.* SCHOLASTIC and associated logos are trademarks and/or registered trademarks of Scholastic Inc.

The publisher does not have any control over and does not assume any responsibility for author or third-party websites or their content.

No part of this publication may be reproduced, stored in a retrieval system, or transmitted in any form or by any means, electronic, mechanical, photocopying, recording, or otherwise, without written permission of the publisher. For information regarding permission, write to Scholastic Inc., Attention: Permissions Department, 557 Broadway, New York, NY 10012.

This book is a work of fiction. Names, characters, places, and incidents are either the product of the author's imagination or are used fictitiously, and any resemblance to actual persons, living or dead, business establishments, events, or locales is entirely coincidental.

ISBN 978-1-338-32617-8

10 9 8 7 6 5 4 3 2 1   20 21 22 23 24

Printed in the U.S.A.   23

First printing 2020

Book design by Katie Fitch

What is hell? I maintain that it is the suffering of being unable to love.

—Dostoevsky

GREENDALE

IF THE PRESENT WORLD GO ASTRAY, THE CAUSE IS IN YOU, IN YOU IT IS TO BE SOUGHT. —DANTE

I woke with daylight transformed to golden prisms through the diamond panes of my windows. I rolled over toward the velvety-black curled-up shape of my sleeping familiar, tucking a smile against my pillow. Through the tangle of dreams warm as bedsheets, a single cold thought intruded.

Something terrible has happened to your boyfriend.

My eyes slammed open. I sat up, spine broomstick-straight, hands closing into fists around my fat, ruffled pillow.

I was safe and warm in my bed this morning because of Nick. Lounging around drowsing felt like a betrayal of him.

I stared around at my wrought-iron headboard, my mirror with roses in the frame, the bedroom I'd had my whole life. Every inch of my room was familiar, but every detail felt alien because there was no chance of Nick teleporting into any of the sunlit-gold corners, dark and handsome and shocking. I'd scolded Nick for doing that a hundred times. Now I'd give anything for him to appear again.

Salem yawned and stretched, kneading the star-patterned comforter with his claws.

"It's too early for intense angst, Sabrina."

He leaped off the bed and trotted away, nosing the bedroom door open and heading in search of food. The savory scent of Aunt Hilda's cooking filtered up the stairs and through the open door. With my luck, Aunt Hilda was making something featuring eyeballs.

I sighed, climbing out of bed. I knew I wasn't getting back to sleep. I pointed to myself and was instantly clad in a light sweater and short skirt, but I didn't twirl in front of the mirror the way I used to. I was only getting dressed because we always had company these days.

"My love, you're up early." Aunt Hilda glowed as I walked into the kitchen.

Her hair was a golden cloud from bending over her steaming pots, and she wore an apron bearing the legend SEXY WITCH. Her boyfriend, Dr. Cerberus, had given it to her. Her smile dimmed slightly when she saw my face.

Aunt Hilda liked having guests, since it meant more people to appreciate her cooking. And Aunt Hilda was the only Spellman whose love life was currently thriving. My cousin Ambrose's boyfriend had been killed by witch-hunters. Aunt Zelda's husband,

Father Blackwood, had fled the country after attempting to assassinate our entire coven. My boyfriend was trapped in hell.

No matter how screwed up my life was, I wanted Aunt Hilda to stay happy.

With an effort, I smiled back. "Morning."

She enfolded me in a hug. Aunt Hilda smelled like rosemary and mugwort, witch's herbs and childhood love. She stroked my hair. "Sit down and I'll whip you up some waffles in a jiffy."

I sat at the kitchen table, feeling soothed despite myself. It was nice to have time alone with my aunt.

Even as I had that thought, the kitchen door slid open. I sighed, then brightened.

In this house brimful of witches, there was a mortal.

Harvey, one of my three best friends in the whole world, walked into my kitchen carrying a teenage witch in his arms. Elspeth was wrapped in a blanket and had her hands clasped around his neck.

He smiled when he saw me. "Hey, 'Brina."

Only when I told myself sternly to force another smile did I realize I was already smiling at the sight of him. His green flannel shirt and brown hair were sleep-rumpled, and his always small, always sweet smile was drowsy.

"Hey. Didn't know you were here."

Harvey settled Elspeth into the rocking chair, tucking the blanket around her. "Elspeth didn't want to be alone, so I slept over. Miz Spellman said I could," he added, too embarrassed not to call her *Miss Spellman* even though Aunt Hilda had been insisting on *Hilda* for ten years. "Hope that's okay."

"Always," Aunt Hilda and I chimed, as one.

We grinned at each other and him, three points of light each catching brightness through reflection.

Harvey knelt by Elspeth's rocking chair. "I'll get you your pillow to lean back on, okay?"

"Very well, beautiful mortal," said Elspeth happily.

"That's a weird thing to call me." Harvey patted her hand and left the room on his pillow quest.

When Father Blackwood tried to murder our coven, his daughter Prudence saved all the witches she could. Those who lived were the few remaining students of the Academy of Unseen Arts, my witch classmates. They were living in my house now, sleeping on floors and recuperating from Father Blackwood's poisoning attempt. My mortal friends had raced to help me out. Harvey especially was stricken by the sight of suffering, and swooped in to bring meals and medicine to the witches and, if requested, carry the invalids anywhere they wished to go.

Most of the witches were fully recovered. I suspected Elspeth was too, but she was milking the situation for all it was worth.

When the door shut behind Harvey, Elspeth rocked her chair vigorously.

"You wouldn't believe the freaky things I did with that mortal last night!"

Aunt Hilda dropped her wooden spoon on the floor.

"Oh, yes?" I asked.

Elspeth fixed me with a wide-eyed stare. "I asked him to spend the night with me."

"Oh, yes?" I repeated, hearing the edge in my voice.

"He said okay. So I thought, 'Finally!' I was about to take off my dress when he said, 'You don't have to be alone if you're scared' and he fetched me blankets and hot chocolate!" Elspeth's voice was outraged.

I hid my smile with the back of my hand.

"He put marshmallows in the hot chocolate." Elspeth brooded over her wrongs. "Never in my life have I been treated like this by a man. Even the way he talks would shock my mother to her very core. Who knows what other strange deeds he wants to do in the dark of night?"

Harvey, coming back in with the pillow, caught the end of this and made a scandalized face. "Whoever that is, he sounds horrible."

Elspeth collapsed back against the pillow with a dramatic sigh, as though too weak even to keep her eyes open.

Aunt Hilda clicked her fingers so her spoon flew up into her hand, and busied herself at the stove. Harvey gravitated toward her.

"Something smells great."

I twisted around in my chair and made frantic silent gestures to warn Harvey, but he was already peering beneath the pot lids. I watched as the inevitable unfolded.

"I'm making enough satanic shepherd's pie for everybody. Try some of this, sweet Harvey."

"Happy to." Harvey accepted a small bowl with alacrity. He wasn't as starving-intent as the Academy students, but he was a teenage boy, and he had to do all the cooking at his place.

"I wanted to make the kids a special treat," Aunt Hilda confided, while Harvey nodded and dived in. "So I didn't use grass snake intestines for the mince, or anything inferior like that. Only ball python. Nothing but the best!"

Harvey's face froze around the spoon.

Aunt Hilda beamed. "Is it good?"

"Delicious," Harvey answered in a small, horrified voice.

"Oh, wow." Elspeth's eyes snapped open. "Snake intestines, for real?"

Harvey moved with the speed of, ironically, a snake. He scooped Elspeth from her rocking chair, deposited her at the table, then placed his bowl before her and his spoon firmly in her hand. "You have it."

Elspeth hesitated. "Do you mean you want to share?"

"No! You should keep up your strength," Harvey urged. "I want you to have the whole thing."

"Truly?" asked Elspeth.

Harvey nodded with conviction.

Elspeth clutched the bowl and whispered: "Is this what love feels like?"

Harvey patted her on the back. "Nope. That's the snake intestines talking."

He went to make coffee. Elspeth began to eat, kicking her feet happily under her blanket. *Better her than me*, I thought, though since my dark baptism I was more able to swallow witch's cooking. Not that I got much of a chance these days. The Academy of Unseen Arts students ate like a pack of starving hyenas. It made me hate Father Blackwood even more, to think he hadn't been feeding them properly. *Nick* had lived at the Academy. I should have invited him for dinner every day.

"Here you go, 'Brina." Harvey set coffee down by my elbow.

I leaned against his shoulder, then he drew away and sat in the chair beside mine. He unslung the gun he often carried these days from his shoulder and propped it between us. I took a deep draft of coffee.

Salem, the goblin cat who'd got the cream but demanded more cream, came up onto the table and was disappointed to see I was drinking my coffee black as the path of night. Harvey petted him. "Hey, kitty cat."

"*Fool mortal*," said Salem. "*Ingrate. You should have shared the snake intestines with me. More ear skritches, I say, more.*"

Harvey didn't understand Salem. Sometimes I felt that was best. He smiled as Salem tipped his head imperiously into Harvey's hand and gave Salem more ear skritches. "Who's a sweet kitty?"

"Not Salem." I grinned, then yawned against the rim of my cup.

"Must get lashardia," murmured Aunt Hilda. "I'll make you some soothing tea for tonight, Sabrina."

"Lashardia?" Harvey asked.

"Corpse plant," Aunt Hilda told him in her sunny way. "Feasts on flesh and blood. I grow it on graves. Once Sabrina drinks lashardia tea, she'll rest in peace all night. Mind yourself around lashardia fruit, though, Harvey love. The seeds are deadly poison!"

"Oh," Harvey said quietly, as Aunt Hilda whisked out. "Is she gone?"

When I nodded, Harvey scrambled up and drank water right from the tap. Then he ducked his head underneath, emerging with drops sparkling like rain in his untidy hair.

"Snake intestines, wow. Uh, could I have some cereal? Just to get the taste ... out of my mouth."

"Do you not *like* snake intestines?" Elspeth sounded amazed.

Harvey acquired cereal. The Academy students were suspicious of mortal food that came in packets. Nobody else was eating Ambrose's cereal, and my cousin wasn't here to eat it. He'd gone with Prudence to track down Father Blackwood and make the former head of our coven pay for his crimes.

Ambrose had been magically confined to our house for years. I was used to seeing my cousin every day, whenever I wanted. I missed him a lot.

He wasn't the only one I missed. At least I knew Ambrose was out in the world somewhere. Not suffering in hell, in who knew what terrible ways.

I reached for my coffee cup with trembling hands, and missed. Harvey put down his spoon and reached for me, linking our fingers together. I let myself cling.

"Oh no, Sabrina," remarked Elspeth. "Are you being sad because Nick is in hell?"

The Academy students didn't know exactly why Nick was in hell, but they'd absorbed that he was. Most of them were tactfully not mentioning the issue, but Elspeth wasn't a tactful person.

"You're not helping, Elspeth," Harvey warned.

"Nothing will help, will it?" Elspeth asked. "Nick's gone! Poor Sabrina. Here you are with only one boyfriend left. And he's mortal, so—no offense, mortal, I'm sure you're doing your best— but you must miss the warlock sex. Nick Scratch was balefire in bed."

Harvey and I dropped each other's hands with extreme swiftness.

"Good for him," Harvey said distantly.

I took a fortifying sip of coffee. I'd gone to mortal school, which meant mortal peers and mortal sex ed until I was sixteen, and I was still growing accustomed to the ways of witches.

I didn't miss the warlock sex because I'd never had it, or any other kind of sex. Nick always made it clear going further was my choice, because he was the best. We hadn't been dating that long and he was very experienced, which was intimidating. And we kept getting interrupted by murder trials and werewolves.

I'd believed we would have more time.

With determination, I ignored this and addressed the other issue Elspeth had raised.

"I only have one boyfriend."

Elspeth nodded. "Right, because you lost the other one to hell."

"I only have one boyfriend, *Nick Scratch*, who is currently in hell," I clarified.

Elspeth frowned. "What do you mean, currently? Nobody comes back from hell."

I exchanged a glance with Harvey, then trained my gaze on my coffee cup.

"Sabrina and I aren't dating," Harvey put in hurriedly. "We're just friends."

Without looking up, I nodded. I heard Elspeth push her empty bowl away.

"Weren't you in love with this mortal, Sabrina? Everybody

was talking about it. Have I got it wrong? Were you in love with the other mortal, um, Theo?"

She sounded genuinely puzzled. Now I had to contemplate a universe in which I'd dated another of my best friends.

"Er, no. I wasn't dating Theo. I was…I was dating Harvey. But not anymore."

I had been in love with Harvey. But not anymore.

"We broke up," said Harvey. "Amicably."

Sure. If you wanted to describe me raising his brother from the dead, resulting in Harvey finding out about the world of magic and laying his brother to rest, then dumping me, as "amicable."

"But why?" I started to daydream about transforming Elspeth's head into a turnip. "Didn't Nick suggest you could have two boyfriends, Sabrina? I heard from the Weird Sisters he was planning on it."

"He *most certainly* was not," snapped Harvey. He gave Elspeth a disappointed look and took a huge, horrified bite of cereal.

"He may have suggested something like that," I admitted. Harvey choked on his cereal and began to cough violently. "But I said—" Well, I hadn't said no, because I was so stunned. "But that's not the way it worked out!"

Elspeth regarded me with sympathy. "Bad luck, Sabrina."

I drained my coffee and glared at the bottom of the cup. Harvey had abandoned his cereal and was running his hands through his hair.

"Thanks, Nick," Harvey muttered to the floor. "Thanks for making everything super awkward, *from hell*. However witches and sometimes people in the big city do things, and whatever freaky jokes Nick may have made before we met—because that dude hates me—I hope you understand the situation, Elspeth. Sabrina and I are good friends! Everything is very simple! There's no need to make things weird. I hear Sabrina's aunt Hilda coming back, so we need to shut up about embarrassing stuff."

I too could hear Aunt Hilda singing softly. She entered the kitchen, her arms filled with fruit and blossoms that were either bloodred or lavender with dark hearts.

"Are mortals embarrassed by discussing sex in front of authority figures?" Elspeth asked.

"Oh my God," exclaimed Harvey.

Elspeth regarded him with dismay. "Don't call upon the false god in front of ladies!"

"Sorry," Harvey mumbled.

We collapsed into silence. In the quiet, I heard the front door swing open. Everybody tensed. We'd laid many protection spells upon our threshold since vulnerable invalid witches lived here. We'd learned caution after attacks by witch-hunters, countless demons, and Satan himself. There were only so many people who should be able to enter.

The fruit and flowers of the corpse plant tumbled from Aunt Hilda's arms onto the table like blood rain. Salem's shadow loomed against the salt and pepper shakers. Aunt Hilda turned toward the door, a vision of golden rage in a Sexy Witch apron.

"*Salus!*" she murmured.

Elspeth rose, blanket falling from her nightgown-clad figure. "*Salvus.*"

We were three. Though I couldn't say I felt any particular mystical connection to Elspeth.

"*Ardens*," I whispered.

Tiny lines of blue lightning wrapped around the silver rings on my fingers. Hellfire came to me so easily.

"*Dracarys*," murmured Harvey, and shot me a smile. "That's from a TV show. Just trying to be supportive."

Despite the smile, I saw he'd reached for the gun propped beside his chair. I laid a hand on his shoulder and aimed my other hand at the door. The faint glow radiating from my palm moved as the door swung open, falling like a spotlight on Roz's startled face. Theo was right behind her.

"Oh. Sorry, guys."

Roz and Theo were two of the very few people I trusted unconditionally. My protection wards would always let them pass.

The scrape of Harvey's chair made me glance toward him. My hand fell away from his shoulder as he rose, face alight with quiet joy.

"Hey, it's my man." He fist-bumped Theo. Then he cupped Roz's face in his hands. "Hey," he said, soft. "It's my girl."

Harvey kissed my best friend on the mouth. He lingered over the kiss, staying close to Roz's smile as though he liked to be there. When they strolled over to the table, Harvey's arm was around his girlfriend's shoulders. He picked up one of the lavender blossoms from the table and drew the petals down Roz's glowing brown cheek. He kissed the flower and then folded Roz's fingers over the stem. Harvey was always offering tokens and gestures, small tender proofs that love never left his mind. I remembered.

"Thanks," Roz murmured, rewarding him with another smile.

"Don't touch the fruit," Harvey cautioned. "They're poisonous."

Roz edged toward the table so she could lay the flower discreetly down. She waggled her fingers at me in greeting.

I waved. "Wasn't expecting you guys until later."

"I woke early," Roz said. "And Theo always rises at some awful hour with the chickens, so I swung by to get him on the way."

"Two words for you, witches," said Theo. "Farming hours."

He rubbed a hand over his buzz cut and wandered over to the table, where he gave Elspeth an uncertain nod. Even sitting down, Elspeth was taller than Theo. Most people were taller than me and Theo, but I liked to think we made our presence felt.

I gave Theo a fist-bump as Harvey had, the light twined around my fingers giving a final glimmer before going out. "We run a funeral home, so we're in the clear."

A joke occurred to me about corpses rising late, but Harvey wouldn't enjoy necromancy humor. Even now, we heard the patter of tiny incorporeal feet on the stairs and I saw Harvey flinch.

"Don't worry, Harvey," said Aunt Hilda. "It's only the ghost children."

The restless shades of children who'd died at the Academy lingered on in their halls. It turned out the living students who attended the Academy counted as the spirit of our school, because even the ghosts had relocated to our home. As if we didn't have enough house guests.

"The ghost children haunt me," Harvey muttered, then

blinked in a worried fashion. "Uh, not literally. I just think about them a lot. But I'm not scared of them!"

Aunt Hilda tucked a comforting hand into the crook of his elbow. Harvey looked at the top of her head with pleased surprise. He always seemed startled that she liked him. This was absurd, since Aunt Hilda made it clear Harvey was her favorite.

"I thought we could get a head start on our Fright Club meeting," Roz said, leaning against my chair.

I smiled at her gratefully. "Good idea."

Theo was eyeing Aunt Hilda's cooking with interest, but Harvey drew him protectively away. He mouthed *snakes* and Theo stared in confusion.

"Why did you kids change your club name from, what was it, WICCA?" Aunt Hilda wanted to know.

"WICCA was a school organization," Roz explained. "Dedicated to supporting women and fighting systemic injustice. Our Fright Club is more a personal quest."

Aunt Hilda offered Theo a spoonful of mince, but Theo glanced at Harvey and wisely shook his head.

"How do you mean, a quest?"

Aunt Hilda liked to take an interest in my mortal friends. Partly because my aunt Zelda made it clear she wished I didn't have mortal friends. I didn't think she was suspicious.

"Well…" said Roz. "The Fright Club is just the four of us, researching evil and trying to do good."

None of my mortal friends were great liars.

I gave Aunt Hilda a mischievous grin. "Maybe someday we'll have a bake sale. Let's go to our club room!"

"You don't want waffles?" Aunt Hilda inquired.

Harvey and Theo looked conflicted. Roz valiantly resisted the waffles temptation.

"*I* want waffles," said Elspeth. "And I want the heaven-sent one to carry me back to my fainting couch, where I will eat waffles."

"What do we call me?" Harvey asked.

"Witch-hunter," said Elspeth, grinning. "Mortal."

Harvey shook his head.

"*Harvey*," Elspeth obliged.

"See, it's not hard." Harvey scooped up Elspeth and carried her toward the door.

Roz seemed unmoved by the sight of her boyfriend princess-carrying another girl around. I guessed she knew she had nothing to worry about. Harvey so transparently adored Roz.

Theo and Roz made for the door. Before I could follow, Aunt Hilda caught my hand.

"Sabrina, can I have a word?"

My heart thumped hard, a telltale sign of guilt. "Sure."

When I dared look at my aunt, she was gazing at me benevolently, with no sign of accusation.

"I'm so glad you're spending time with your mortal friends," Aunt Hilda whispered. "I know they'll take your mind off...that awful business with poor Nick. You're doing the right thing, my brave girl."

"I hope so." I averted my eyes. My aunts had no idea what my friends and I were really up to.

I gave Aunt Hilda a quick hug and fled, out the door and up the stairs after the others. We made our way to the attic that was my cousin Ambrose's bedroom. Even though he'd been gone for weeks and we were badly off for space, we tried to keep the room set apart and ready for Ambrose to return to. But I knew my cousin would want me to use the space, if I needed it.

And I did.

Harvey was the last inside. He closed the door carefully, then turned the lock. I stood in front of the Fright Club. My best friends, ever since we were little.

Now they were my team, assembled on the cushions we'd piled up on the floor. Roz, her legs tucked under her and her corduroy skirt smoothed under her nervously moving hands. Theo, arms looped around his legs, his face bright with determination. And Harvey, gun laid down by his side, hunching forward with his elbows on the worn knees of his jeans and dark eyes steady on mine. Every one of them was inexpressibly dear to me. Every one of them was intent on our secret mission. I'd asked them to help me, and they'd sworn they would.

"All right, Fright Club," I said. "Let's review."

I lifted a hand and the whiteboard sheet Roz used for projects slid down over Ambrose's British flag. The sheet was covered with writing, Roz's neat print, Theo's slapdash scribble, and my script, flowing and dramatic because Aunt Zelda had taught me calligraphy when I was five. Harvey had drawn the pictures.

Each scribble and drawing were connected by a web of lines drawn in marker. Every black line across the whiteboard looked, in my eyes, like a road to hell.

Aunt Hilda wanted me to forget what had happened. I couldn't.

It didn't matter that I was Lucifer's daughter, not Edward

Spellman's as I'd always believed. Not a Spellman at all. Who cared? I'd decided I would be a Spellman. I would be a witch, and I would live half in the mortal world and half in the witch world with my chosen friends and chosen family, and I would never use my strange powers ever again. I'd be happy.

But before I could be happy, I needed one more thing.

I needed Nick.

Nothing mattered, except finding a way into hell. I had to devote myself entirely to Nick. That was what he'd done for me.

I smiled at the drawing of Nick, gorgeous and grinning in a tuxedo as though nothing bad could ever happen to him. His picture was placed in the center of our winding paths.

Nick had used his own body as an enchanted cage to imprison Satan, foiling Lucifer's plans for the world and his daughter. Nick cast the spell for me because he loved me. Lilith, the Mother of Demons and the new Queen of Hell, carried Nick away into the depths of her kingdom so Satan could never escape and take back the throne.

That was why Nick was trapped in hell. That was why I would risk anything to free him.

I couldn't stand the thought of what might be happening to him down there.

HELL

THAT BRUTE WHICH KNOWS NO PEACE CAME EVER
NEARER ME. —DANTE

Lilith, Queen of Hell, was aware of the importance of appearances. The world impressed on women early that their surfaces meant more than whatever seethed beneath.

Now that she was a public figure, with the eyes of hell upon her, presenting a darkly serene image to her subjects was vital. Lilith spent a great deal of time each morning carefully putting on her face.

There were many faces to choose from.

Lilith spun in the cavern that served as her walk-in closet. More than a hundred wounds had been slashed into the stone walls. In the roughly hewn recesses were golden plinths. On each plinth rested a face torn from one of the lost souls of hell. The faces awaited Lilith's pleasure, tucked away in the dark until their turn might come to suit Lilith's fancy. She could wear faces men had killed for, faces that launched a thousand ships and burned towers. This power was hers now.

As Lilith surveyed her kingdom of beauty, she paused, arrested by the sight of one face. Placed down low, it shone in the shadows like a pearl.

A cloud of dark hair, cheekbones for days, and a mouth that was slack now, but Lilith knew how it curved. The eyes tilted, catlike, so people saw them as green. Lilith remembered they were truly blue. A face she'd put aside after her descent to rule in hell but had kept for sentimental reasons. Mary Wardwell's face.

Adam loved that face. Not her first Adam, but her last. Mary Wardwell's Adam, who came to his fiancée's cottage with gifts. Adam, whose love was kind. The taste of kindness was so strange, Lilith almost found it sweet. But Lucifer had killed Adam and left a different taste in her mouth.

It didn't matter. What was that mortal Adam's love worth? He'd never even realized the woman he'd returned to was not the woman he'd left behind, but a murderously evil demon who'd stolen Mary Wardwell's life. Like every man, Adam saw only the face.

So much for love.

The Queen of Hell turned away from Mary Wardwell's face and selected another. This one was smooth as ice, the hair pale gold. A snow queen's face, cold as winter, feeling nothing. It was exactly the face she wanted in case a lord of hell visited the palace. Lord Beelzebub in particular was judgmental of his new queen, and Beelzebub's heir, Prince Caliban, had the distinction of being the most annoying soul in hell.

Lilith left the cavern of faces. She dropped by her office on the way to her throne room.

Pretending to be Mary Wardwell in Greendale, she'd been promoted from teacher to principal, and discovered her new high position meant far more administrative work.

Oddly, this was also the case in hell. When Lilith had spent centuries dreaming of ultimate power, she hadn't imagined documents from infernal officials. Lord Beelzebub wrote endless insulting missives about war in the borough he ruled, and about the impossibility of quelling unrest with Lilith upon the throne. Beelzebub had a definite idea of how power should look. He thought it should look male.

Prince Caliban wrote Lilith exquisitely polite letters. Somehow, that was even more vexing.

Dealing with the lords of hell was almost enough to make Lilith miss the days when her worst problem was attempting to corrupt Sabrina's annoying soul. Little Miss Snow-White Hair was irritating beyond belief, but there was only one of her, and she wasn't a man.

Lilith must be careful if she wanted to keep the power she'd won.

Men might look down on an ambitious woman, but they felt comfortably secure assuming she'd never reach her goal. They hated a woman who'd achieved her ambition. Not only was she in their way, she taught other women it could be done.

The dark lords of hell were in eternal opposition, but now

they'd united. She was sure they were plotting to crush her.

Lilith had faced worse. She'd spent centuries with their master's boot on her neck. There was not a soul in hell Lilith feared, save one.

And Lucifer, Prince of Lies, was tormenting someone else now.

Lilith departed, tossing Lord Beelzebub's latest letter high above her head. Pages fluttered to her bone chandelier. The papers caught fire, curling like black roses in midair, then falling to dust at Lilith's feet. As all empires would, in time.

That was the paperwork sorted.

Lilith flung open the golden double doors. Here was her throne room, the seat of her power. Here the Infernal Pedestal, there the tasteful satyr statues crushing humans under hooves. She'd schemed to achieve this through all the long, weary days of her life.

A demonic minion hurried to her, uttering an oily whisper: "Can I serve you in any way, my queen?"

"Bring me Lord Beelzebub's head on a platter, and Prince Caliban's tongue in a salad," drawled Lilith. "Can you do that?"

"Defeating their infernal armies could be tricky," mumbled the minion. "I'm only a minor imp...I meant, can I bring you a refreshing beverage or a fresh soul to torment. Can I serve you in any *petty* way, my queen, that sort of thing..."

Lilith had lost her patience in the fourteenth century and never bothered to find it. Today she was in an even more restless mood than usual. Lilith felt her unfamiliar mouth twitch into a smirk as she thought: *No rest for the wicked, and who was ever more wicked than I?*

Lilith came to a decision. She turned her back on the Infernal Pedestal and snapped her fingers at her minion, gesturing to an elaborate fan, wrought gold and festooned with the feathers of peacocks and ravens. "You may escort me. Fan the sparks of hell to light my passage. I go to visit our guest."

She had to monitor the situation. Lucifer was bound to break the boy shortly. Action must be taken when he did.

Nobody knew her lord's wrath better than Lilith. The arrogance that could not endure serving in heaven, the pride that had created hell, must be outraged at being tricked and jailed. He must be seething at the betrayal by his own daughter. Her god was the most vengeful god. Lucifer was exercising his worst wiles and all the dark fury at his command to rip apart the prison that held him. The boy's soul would soon shatter into a thousand pieces.

Lilith was surprised Nicholas Scratch had lasted this long.

GREENDALE

THE TERRIBLE THING ABOUT THE QUEST FOR TRUTH IS THAT YOU FIND IT. —REMY DE GOURMONT

A t the top of our plan to free Nick from hell I'd written, in capital letters, the words *OPERATION EURYDICE*.

I felt the name was fitting. My Nick, who was passionate about books, would like that it was taken from a story. If he didn't know the legend, when we reclaimed Nick I could tell him: how Orpheus the musician went into the underworld to rescue his love, Eurydice. He charmed the lost souls and won her passage out with the beauty of his song. I believed Nick would approve of gender-bending the classics.

"One thing we're trying is unlocking the configurations that bind the gates of hell." I pointed to Harvey's sketch, gates hanging ominously open in the corner of our whiteboard. "If we work out the right combination, the gates should open. Roz is keeping track of the different combinations I try and calculating which might have the best chance."

"Harv and I can't help with that," contributed Theo. "Because math."

Theo and Harvey nodded, bros united against math. Roz and I gave them a reproachful look for being math delinquents.

"Next up!" I pointed to a drawing of an angel blowing a trumpet. "The horn of the Archangel Gabriel will make the gates of hell open. We should acquire it. Harvey and I were discussing this last night."

Harvey leaned forward eagerly.

"You know how some of the witches call me *heaven-sent* and it's very weird? I think it's their less offensive way of saying *witch-hunter*. When a bunch of witch-hunters came and tried to murder the witches that one time, Sabrina said they were... basically angels. There might be a connection to heaven I could use to summon the Archangel Gabriel."

Harvey came from a long line of witch-hunters. Many witches were suspicious of him for that reason. They didn't know him as I did. I was certain there had never been a witch-hunter like Harvey before.

Theo didn't sound as impressed as I'd hoped.

"Harv, what's the next step? After you... summon the Archangel Gabriel."

"Ask him to let us borrow his horn."

"Have you guys considered that the archangel might not want to loan you his, like, sacred horn?"

"'Course," Harvey answered, clearly relieved that was the objection. "Sabrina's researching ways she could use her power to threaten the Archangel Gabriel after I summon him, so he'll give up his trumpet."

I nodded confirmation.

"Failing a spell," Harvey added thoughtfully, "I guess I have my gun."

Theo's and Roz's stares suggested they weren't completely on board.

"Whoa," said Theo eventually. "That's a banger of a plan."

"Harvey," said Roz in a high voice. "I implore you not to mug an angel!"

Harvey reached for her hand. "Not if you don't want me to."

"I don't want you to!" Roz exclaimed. "I'm literally the daughter of a preacher man, and I'm not comfortable with this idea."

I'd gone to sleep last night reading up on ways to menace the heavenly host and trying to recall what I'd done to the witch-hunters we'd encountered once. It was a blur, but I remembered shouting that I was the Dark Lord's sword and reducing the angelic witch-hunters to ash. I'd thought I could refine the process, but obviously we didn't want to make Roz uncomfortable.

She was the reverend's daughter. I was the spawn of Satan. Roz was already putting up with a lot.

I nodded. "We'll put down shooting archangels as a last resort."

Shooting archangels probably wouldn't work. My plan to menace the archangel was an intricate infernal ritual, but there were other things I could try first.

"Cool," said Theo. "I support you guys mugging angels if it comes down to it."

Harvey gave Theo a grateful grin. I gestured toward the far side of the whiteboard, where Harvey had drawn a large blue lake. "Which brings us to our next idea."

I clapped, and the whiteboard whisked itself out of sight. Harvey unlocked the door. A red-gold head appeared, adorned with a piece of black spiderweb lace and a disdainful expression.

"Please welcome to the Fright Club our first guest speaker, my aunt and the new High Priestess of the Church of Night, Zelda Spellman."

Zelda, Lady Blackwood, the Academy students called her. But there were those who called me Sabrina Morningstar. Father Blackwood wasn't worthy to touch her, any more than Lucifer was worthy to touch me. We were Spellmans.

The tight corners of Aunt Zelda's mouth relaxed infinitesimally when she looked at me. Her mouth set again when she surveyed my friends.

"I'm far too busy to waste my time in this manner, but Hilda feels it's important you engage in bondage with the mortals."

A pause followed this announcement.

"Pretty sure Aunt Hilda said 'bonding,'" I muttered.

Aunt Zelda waved this off with a regal air. "Either seems misguided. However, against my better judgment I came here to tell these unworthy mortals the story of the Lady of the Lake."

"We appreciate it, Lady Blackwood," piped up Roz. "The Fright Club is very dedicated to our academic interest in legends that put women in the foreground."

Theo contributed: "Not a woman personally, but interested in women's untold stories."

"Herstory as well as history," Harvey murmured, with a covert glance Roz's way to see if he'd gotten that right. She gave him a thumbs-up.

Aunt Zelda moved in front of Ambrose's British flag as though it were the backdrop to a play, and she the star of the show. She lifted her voice authoritatively. My aunt wasn't overly fond of mortals, but she'd been mistress of the Infernal Choir at the Academy. Plus, she'd spent my whole life admonishing me and Ambrose. Lecturing was an area in which Aunt Zelda excelled.

"I realize mortal children are ill-educated. Have you even heard of the Lady of the Lake?"

"Arthurian legend," said Roz.

"Monty Python." Harvey nodded.

This caught Aunt Zelda's attention. "Is Monty Python a warlock?"

"Um," said Harvey. "Could be."

"I know the Pythons," said Aunt Zelda. "Good witch family. But I don't think I know a Monty. How do you know him?"

"Oh, like . . . around," said Harvey.

Theo intervened to rescue Harvey. "I don't know anything about the Lady of the Lake!"

Aunt Zelda went back into lecture mode. "The Lady is a minor goddess witches worshipped before they devoted themselves exclusively to the service of Satan. Our Lady was often approached by pilgrims who sought strength on a quest. The stories say the

Lady's hundred silver eyes are always watching. The Lady can see you. She will know if you are unworthy."

Aunt Zelda watched the effect of her creepy whisper on the mortals with satisfaction. Aunt Z enjoyed making an impression.

I'd fought a river demon once, an incident I remembered with no fondness, but Aunt Zelda was talking about a goddess. Surely a goddess would be different. A goddess would help.

"Any witch can summon the Lady, but every witch knows it is not safe. When the warlock Merlin summoned her, the Lady tested Merlin and his mortal companion Arthur, and did not find them wanting. She gifted Arthur with a magic sword, which Merlin and Arthur used to create a kingdom and change the world. The legend goes that any who quests for truth with a pure heart will obtain the Lady's aid, but those whom she does not find worthy, she consumes."

A smile illuminated Aunt Zelda's countenance. Theo appeared to be going cross-eyed.

"It is almost April. We approach the celebration of your false god's son."

Roz made a face of agonized protest.

"Some witches believe this is a dangerous time for us, but I don't think we should permit the mortals to take our feast days. The Lady is also called Eostre. Before this month was called April, it was Eostremonath, and it was dedicated to our Lady's honor. We witches once chanted her names as we danced with bright swords and leaped toward the dawn. Eostre, Freyja, Kaguya, Austra, Lady of a Hundred Eyes, Shining Princess, Lady Star. She is the white maid of the water who cannot be fooled or denied.

and your best friend? How much they wanted each other and secretly resented you? How much more do they resent you now, when you lead them into danger?"

I leaped almost a foot in the air, casting a wild look around. Everybody's eyes were fixed on their own shoulders. I didn't dare study Harvey's or Roz's faces. Instead, I turned to Theo.

"Guys!" Theo said urgently. "Do you hear your birds talking, or am I having a poorly timed break with reality?"

His buzz cut was growing out. It seemed to bristle, as if Theo was a freaked-out cat.

I was the expert on magic. I had to stay calm. "It must be like when my familiar talks to me," I said, in as reassuring a tone as I could. "Other people won't be able to hear. The Lady said the birds could speak to our souls."

"There's a play about a quest and birds," Roz said softly. "In the play, the kids search for the Bluebird of Happiness."

"But we get the Bluebirds of Self-Doubt?" Theo swallowed. "Sounds like our luck."

He seemed the most disturbed of all. I wondered what his birds had said to him.

"Come on," Roz said. "We should get to school."

"Can't believe we have to go on death-defying quests and worry about missing first period," Harvey muttered. "The universe should write us a note."

We headed toward Baxter High. Billy Marlin met us at the bottom of the school steps.

"Hey, uh, Theo."

Theo cast him a harried glance. "Hey, Billy. I'm at peace

with the fact you exist. That's as good as you're getting from me today."

Billy clearly didn't see the silver birds on our shoulders, which was a huge relief. We were still the weirdos of Baxter High, but not more notably weird than any other day.

After school, the Fright Club walked to my house. As soon as Harvey walked through the door, the little-girl ghost materialized in front of him. Harvey almost tripped over her.

"You can just walk through her," I advised.

"I can't. It's rude. Hey," Harvey said softly to the ghost. "Can I try something?"

He stooped and picked Lavinia up. Over Harvey's shoulder, her face was small and pale as a cameo with the eyes bored out, but she was smiling.

I wondered how it felt, taking the dead in your arms.

Aunt Hilda beamed when she saw us. "Do you want to stay for dinner, children?"

Roz and Theo murmured unconvincing excuses.

"Happy April Fools' Day, anyway," said Aunt Hilda. "You know, for witches the first of April means the beginning of an uncertain time. Any witch who makes a big decision on April Fools' Day is a great fool who has made a great mistake."

My friends stared at one another.

"Sometimes I think you and Aunt Zelda could've told me more about witchcraft, growing up!" I said in a strangled voice.

Aunt Hilda shrugged airily. "We didn't want you to disturb the mortals."

"Yeah," said Harvey. "Be a shame if we were disturbed."

Roz seemed worried, but she still kissed Harvey goodbye when she went home for dinner.

"I wish you didn't have to go first," he murmured to her.

"I'll be all right," Roz promised, but Harvey stood at the door watching her and Theo walk away into the woods, his face creased with concern.

Tomorrow, the quest would begin, and it was Roz's turn first. Roz was safe for tonight. Tomorrow was another story.

"Who's that girl?" Lavinia's voice was grating stones. "Do you like her specially?"

"That's Rosalind," Harvey told the ghost proudly. "I love her."

Sometimes I *did* wonder whether Harvey ever liked Roz when we were together.

What did it matter? Roz was his favorite person in the world now. She'd never rained horrors down upon him. She healed him after I hurt him. She was honest. Harvey probably wondered what he'd ever seen in me.

Oh, Nick, I thought with despair. If I could see Nick, I'd feel better. He'd made me feel better when the pain of breaking up with Harvey was brand-new. Even saying Nick's name used to make me smile.

The memory of Nick couldn't console me now. Whenever I thought of him, I was miserable imagining what he might be suffering.

"Because of you," murmured the birds on my shoulders, a silver Greek chorus.

I found my mind turning in desperation to my oldest and

sweetest comfort, the brightest memories that meant home.

Running past the yellow sign and down the curving path to my house and my cousin. Ambrose would smile his wide, wild smile at the sight of me. I recalled a time I'd fallen and gotten hurt in the playground. Aunt Hilda healed me on the way home, but I was shaken. I'd tumbled through the front door and launched myself at my cousin, arms wrapping tight around his waist.

That was the day Ambrose taught me to dance properly, humming a waltz and beaming down into my face. I laughed with him, felt graceful and grown-up, and forgot pain.

Now I ignored the cold voices in my ear, the weight on my shoulders, and remembered dancing with my cousin.

Wherever you are in the world, Ambrose, I thought, *I hope you're getting up to wonderful mischief.*

ON THE ROAD

THE WAY AMONG THE LOST . . . —DANTE

A mbrose Spellman was sitting across from Prudence Blackwood at a dainty wrought-iron table in an Italian courtyard, feeling well satisfied with life. Day was sinking deliciously down into night in Florence, the shadow of the Duomo cast across the cobblestones. Above him, Ambrose saw the marble panels of the basilica, inlaid green and the delicate blush pink of the inside of a seashell. The building was beautiful, Gothic peaks and swoops made pretty as confectionery and immortalized in stone. As if a small girl had built a castle of seashells on the shore, only to have her wish granted and her wild dream of a seashell palace come true.

When he looked at Prudence, that was even better. Her bleached hair was a white glimmer in the great dome's shadow, capturing the eye. Once captured, you couldn't help but appreciate the flawless lines of her face and the wicked delight of her eyes. Like seeing a pretty girl, then noticing her draw a sacrificial dagger from a thigh sheath. Great at first sight, but marvelous on the second.

Ambrose asked Prudence, his voice caressing: "What are you thinking about?"

"Bloody vengeance," Prudence answered.

Ambrose hid a smile against the gilt rim of his coupe glass. "Sure."

He took a sip of champagne, the taste fresh and delicate as spring flowers, filling his mouth with a promise of unfurling blossoms.

In the darkened courtyard there was a sudden rain of small spheres, all the colors of a rainbow, onto the cobblestones. Turquoise and crimson, gold and silver, the bubbles gleamed and couldn't be burst. The mortals thought they were only plastic, a shower of radiance meant to entertain tourists. Ambrose and Prudence knew better. They were magical messages.

But not the one they were waiting for. Not yet.

Ambrose directed a fond grin at the shining spheres, thinking of someone else who was small and bright.

"What...are you...thinking about?" Prudence asked, her voice slightly rusty, as though she was unaccustomed to simple pleasantries and not sure if she was getting them right.

There hadn't been much pleasantness for Prudence in the Church of Night under Father Blackwood. That could change now. As soon as they hunted down her father.

Ambrose was on board with the plan for bloody vengeance, but he felt there was no reason they couldn't combine revenge and romance. It was a nice night.

"I'm thinking about my cousin," he said honestly.

Prudence gave an irritated sigh. "What about Sabrina?"

"Nothing in particular." Ambrose took a deep breath and committed sacrilege. "I love her, so I think about her a lot. Wondering how she is, if she's happy, whether she's back at mortal school or broken up about Nick. Pour one out for Nick Scratch."

He poured Prudence a fresh glass of champagne. The golden bubbles in her glass glided upward as the faerie spheres cascaded down around them.

I love her. It wasn't the kind of thing witches said. It felt like confessing a crime.

Luckily, Ambrose was comfortable with crime.

Prudence took a long sip of her champagne. "Are you sorry about Nick?"

"Sure. I liked Nick. What's not to like? He was hot, he cared about Sabrina, I'm a simple man," said Ambrose. "Seemed horrified to find himself in a love triangle, which: strongly agreed. So much fraught emotion when there's an obvious solution. Calm down and come to an arrangement, people in love triangles!"

Prudence made a small face, like a kitten whose nose was being shoved in a dish. "Then you're in an arrangement with *Harvey*."

"Therein lies the beauty of my plan," said Ambrose. "Suggest an arrangement to Harvey, watch him die of horror, find someone else to have an arrangement with."

Prudence's laugh was as lovely as the sound of bells over Florence.

Ambrose laughed with her. "Shame Nick didn't get the chance to initiate Sabrina into a world of carnal delights, but them's the breaks. Guess it's Harvey after all. Brace yourself for potentially days of tender cuddling, cousin! Those will be some amateur fumblings, but Sabrina loves him. Always did. Don't think she knows how to stop, though I expect she's trying."

Ambrose checked in on where Prudence was at, with this scandalous talk of love. Prudence was scowling.

"I don't like cuddling."

"Oh, no?" Ambrose asked.

Pity.

Prudence propped her chin onto her fist. Her voice was gloomy. "Nick Scratch tried to cuddle me once . . . I think. It was a horrible experience."

Ambrose raised his eyebrows and grinned, knife sharp. "How bad could it have been?"

Prudence, lost in awful reminiscence, didn't grin back.

"He had no idea what he was doing. It was like being attacked by an awkward coatrack. I lay still and thought of the Dark Lord. After five minutes I threatened Nick with a knife. He leaped back. My hair got caught in one of his shirt buttons. I had to cut myself free. Later I hacked off my hair and bleached it to make the memories go away."

"Wow," breathed Ambrose. "That's much worse than I was expecting."

He recalled his childhood, carriages rattling down the streets of London and lamps barely able to burn through the fog. In his nursery, there was always a fire burning in the grate. There was his auntie Hilda, holding him and cooing at him about who was the sweetest, most handsome boy in the whole world?

Then and now, that was Ambrose. But the witch orphans of the Academy hadn't had his advantages.

"I wouldn't give up on cuddling just yet." Ambrose shot Prudence a provocative smile. "The best way to experience new things is trying them with someone who has experience."

Prudence shook her head obstinately. "I don't like it."

"I'm a fan, personally," Ambrose observed. "Chains and cuddling. Girls and boys. I like it all. But you know that. I always wonder why so many mortals are obsessed with monogamy when there's beautiful variety in the world."

He tilted his head to see the effect of this on Prudence.

"What's monogamy?" Prudence asked lazily. "A mortal game, is it not? You get all the hotels and you win?"

Ambrose opened his mouth to correct her, then recalled the time Prudence was staying over in Sabrina's room. He'd found her running her fingertips lightly over Auntie Hilda's books and the stacked-up games he used to while away evenings playing with Sabrina. He knew she'd seen the Monopoly box.

Prudence was making a joke. Ambrose smiled, thrilled with her, and Prudence smiled a naughty little smile back.

"Best way to win that game is not to play," remarked Ambrose.

"Doesn't seem like a game I'd be interested in, no," drawled Prudence.

So that was settled. Fantastic.

"But I've been thinking," began Ambrose.

His eye was caught by the glitter of a midnight-blue orb falling from above. The bubble was almost lost against the night sky, but notably dissimilar from the globes of white and crimson, green and gold.

This was what they were waiting for. Ambrose clocked the gargoyles creeping across the roofs.

No rest for the wicked. For the wicked it was all sexy adventures, strange magic, and duels to the death, which Ambrose personally found to be terrific. He indulged himself by reaching out and taking Prudence's hand in his, the same brown as his own but ringless and with the nails painted dark.

"What do you call this color nail polish?" he asked idly.

"Eggplant," Prudence responded, her eyes sparking and intent.

Ambrose kissed her hand. "I call it aubergine. Americans are a ghastly people who speak a brutish tongue."

"We speak the same language." Prudence rose. "Try saying something in English that I couldn't say."

Eggplant and *aubergine* were their code words.

The gargoyles dropped from the curved-eggshell dome of the Duomo, the hard claws of stone monsters scraping against the cobblestones. One gargoyle looked to Prudence, and its gray lips curled back from granite fangs.

Ambrose grinned as Prudence drew her twin swords. "Darling, I rather fancy you."

While they were in Italy, Prudence wore long, floating dresses. Usually she dressed to match her sisters, in a witch uniform of prim lace collars, dark colors, and short skirts. Ambrose liked to imagine that Prudence sometimes saw this murder quest the way he did. As an opportunity to be who they were when not bound in a web of complex loyalties. Escapism got a bad rap. Who couldn't use an escape now and then?

Prudence's long dresses showed cleavage in which a man could plunge to his glorious death.

As Prudence spun over the darkened cobblestones, her skirts and her swords were a luminous whirl. Ambrose drew his own sword, tipped his straw hat to a table of mortal tourists, then flung his hat onto the table, where it landed spinning between their champagne flutes.

"I challenge you to a battle of wits," Ambrose told a gargoyle.

The gargoyle grunted.

"I can see in the battle of wits you are unarmed," said Ambrose. "Battle of battle it is!"

He joined the fray. The legend went that the last star to appear at evening in the warlock Galileo's city would show you exactly where you wished to go. Being guided by the stars was something even the mortals knew how to do.

But there were other warlocks and witches hunting for the star's answer. Or perhaps someone was trying to prevent Prudence and Ambrose from reaching their goal. For whatever reason, these gargoyles had been sent to stop them.

Their enemies hadn't yet realized that Ambrose was with an unstoppable girl. Prudence reached out and grasped the midnight-blue bubble. The gargoyles closed in.

Prudence circled their enemies, skirts swaying like a country girl dancing around a maypole, and lopped off a gargoyle's head.

"Do not make puns about how everyone loses their heads over me," warned Prudence. "You already did that with the ghouls last week."

"Yes, dear," said Ambrose. "But consider this. We are gorgeous immortal creatures with cool weapons and killer fashion sense. The world has a right to expect witty repartee."

A gargoyle lunged for Prudence, and Ambrose buried his sword in its stone breast.

"*O, if no harder than a stone thou art*—" Ambrose began, then was rudely interrupted by another gargoyle, stone claws sinking into his sword arm. Prudence hurtled through the air like a silver shrike, landing on the gargoyle's back and cutting the creature's throat. Ambrose admired her narrowed eyes and the lethal twist of her mouth, her face set harder than stone over the monster's shoulder.

She had more killer instinct than he did, but he could usually keep up. Even when he couldn't, he had fun trying. Ambrose took a knee and scythed the legs out from another stone monster. When three came for Prudence, stone teeth raked her shoulder, and she let the orb drop. Ambrose rolled across the cobblestones, caught the star's message, and came up swinging. Their swords kissed with a victorious ring as they cut off the last creature's head together.

He and Prudence stood with their blades bared as the stone flesh of their enemies crumbled to dust at their feet. Moonshine made their pale clothes glow silver, so they seemed beings garbed in light.

Ambrose was wearing a white linen vest and trousers. He felt no need to wear a shirt on holiday. He was cheerfully confident that he and Prudence made a handsome pair.

The table of mortal tourists applauded enthusiastically. Ambrose bowed with a flourish.

"What a fun cabaret!" called out a woman. "Do you do private performances?"

"I'm just as sensational in private," Ambrose called back.

"Ambrose," said Prudence, her voice arch but firm.

She caught his hand to attract his attention. Ambrose gave her a swift, fond glance. Prudence gestured to the midnight-blue orb in his palm.

"The star's message?"

Ambrose turned away reluctantly from his adoring public and passed a hand over the orb, the metal of his rings sparking and suffused with light. The shimmering blue turned to water, and he pulled out a message written in blood on a broad white feather. The message read: *Ask Urbain Grandier at Marche d'Ailleurs in Paris.*

Prudence nodded. "This is our last night in Italy."

"Then we should enjoy it!"

She started to release his hand, but Ambrose pulled her around the curve of the domed building, glowing pink marble on one side and a glittering Florence on the other. Prudence's skirt flared, and her laugh came pealing behind him. Better than bells, filling the whole city with music.

"You enjoy yourself too much," Prudence told him breathlessly.

"No such thing," Ambrose returned.

"Doesn't that attitude get you into trouble?"

"Sure," said Ambrose. "I was put under house arrest for trying to blow up the Vatican. I go big *and* I go home … and stay there under occult house arrest. I do it all. All's a lot more fun than nothing."

Prudence laughed. This was going considerably better than Ambrose's confession of misdeeds on his first date with Luke, Ambrose thought.

Thinking of Luke made melancholy drag down Ambrose's buoyant mood.

His boyfriend Luke Chalfant, lost in exactly the same way Ambrose's father had been. Killed by witch-hunters. Only, unlike Ambrose's father, Luke had loved Ambrose. Luke had told him so.

Ambrose was flattered, and fond of him. Luke was cute and had appeared on Ambrose's horizon when Ambrose was almost despairing. Luke offered him freedom from house arrest, and Ambrose had dreamed of nothing but freedom for decades. Ambrose *owed* him. Luke had no reason to help Ambrose. He'd been purely motivated by affection. Ambrose thought, surely if he was capable of loving anyone besides his family, he should love Luke.

But Ambrose hadn't. Ambrose thought maybe it would come. And he'd thought maybe he couldn't love anyone. Not in that way. Perhaps love was only for his family, for Auntie Hilda, Cousin Sabrina, and Auntie Z, not that Zelda or Ambrose would admit to feeling that way about each other.

Maybe Ambrose couldn't ever fall in love.

"If you've forgotten the way to our hotel," said Prudence scornfully, "I shall lead you."

And maybe he could.

She led him past Gothic towers and cathedrals, over the Ponte Vecchio with its medieval arches and jewelry shops where mortals bought diamonds for their beloved ones. There was a stone plaque on the bridge, worn to illegibility with time, saying this bridge had been rebuilt after a flood seven hundred years ago. Prudence didn't let go of his hand.

"You said earlier you were thinking of something," said Prudence.

Ambrose hesitated, but if not now, when?

"I was thinking about having a partner in crime. How it would be to go on all the adventures of the world together."

Prudence's glance was half startled, half disdainful. "You're a romantic, aren't you?"

It seemed like a night for confessions.

"I used to be. I wrote poetry. Even had a book of poems published when I was at Oxford—a mortal university. Quite old."

Prudence didn't seem impressed by Oxford. She was difficult to impress. It was one of the things Ambrose liked most about her.

"You can tell me one of your poems," she said. "Please don't pick an overly sentimental poem."

Ambrose began to smile. He stopped by the ancient witch's moondial on the bridge, pressed their joined hands to his heart, and declaimed:

"The lioness, you may move her
To give over her prey;
But you'll ne'er stop a lover—
He will find out the way."

"Catch *this* lioness giving up her prey." Prudence's lip curled. "I never would. Lions don't belong in love poems."

"That's nonsense," said Ambrose. "All the best love poems have lions. The oldest love poem in the world, four thousand years old, has a lion. *'Lion, dear to my heart. Goodly is your beauty, honeysweet.'*"

The river Arno washed under the stone arches, waters new every minute under old shadows.

"You used to write poetry," Prudence observed. "But you stopped. Why?"

"Lucifer came to me in my dreams," said Ambrose. "He asked me to perform a dark devotion. To write a certain letter to a mortal I knew in Oxford, a tender mortal boy who...liked me. Among mortals, caring for someone of the same sex is sometimes seen as a crime. He was only a mortal. But somehow, after I did the Dark Lord's bidding and ruined that mortal's life, I didn't have the heart to write poems any longer."

They weren't meant to speak of the devotions. They were meant to obey.

"The Dark Lord never wanted us to have the heart for much," Ambrose murmured, soft as the sound of the river. "Did he?"

The Dark Lord, and his darker devotions. Asking them all to shut up their hearts, hurting themselves by being willing to hurt others. Until your ability to care for anyone became something that crawled in chains when it used to fly.

And they'd gone along with it, every witch soul, Ambrose included. Without even seeing that their lord had them trapped.

Nick Scratch saw it. Nick Scratch stopped it.

For love of Sabrina, a motive Ambrose entirely sympathized with.

He'd misjudged them, the students of Blackwood's Academy. He'd been trapped so long away from witches and warlocks, he'd seen the Academy orphans as nothing but new amusements. He hadn't taken Nick Scratch seriously. Not until the last second, when everything Ambrose had seen of Nick added up to more than he'd thought. Pretty boy who liked to have fun. Sharp guy who liked books and Sabrina. The curious sort, with his pleased, puzzled interest in mortal things like school dances and frozen drinks. None of that prepared Ambrose for the moment Nick stepped up to face down the Dark Lord and did what Ambrose would have died to do. Nick kept Sabrina safe.

"You're thinking about Nicky," remarked Prudence.

"I was thinking he was a brave boy. Raised by wolves and witches, but reaching for something else. I didn't know."

"He was a fool to do what he did," Prudence announced. "He was always a fool. We used to date. He dumped me and my sisters, saying he wanted something real. As if we weren't real. I should have stabbed him and saved him some pain."

"Forget what I said just now," Ambrose told her. "I didn't like Nick that much. He dumped *you?* The man was an idiot."

That made her smile.

Worse than misjudging Nick, Ambrose had misjudged Prudence. She'd turned up one day and he'd thought, *Why, hello there.* She was perhaps the most stunning woman he'd ever seen, and from the first minute it was evident she thought Ambrose was cute too, so she was a stunner with great taste. The night they met, she knocked on his bedroom door with her hot friends in tow.

Months later, when Prudence approached him at the

Academy to make her interest in further encounters clear, they had more great times. She was as fun to be with as she was to look at, and Ambrose never once thought about what she might feel.

But then Prudence rebelled against her father, the High Priest. When Blackwood hurt her sisters, she rose up against him in fury.

We are more than our dark god ever knew, Ambrose thought. *We are more than we ever knew. The Morningstar was defeated because he believed we would turn over Sabrina to him without a fight.*

Lucifer was sure love didn't matter. But love mattered in spite of him.

They walked back to their hotel hand in hand. Ambrose had reserved separate rooms, but their chambers were linked by a marble balcony overlooking Florence. The balcony ceiling was red-and-blue encaustic tile. A chandelier sang in the breeze above them.

Ambrose left Prudence at her door every night with a promise they would get vengeance in the morning.

"Wait," she said tonight, just before their hands parted.

Ambrose waited.

"Why are you here?" Prudence asked abruptly. "My father framed you for murder and threatened your family. I understand why you want to kill him. But that's not the same as a hunt across the world. You're not the kind of man who chases revenge."

No. But he used to be a poet who chased beauty.

Ambrose opened his mouth to say: *Because you wept and begged for your sisters, then wielded swords with deadly, furious precision. Because you were so many different kinds of beautiful I couldn't look away.*

"Never mind," Prudence told him. "It doesn't matter. You're here."

Prudence stopped his open mouth with a kiss. Ambrose went still. Then, because his auntie Hilda hadn't raised a fool, Ambrose kissed her back with wild abandon. Prudence seized hold of his vest and began to drag him, a willing captive, to her bedroom.

Ambrose halted, catching Prudence's gloriously merciless face in his hands for more kisses, and found himself surprised by tenderness. He didn't know how old Prudence was. Such distinctions weren't meaningful to witches, since they lived so long and didn't mature fast. But he knew she was younger than he, still a student of the Academy. She'd hoped for something from her father, so recently. Blackwood had crushed Prudence's dream. Ambrose wanted to kill him for that alone.

Once, when they thought Prudence doomed to die, he'd made a crack about missing her body. As though a body was all she was.

Ambrose didn't want to make the mistake of acting like she didn't matter. Not ever again.

"Lioness," Ambrose breathed. "Stop. Perhaps we shouldn't."

Prudence wrenched herself away from him, eyes outraged black holes.

"Wait," Ambrose said. "Let me explain."

"There's no need." Prudence's voice was very calm. "I understand you perfectly. And I don't care much, either way. Why should I? You don't matter to me."

"I never believed I did," Ambrose murmured.

What he had seen, and believed, was that Prudence loved her

sisters in the same way Ambrose loved his family. Enough to fight and die for them. Seeing that, Ambrose had suddenly wanted her fierceness for his own.

She retreated from Ambrose as she hadn't from stone monsters, shaking her head.

"I'm not Sabrina, who has to try not to love someone," Prudence spat. "I don't even know why she tries so much about love."

Ambrose tried to explain romantic love for one of the lost orphans. Prudence might have learned a way to love her sisters on her own, but she had read no poetry and received no tenderness. She had probably never even imagined being in love.

"After what Nick did for Sabrina, she'll want to do everything for him. Be loyal, in all the ways witches and mortals know how to be. It's a mortal notion, the idea of the only one, but she grew up among the mortals. She will love Nick as ferociously and completely as she can."

Prudence gave a brittle-sounding laugh. "How absurd."

"Is it?" Ambrose asked. He took a step toward her.

"Love always is. It won't do Nick any good, her loving him," sneered Prudence. "Not where he's gone."

She slammed her bedroom door in Ambrose's face.

Ambrose was forced to admit that hadn't gone particularly well, but tomorrow he and Prudence were going to a city made for lovers. He'd never been the type to back down from a challenge.

Ambrose stayed on the balcony, thinking of songs and lions, hope and Paris, and poor lost Nick. "You never know. Perhaps love might do him some good," Ambrose murmured. "Even where he's gone."

HELL

LIVING IN DESIRE, BUT HOPELESSLY. —DANTE

In hell there were dark shores and woods with leering shadows, chambers for torture and chambers for sinister pleasure. Nick was sauntering by when an attractive demon leaned out of a doorway, snakes in her hair reaching past her arms toward him.

"Child of earth and fire," she murmured through sharp teeth. "Aren't you beautiful?"

"Don't I know it," returned Nick. "What's up, snake demon?"

The forked tongue of a snake flickered against the inside of his wrist. "Let's find out."

Nick paused, then shook his head. "My girlfriend wouldn't like that."

The lady and her snakes stared in genuine bewilderment.

Nick shrugged. He didn't fully understand Sabrina's objections himself, but it was a small price to pay, to be with Sabrina.

"You're not with her, though, are you?" murmured the treacherous voice in his mind, growing louder every day. One of the last things Sabrina had said to him was that she hated him. She'd spoken to him of hate, never of love. She probably didn't think she was his girlfriend anymore. Nick would never see her again. No matter what Nick did, Sabrina wouldn't know or care.

Drowning out misery in whatever entertainment offered was something Nick did plenty. He was great at being cruel and out of control.

Nick wished he could be sure he wouldn't give in to temptation. He couldn't. Nobility wasn't really his style.

But he told himself: *Not today. Hold out a little longer.*

Long after passing the demon's chamber, Nick came upon a stone tower nestled in the midst of a wilderness. In the window set above his head, there was a light burning.

He remembered this place.

In the days when Nick ran with the wolves, they stayed away from the covens, but the world was crowded by mortals and Nick was human enough to require some necessities. Nick and Amalia occasionally stole food and clothes from mortal villages.

Nick saw a mortal mother once. She had shining hair, and she sang to her child. Nick followed the sound. Amalia padded after him, inescapable as his shadow. They watched as the mortal mother chased her little boy, caught him, and made a fizzing noise against his cheek. She wasn't trying to hurt him. "They're playing," Nick whispered. "Do humans do that?"

"They all play with their young," said Amalia dismissively. *"The mortals."*

"Oh," said Nick. "I didn't know."

The only one who ever played with him was Amalia. Later, Nick was sure Sabrina's family played with her when she was small. At the time, he believed it was only mortals.

After that, when the wolf pack ventured near mortals, Nick would...look. The mortals were fascinating, inventing substitutes for magic, using nonsense words like *love* and *grace* as though they were spells. Living with each other in little homes with false light that burned so bright.

Nick discovered a mortal girl living in a stone tower. Light burned in her window like a small sun he could, just possibly, have for himself.

He would sneak away from the pack at night and listen to the girl singing in her tower.

"Just a song at twilight, when the lights are low,
And the flick'ring shadows softly come and go,
Tho' the heart be weary, sad the day and long,
Still to us at twilight comes Love's old song,
Comes Love's old sweet song."

She had long dark hair, with gold in it. There was always something bright about the mortals. Nick thought she might like someone to sing to.

By day she wandered the hills, guarding a flock of animals. Nick couldn't remember whether they were sheep or goats. They were food. The wolves pulled some of them down.

He tried speaking to her. The first couple of times hadn't gone well, but you could always memory-charm mortals, then get another chance to make a good impression.

Later, Father Blackwood and his society would complain in Nick's presence about the unreasonable demands of females. Nick found this tiresome. In his experience, women's requirements were that you be basically clean and interested in what they had to say. That wasn't hard.

The third time Nick had a first meeting with the mortal girl, he'd scrubbed himself in a spring, found the right clothes, and talked to her about her dreams of seeing the city one day.

"You're a charmer, aren't you?" the girl asked.

Nick wondered how she knew. The girl laughed a musical laugh.

"My heart's not safe! Are you a big bad wolf?"

Nick saw she liked the idea of a little wickedness. "Something close."

They sat on a low stone wall together. She wore daisies in her hair.

When Amalia found them, Nick was smiling, looking at the girl. He had only a split second to notice the gray shape slinking low on the winter ground, covering the space between them too fast. The mortal girl had less time than that. She never saw her death until it was on her. Her laugh broke apart and became a scream before her throat was torn out. Nick should have tried to save her, but he was frozen with horror. He watched as his familiar ripped the girl limb from limb.

"*What did you want?*" Amalia snarled. "*A little mortal love to call your own? The mortals don't matter.* This *is where mortal love ends.*"

Blood on the snow, and the silence after a scream. Nick threw up.

Later Nick stood at the mouth of the cave where they sheltered, murmuring the spells from his mother's books so he wouldn't forget. Amalia came to him, in her transformed werewolf form—walking on her hind legs, human shaped, dressed in a long nightgown she'd stolen, but still with fur and wolfish teeth. Nick found her pretending grotesque. It made him feel more trapped than anything else.

"*Look at me,*" said Amalia. "*I'm like a human. Better. You're happy to be with me like this, aren't you?*"

"Yes," Nick assured her.

Wolves couldn't tell when you lied to them. People rarely could either.

Nick never tried again, with a mortal. They could take their brightness and warmth away so easily and leave you out in the cold. Amalia was right about them.

Now Nick was in hell, listening as the song drifted down from the tower top. "*Tho' the heart be weary, sad the day and long…*" There was a hollow echoing place under his ribs, cold as an empty cave. Heartsick. Homesick. He'd felt this way his whole life.

He could follow the melody of radiant mortal sweetness up the stairs.

The door in the tower was a cage door.

"Come *on,*" Nick told Satan and the flickering shadows. "I learned better than this long ago."

Mortals weren't for him.

Across icy fields in hell, through trees that sprang from the earth like mushrooms, Nick glimpsed a building that hadn't been there before. A darker gray than snow in shadows, solid and reassuring. Built to look like a mortal tomb, with a flight of stone steps where witches could pass back and forth, and a broad stone banister where Nick sat outside in the sun and read. *Invisible Academy*, the mortal called it, because he was dumb.

Nick always remembered the first time he saw his school. He'd been in the mountains with the wolves, days before his dark baptism. Amalia roamed far afield, and Nick saw his chance. He didn't hatch any plan. He only realized, with a shock, how long she'd been gone. His head jerked up, and he thought: *I cannot live like this for a moment longer.*

He ran. Amalia caught him. She tried to drag him back, but he fought. It felt like his last chance. She snarled and hurt him, werewolf red in tooth and claw. For a blurred, desperate moment Nick was sure she'd kill him. His mind seized on a spell he'd read years ago, sitting by his mother.

With a mouth full of blood and trembling hands, Nick teleported away.

Teleportation was advanced magic, the witches and warlocks of the Church of Night told him later. Far too advanced for a boy who hadn't even signed the Book. It should have killed Nick. They were impressed that it hadn't.

Nick teleported to the foot of the mountains in the wild woods of Greendale. Through the trees, the Academy of Unseen Arts stood with its dark doors open wide.

The witches welcomed him. He'd been so alone, but now he

was surrounded by people like him. They showed Nick the Academy, soothing scarlet light safe behind stone walls, and brought him to a huge room with wonder on all sides. After years of words lost to the wind, Nick found again—at last—his mother's books.

Nick wasn't like Sabrina, unwilling to trade her soul away. He signed his name in the Book of the Beast with total readiness. It made sense to Nick that a book would offer him refuge.

Nick spent several days in the library, where he discovered the works of Edward Spellman. Then he emerged to explore his new home. The first students Nick met wanted to attack him, which went badly for them. Next was a guy with blond hair who wanted something else.

"Hello," he said. "I'm Luke Chalfant. And *you* are gorgeous."

Nick smirked. "Yes, I know."

"I'm on my way to a club run by Father Blackwood. No girls allowed. Good for witches to be locked out of a few things, am I right?"

You're trash, Nick thought, looking anywhere but at Luke. He chanced to see down a low stone passageway to a red velvet sofa and two girls. One was sleeping with her head in the other girl's lap. The girl still awake was smoothing a hand over the sleeper's coal-black hair, unaware anyone could see her. At the time, Nick didn't know how rare it was, to catch Prudence in a moment of tenderness.

"Would you like to join our society?" asked Luke. "You'd fit right in."

That was insulting, but no matter how much Nick disliked someone, he wanted everybody to approve of him.

"Maybe later," Nick said with a charming smile, meaning *Never, please die.* He went toward the girls.

They noted his approach.

The girl with marvelous cheekbones and even more marvelous sweetness in her face, who Nick would find out later was Prudence, raised an eyebrow and said: "Sister?"

Dorcas came fluttering from a corner of the room to sit beside Prudence, red head tilted against Prudence's shoulder.

There were *three* of them, Nick noted approvingly. Like a pack—no. Like a family. They would be safer in a group. And they could do magic. They would protect each other.

He leaned forward, reaching up to catch the stone lintel so he was framed in the doorway, and let them take a long look.

"Hello, ladies," he murmured. "I'm Nick Scratch."

After some time, Nick proved his prowess in all areas, and was officially their boyfriend.

Except being with the Weird Sisters wasn't how Nick thought. Prudence never looked at him with that sweetness in her face. He slowly understood it wasn't for him. There were occasions when the Weird Sisters said it was girls' time and shut the door in his face.

There were the illusions they created too. Illusion was second nature to witches. It shouldn't have reminded Nick of Amalia, pretending to be human with her wolfish teeth. But it did.

After Amalia, Nick's world was his school and his spells, witches and books. Everybody said he was the guy who had it all.

Only in his latest and loneliest hours did he admit to himself that nothing felt real.

The Weird Sisters harassed the half mortal who lived nearby whenever they caught her alone. Nick had never seen her, but he paid attention when the Weird Sisters talked about Sabrina Spellman, his favorite author's daughter. Nick was curious about Edward Spellman, the man who'd written those wonderful books and married a mortal wife.

Once, the Weird Sisters were discussing how much they dreaded Sabrina coming to the Academy. Father Blackwood and the coven had never permitted the half mortal to even attend unholy service at the Church of Night. She'd been raised away from other witches.

"She must be lonely," Nick mused.

Prudence heard. "*Her* lonely? Her family fusses over her as if she's the only girl in the world. She goes to a mortal school! She collects mortals. She's got one of her very own. They walk around the woods holding hands as if she's afraid she'll lose him."

Nick hesitated. "Is he trying to get away?"

Prudence scoffed. "She treats him like gold. She's soft, if you ask me. Like Edward Spellman."

"Oh," said Nick.

At the next opportunity, he got eyes on Sabrina and her mortal. He grabbed a chance to talk to the mortal. Naturally Nick memory-charmed him after, but he learned what he wanted to know. The mortal was happy to stay with Sabrina. The mortal was in love.

Nick saw Sabrina from afar, and liked what he saw.

He went home and broke up with the Weird Sisters.

Cold in hell, Nick remembered seeing Sabrina in summertime.

He turned away from the illusion of the Academy of Unseen Arts. He knew it wasn't real. The doors of his school hadn't looked like cage doors.

Nick had waited for All Hallow's Eve, for Sabrina to come to the Academy. But Nick worried. Perhaps pretty Sabrina was *too* like a mortal. The harrowing at the Academy was brutal.

A girl from the mortal world might be frightened. She might be killed.

Then Sabrina walked into their Infernal Choir. She sang under the furious gaze of the Weird Sisters, and everybody understood she feared nothing. She actually *was* as daring as Nick pretended to be. He stood silent amid the chanting, stunned.

It felt like recognition, Nick's burst of joy and relief at seeing her face, hearing the ring of her voice.

Oh, there you are, Nick thought. *I've been looking for you everywhere.*

He asked to sit with Sabrina at lunch that day. That night, the Dark Lord came to Nick and demanded the obedience Nick had promised. Lucifer told Nick to make Sabrina trust him.

Deceit was easy for Nick.

He liked doing things for Sabrina. He could tell she liked him too. Nick had hope.

Until Amalia came back, as Nick always knew she would, deep down. Amalia sensed Nick might finally be happy.

Nick should have killed Amalia, for Sabrina. But he didn't, because he was weak. He lured another of his wolves to him, and gave Sabrina the heart as though it was Amalia's. A false heart, like Nick's own.

He chained Amalia in a cave. He didn't want either of them to die.

"Please understand," Nick begged Amalia as he chained her.

She turned her face away. *"I understand you grew up to be the kind of man who cages."*

Amalia broke free, and Sabrina got hurt because of him. Then Amalia was dead on the forest floor, and to his horror and shame Nick was crying, and Sabrina forgave him. She put her arms around him and kissed him on the forehead, touched him, and spoke to him in the tender way mortals touched and spoke to one another. She told Nick he'd loved Amalia, and that wasn't weakness.

That was the moment Nick was sure he loved Sabrina. Really loved her, as mortals did, in a way he hadn't known he could love anybody. And how did he show it? Nick lied.

GREENDALE

BE AFRAID OF THE ONE WHO CAN DESTROY BOTH SOUL AND BODY IN HELL. —MATTHEW 10:28

Every day in school Sabrina sat listless at her desk, face as white as her new hair, clearly lost in hideous private visions. Roz fretted Sabrina's grades might drop.

The day after they made their bargain with the Lady of the Lake, Sabrina caught Roz slipping her class notes into Sabrina's bag. For a scary moment, Sabrina stared at the notes and the bag and at Roz, as though she didn't know how any of them might be relevant to her.

Then she smiled, and was Roz's best friend again.

"Come on, 'Brina," said Harvey, putting his arm around her. "I'll walk you home."

Roz had a music lesson. She watched them go. Before,

during the months when Sabrina was devoted to witch school, Harvey would wait outside Baxter High so he could walk Roz home.

"He loves her more than he loves you," said the silver bird on Roz's shoulder. *"He always did and he always will."*

Roz walked down the passage toward her music lesson, steps slowing over the blazoned legend of the Baxter High Ravens painted on the floor. The school was shadowy and quiet after hours. Like one of Sabrina's horror movies.

Roz's cunning gave her a split second's warning. A vision flashed before her eyes, of smoke coiling to leap at her. Out of the corner of her eye she saw a smoke demon sliding from behind a row of lockers. The demon was a piece of cloudy darkness with teeth and watchful eyes. Like the mist that used to obscure Roz's vision, shaped into a monster.

She started to run, stumbled and fell, and the demon almost had her, but her vision had bought her just enough time. She dodged into a classroom, catching the demon as it slid its long smoky neck around the door. Roz slammed the door repeatedly on its head, sobbing.

Once the smoke demon was dead, she smoothed down her paisley scarf, then went to tremble in a bathroom stall.

Every time she had a flash of the future, Roz remembered how it felt to be blind.

Roz had kept calm when the final darkness descended. She talked to her parents about braille and audiotapes. She held on, until she had her first vision when blind. Then she collapsed in class.

It wasn't being blind that terrified her. It was that the only thing Roz would ever see now were nightmares.

Behind a vision of snarling monsters and cackling witches, she'd heard a hiss of whispers and uneasy giggling from her classmates. They were hanging back from the demented creature prostrate on the floor. Roz was screaming, alone in the dark.

Then she heard the door bang against the wall. She was lifted up from the floor and held. There was someone with her in the dark, and he wouldn't let her go.

"Rosalind," Harvey murmured in her ear. "I'm here."

Harvey carried her out of the classroom, Theo trotting beside them, talking in his loudest and most determined voice.

Roz would've gone mad without Harvey and Theo.

The night after she collapsed, Roz slept fitfully in her narrow hospital bed.

"Harvey, are you there?" she kept whispering.

Every time she asked, Harvey answered: "I'm here."

Whenever Roz cried out, he held her hand. When she cried and curled up in terror of the visions, he murmured comfort, then paused. Harvey began to sing, tender and sweet. Roz was finally able to rest.

"I didn't think much of your white boy at first," Roz's favorite nurse remarked the next morning. "But I get it now. Were you childhood sweethearts?"

We've been together three weeks.

Roz cleared her throat. "I met him for the first time when we were five, and we both knew right away. He's walked me home from school every day of our lives. It's a joke among our friends, how much he loves me."

It wasn't really a lie. That's how it would have been, if there was no Sabrina. And there was no Sabrina. She'd flown off to witch school and left her mortal friends behind.

Roz hadn't seen her best friend in weeks. She wasn't going to see anybody ever again. This was the worst time of Roz's life, and Sabrina didn't know or care.

When Sabrina came back, Roz accused Sabrina of hurting her with magic.

Then Sabrina used magic to heal her.

Now Roz was sitting in the bathroom, shaking but seeing. It didn't matter how much Roz hated demons and visions.

I owe Sabrina a miracle, Roz thought. *She gave one to me.*

From outside her stall, she heard some of the girls from her music lesson discussing why she hadn't been there.

"Off making out with Harvey, I expect," drawled Susan.

"Hate to judge," said Catie, sounding as though she loved to judge, "but can you imagine? Your bestie *snaps* up your man like he's the last hot dog on the Fourth of July."

"Sabrina's not doing badly for herself," said Susan. "She's got that guy she brought to the sweetheart dance. I bet she found Nick, dropped Harvey like a bad habit, and Roz caught Harvey on the rebound."

"Still against girl code," argued Catie. "Harvey is *not* the last hot dog. There's always another hot dog your friend hasn't put ketchup and mustard on."

"That metaphor's getting weird, Catie," said Susan.

Catie snorted. "Anyway, the guy at the dance was obviously a male escort Sabrina hired to pretend she wasn't bothered by Roz and Harvey hooking up."

Roz choked.

"Hiring a male escort for a school dance is super extreme behavior!"

"Yep," said Catie. "Exactly. Typical of Sabrina Extreme Behavior Spellman. My aunt runs a casino in Vegas. I know gigolo chic when I see it. That guy Nick was hot, but he was *sleazy* hot. Total tight shirts, too smooth to trust, greased-back hair, gigolo vibes. That guy doesn't turn up out of nowhere desperate to take you to the school dance. C'mon."

"Sabrina said she met Nick at that after-hours genius camp she goes to."

"Sure. Let's pretend the hottie with the body can *read*. I appreciate a sensitive *artiste*, not a club rat. If he was given an extreme makeover, Harvey would be my pick."

"Not mine. How much do you think gigolos cost?" asked Susan. "I would never! But…"

"I'm surprised Sabrina still speaks to Roz," Catie declared.

"Maybe they're a friend group who can be mature about dating," rang out a new voice.

Roz opened the door of the stall out of sheer curiosity to see her defender. She blinked when she saw three cheerleaders staring down the girls from Roz's music class. In front was Lizzie, who everyone said would be prom queen one day.

"Let's not pretend this isn't about your thing for Harvey," added Lizzie. "You've only been crushing hard since third grade."

Roz cleared her throat. "Step off my man, Catie."

The two girls from music class decided to leave. Roz washed her hands so the cheerleaders wouldn't think she was gross.

"Thanks," she told Lizzie softly.

Lizzie shrugged. "No prob. We're used to nasty gossip. Because... we're cheerleaders."

"Hot cheerleaders," agreed Lizzie's friend.

"You should hear the stuff boys say about the two hot cheerladies dating each other in Riverdale," Lizzie continued. "We shut that down too. Nothing but support for our sapphic cheer sisters!"

Roz nodded enthusiastically. She could get behind the cheerleader campaign for social justice.

"You move differently these days." Lizzie gave her a friendly wink. "Try out for the squad."

"I..." Roz opened her mouth to refuse, then realized she didn't want to. "Maybe I will."

All her life, Roz had prepared to go blind. She hadn't done physical activities. She'd studied hard, learned musical instruments, and read as many books as possible. Roz still loved those things, but perhaps there was more she could love. Everything she'd missed out on.

Roz did move differently now that her vision was crystal clear. Trees had distinct leaves, even from far away, rather than being blurs of green. Sabrina had given Roz the world made new.

Now Sabrina had asked Roz for a favor in return. She'd asked Roz to help save Nick.

Roz kept returning in her memory to the terrible night Nick fell.

They'd gathered together, mortals and witches, everybody Sabrina could trust, in a desperate plan to trap Satan. And Sabrina's boyfriend had figured out how to imprison Satan in his own body. Roz didn't know how any of it worked, but she knew what she saw.

One minute Nick Scratch was on his feet, devouring red bleeding into his dark eyes. The next he was down. Sabrina went down too. She collapsed on the floor, her gown a golden pool around her, saying Nick's name in a terrified whisper.

There was an awful silence. Until the woman whom Roz'd believed was their sweet principal, Ms. Wardwell, and whom Sabrina now referred to as the demon Lilith, spoke up.

"All's well that ends in hell," she remarked coolly. "We must move fast to secure the Dark Lord. I'll take the body and—"

"The body?" Sabrina repeated. "*Nick?*"

Nick lay on his face, unmoving. He looked dead to Roz. He might be worse than dead. *They will be thrown into the lake of fire*, Roz remembered from her father's sermons on damnation. *That is the second death.*

Lilith stepped forward with a click of heels. Sabrina gave a wild howl.

"No! Don't come near us. I won't let you touch him! I don't trust you!"

The demoness's demand cut like a whip. "Do you want Mr. Scratch's sacrifice to be for *nothing?*"

"I don't know!" Sabrina shrieked. There were hollow and

discordant notes in her voice, as though her cries were rising from a pit. "I don't care. Get away!"

Abruptly, this seemed like a baroque nightmare to Roz. Everyone garbed in velvet beneath the shadow of a throne. The devil's daughter screaming at the mother of demons. Roz could almost forget she loved Sabrina.

The whole horrific scene seemed like nothing to do with Roz. Then Roz's own boyfriend entered the ring, moving protectively between Lilith and Sabrina. Roz's clutch at his sleeve was an instant too late. Lilith swept him with a contemptuous gaze, but Harvey didn't even glance at her.

"'Brina." He knelt and pressed his forehead to Sabrina's bare shoulder. Roz watched as Sabrina calmed. "Sweetheart. Don't cry. You trust me, don't you?"

Sabrina scraped together the shreds of her composure and answered in a thin voice: "Of course."

Harvey gathered up Nick Scratch in his arms, careful and gentle. He stood, and though Roz could tell it was a burden, Harvey didn't let himself falter under the weight.

"I've got him, Sabrina. I won't let anyone else touch him, unless you say. It's up to you."

Sabrina had let Lilith lead them down to the gates of hell and take Nick away.

But it wasn't long before Sabrina was standing in front of their newly anointed Fright Club declaring: "Let's go to hell and get my boyfriend back!"

Roz froze. Harvey said instantly, "Of course, 'Brina."

Harvey worried so much when any of them was in trouble.

He'd cared for Roz when she was blind. It was natural that now Harvey was desperately concerned for Sabrina.

Roz couldn't help wondering if worry was all it was.

It hadn't been long since Harvey was desperately in love with Sabrina.

Roz sighed as she left school and blinked in surprise as the afternoon sunlight revealed Harvey, waiting for her outside. He pulled off his headphones and bounded up the steps.

"Hey." Roz gave him a quick kiss. "I thought you walked home with Sabrina."

"Sure, I walked Sabrina. Then I came back to get you after your music lesson. Do I look like the kind of fool who misses out on walking his girl home?"

Roz snuggled up. "No fools detected here."

As they walked under the trees, Harvey studied her face. "Something wrong?"

She didn't want to tell him about the demon.

"There were girls in the bathroom saying...Nick Scratch looks like a gigolo."

Harvey burst out laughing. Then he visibly remembered Nick was in hell, and bit his lip. "Oh no."

Roz hadn't enjoyed Harvey's many presentations on the topic of Why Nick Scratch Is a Jackass. She'd worried he might make an illustrative slideshow. Now that Harvey was tenderly solicitous for Sabrina's well-being and determined to redeem Nick from hell, Roz found herself missing the rants.

After walking through the woods in silence for a while, Harvey said diffidently: "You seem...withdrawn."

Roz braced herself to answer questions about demons.

"Were those girls being mean?" Harvey asked. "Not just saying mean true stuff about Nick. Were they being mean about you?"

"Maybe there was some talk about the kind of girl who dates her bestie's ex," Roz confessed.

Harvey's face darkened with protective fury. "I hate that you have to put up with that because of me. It's so unfair. I know you never would've gone for me without the vision you had of us kissing. Never."

"Well," Roz said.

Harvey gave her an affectionate smile. "I'm grateful to magic for that."

Roz couldn't take away the one thing magic had given him. She could only smile back weakly as they stood in front of her brightly painted house, hand in hand. Roz gestured for Harvey to come in.

"We have the house to ourselves."

"Oh." Harvey began to grin. "Well. Sexy words."

"Dad's organizing the church fete," Roz told him. "Less sexy."

She was standing two steps above him on the stairs. Roz had to lean down to rain light kisses onto his smiling mouth.

"Hey, I don't know about that. Keep talking about the church fete," Harvey murmured. "It drives me wild."

Roz felt his smile spread as the kiss deepened. He spun her around as they reached the top of the stairs, then they tumbled giggling into her room and onto Roz's bed.

She'd never let herself think about how kissing Harvey would actually be, until she had the vision of doing so.

If she *had* thought about it, she would've expected something different. Roz had kissed boys before, had done more than kiss them. It was fun, but she'd noticed teenage boys were always in a rush. Too keenly aware they might be interrupted, scrambling for more skin, to get further faster.

Harvey took his time.

Their first kiss at the sweethearts' dance had been achingly sweet but endearingly awkward, Harvey still uncertain of his welcome.

Now he seemed happy to be sure. Always smiling just before their lips met, always wanting to be close. His hands traversed the bends and turns of her body as though he was learning them by heart, fingers tracing the curve of her shoulder with as much reverent appreciation as his palm sliding over the curve of her hip.

The way he kissed made Roz remember Sabrina, starry eyed, talking about the long drives she and Harvey would take through winding roads in the woods last summer, not going anywhere in particular. Taking it slow, on the journey to be together. They would stop by the side of the road, under tree leaves drenched with sunlight, and Sabrina would sing to him.

This summer, Roz thought, *that would be her.*

Roz did wonder sometimes about Harvey's reasons for going slow. If it was love and respect, great.

Roz was a modern girl, theoretically happy to bring up this subject herself, but she'd never had to do it before.

"*He doesn't want you,*" said the bird. "*He was always waiting for Sabrina, and he still is.*"

No, Roz thought. *He's waiting for me now.*

Maybe he was hoping for a sign.

Roz's heart hammered as she undid a button of her blouse. She glanced up to find Harvey's gaze sliding down to the skin she'd bared, then returning to her eyes. She arched in toward him, undoing another button as they kissed, her free hand combing through his soft hair.

Roz leaned back against the pillows. The tan fabric of her blouse parted slightly more, so lace was visible. Harvey's gaze traveled from the newly undone button to her eyes. He undid her little neck scarf, then kissed her throat as the scarf fell away.

From below, they heard the scrape of the front door opening. She heard her father's voice, raised in a manner that suggested he'd noticed Harvey's jacket hanging by the door. Harvey scooted away, and Roz thumped her head against her pillow.

"Rosalind," Harvey murmured.

"Yes?" Roz murmured back.

She thought he might suggest a time his dad would be out, or at least say, *I want to. Do you want to? When might you want to?*

Harvey kissed her brow. "I love you."

"I love you too," Roz whispered, and felt the curve of Harvey's smile against her temple.

"Let's go say hi. I don't want you getting in trouble."

"Ah, what's trouble? I got in trouble with one of the church ladies when I decided to go with natural hair."

"You shouldn't ever be in trouble," said Harvey. "Especially not because of me. And your hair is beautiful."

Roz cuddled up, burying her face into his neck as his hand curved protectively over her hair. Harvey did that often, she'd noticed. She thought to him the gesture meant keeping what he loved safe.

Then she made herself pull away.

"Before we go down..." said Roz, propping herself up on one elbow. "Can I ask you for something?"

"Yeah." Harvey reached out, so their hands lay clasped on the blanket in the space between them. "Anything."

"Can I ask you for two things?"

"Nah, two things seems like a lot." Harvey grinned. "Ask me. Whatever it is, I'll do my best."

"Go home. You can't stay with me. It's my day to do the quest. I have to walk into the woods alone."

She saw the request hit Harvey like a blow. He shut his eyes. But he didn't tell her not to do it.

"What's the other thing?"

"Do you remember when I was in the hospital?" Roz asked. Harvey looked even more pained. "And you stayed with me all night. You sang to me. Will you sing to me again?"

She could read the pure panic and refusal on his face, clear as day. She wished she couldn't.

"Uh. Right now?"

"No," Roz muttered. "Just... sometime."

"*He sang to her, but he won't sing to you. Does he draw you as often as he drew her?*"

Shut up, spooky bird! Roz thought.

Harvey swallowed. "Sure. Sometime. Is there anything else I can do for you?"

"I want to see..." Roz began, and noticed how Harvey tensed.

"Never mind. Let's get through this quest first. I'll ask you later."

They went downstairs to say hello to her dad. Harvey left shortly after.

"How was your music lesson, sweetie?" her dad asked.

"Great," Roz lied.

It wasn't only awkward with Dad when Harvey was there. Roz couldn't forget Dad wanting to send her away when she was blind.

He'd said it would be better for Roz to go to a special school. She knew the truth. Some people you could count on, and some people you couldn't. You never knew, not for sure, until the test came.

Roz had always believed Dad loved her no matter what, but now she felt like he loved her only when he thought she was whole. With Roz's sight miraculously restored, he wanted to keep her.

More people had joined his church because of his daughter's wonderful cure. Roz's dad walked around these days with his chest puffed out like a clerical peacock. Roz couldn't help resenting him for that.

It wasn't your miracle, Dad.

"Think I might go for a healthful walk!" Roz told her father.

Very healthy. Nothing but fresh air and demons.

She walked out alone, shivering at the thought of the demons. The Lady said Roz should go into the woods to find a jewel in the shadows, and Roz had no idea how.

She'd never gone looking for magic.

Except she had. She'd asked Sabrina to cure her.

Roz hadn't been able to count on her family, but her friends had come through for her. Sabrina had restored Roz's sight. Now Roz had to get Nick back for Sabrina.

It was already dark in the woods. Roz felt very alone. She couldn't help thinking of the evening, more than a month ago, when Nick Scratch walked her home.

Roz liked Nick. Most girls probably did, though Roz went more for the sincere type. Years of Bible camp left their mark on a girl. But Nick did seem as if he was trying his best to be sincere with Sabrina.

Roz had been walking through the woods, marveling at all that she could see and worrying about Harvey, Sabrina, and satanic portents. Then she saw Sabrina's new boyfriend moving through the dark beneath the trees.

"Hi," Roz said. "Hey, Nick? I can see you."

"Ah," said Nick. "Yes. Well. Hi. Walk you home?"

"Sure." Roz remembered salacious stories Sabrina had told her about witches. "Platonically! I have an exclusive boyfriend."

"Do you?"

"Yeah," Roz reminded Nick. "Harvey?"

Nick frowned. "Don't think I know anyone by that name."

"He was at the diner with us the other day? He's tall."

Roz held up a hand over both their heads. Nick squinted at her hand.

"Is he? I don't recall." He gave her a glittering smile. "*You*, I remember. Roz, the lovely best friend. Whoever's dating you is a lucky guy."

When a guy made an effort with the best friend, it showed he definitely liked the girl. Roz charitably decided Nick must be bad with names.

"Well. Who knows how long his luck will last."

"Because he's...not smart?" asked Nick.

"Oh no, Harvey *is* smart," Roz told Nick, while Nick made a doubtful noise. "But there are a lot of complications. He used to date Sabrina."

"Did he?" asked Nick. "Gosh. News to me."

Roz worried she'd gotten Sabrina in trouble.

"It's totally over," Roz assured him. "Sabrina's crazy about you! She said you were sexy."

Nick seemed startled. Roz had been startled too. Sabrina was never interested in anyone but Harvey, not in all the years when Roz and Theo had crushes on innumerable guys in movies and bands.

Nick smiled at the ground.

"And—Harvey's with me now," Roz continued. "He said—he loves me."

"Sorry," said Nick, an edge in his voice. "I'm not following. Do mortals not want their mortal boyfriends to love them? Seems the kind of thing mortals would want."

"I mean," said Roz. "Maybe."

"Do you...not love him?" asked Nick. "Maybe you could get to like him? Possibly he has some good points."

He had many good points, as Roz had been uncomfortably aware for years. Tall and kind, sweet to the bone. He was easily hurt, but being hurt never stopped him. When her vision failed and she was sure of nothing else, Roz could be sure of him.

"I do love Harvey," Roz confessed. "He's someone you can't help loving."

"How nice for him!" said Nick. "I don't know him. So what's the problem here? Why don't you think it's going to last?"

"There are a lot of problems. Going out with your best friend's ex is frowned on. Among mortals."

Nick shook his head. "There are so many rules to mortal dating. How do you remember them?"

"I didn't obey that one." Roz felt wretched with guilt. "I should have. It didn't matter if I—liked him. Then there's my dad. Generally I got with guys at camp, where my dad wasn't there to judge. Dad's a minister, and he's not used to me having a boyfriend in Greendale. He's known Harvey all our lives, only—he's never seen Harvey as a threat to me before. But Harvey isn't a threat to me now!"

Somewhat to Roz's surprise, Nick Scratch gave her a reassuring nod.

"Don't break up. I can fix your problem," Nick announced confidently.

"Please don't ensorcel my dad!"

"No need," Nick said. "This will only take a minute."

"What are you going to do?"

Nick winked. "Watch."

Her dad was waiting on the porch. He often did that these days, suspiciously looking out for her.

That evening, Reverend Walker didn't have a glance to spare for his darling daughter. Instead, he was surveying Nick: the much-gelled hair, the fancy boots, the expensive-seeming black clothes, the good looks that were kind of too much. The everything that was too much. The slow, sinful smirk.

"Hey there," drawled Nick, "and Hail Satan."

"WHAT!" said Roz's dad.

"Just walking Roz back," Nick continued. "She insisted on coming home, though I made several suggestions about other... exciting places we could go."

"No, he didn't," said Roz, afraid her father would have an aneurysm. "This is Nick. He's just a friend."

"For now." Nick kissed Roz far too close to her mouth. "Later, babe."

Reverend Walker seemed lost in despair. "What happened to Harvey?"

"Harvey's still around," Roz answered.

"Thank God. Let's have Harvey over for dinner!"

Roz glanced to where Nick was already disappearing into the trees. Nick was looking over his shoulder, smiling his sly smile.

Roz liked Nick as far as she knew him. But she had to admit what she liked most about Nick was that he made her life less complicated.

Getting Nick back from hell was complicated.

None of her friends had faith in entirely the same way Roz did. They didn't realize how hideous Roz found the prospect of going to hell. She kept remembering pieces from her father's sermons.

"*Hell is the second death,*" the silver bird whispered. "*Hell is the eternal fire prepared for the devil and his angels. No boy and no friend is worth this.*"

Roz walked through the woods now, flinching at every movement. She wished Nick Scratch would appear among the trees and solve her problems again.

In the dying light, with her new clarity of vision, Roz saw a shadow that wasn't a demon. It was the shadow of a boy, sauntering away with his back to her.

"Nick?" Roz murmured, wondering if she should step off the path toward him.

"Who's Nick?" asked a woman's voice.

Roz spun around. "*Lilith!*"

The tall dark woman blinked behind her delicate spectacles. "It's Mary Wardwell. Your teacher—ah, principal?" She gave an embarrassed laugh. "Still getting used to that."

"Oh," Roz said. "Hi, Ms. Wardwell! How's life?"

She didn't know how to phrase, *How was dying and being resurrected by the Mother of Demons, who wore your face, tempted Sabrina to darkness, and incidentally got you a promotion?*

"I was taking a walk to clear my head," said Ms. Wardwell. "Life can feel complicated and overwhelming sometimes, can't it?"

"Yes," whispered Roz.

Ms. Wardwell surprised Roz by taking her hand. "For you too? I'm sorry, my dear. Would you like to walk with me a little way?"

Roz nodded. Ms. Wardwell was a frail mortal, like Roz herself, but somehow Roz felt stronger walking beside her.

"Do you want to talk about it? I've had…memory lapses myself lately. It seems like a dream, being principal. I was never even in administration! However strange what's going on in your life is, I might understand."

Roz couldn't betray Sabrina's secrets, and she didn't want to terrify this kind woman. She shook her head.

Ms. Wardwell pressed her hand. "Whatever's happening, at least you have your friends."

"Yes. I have them."

"They're the problem," said Roz's bird.

"I always thought you and Sabrina were a sweet pair," said Ms. Wardwell. "You so grounding, and her striking out for the sky. I—I always wanted a best friend."

"I love Sabrina," Roz said quietly.

"There was a man I was...fond of," Ms. Wardwell confided, in her shy way. "He seems to have disappeared off the face of the earth."

Roz bit her lip.

"I tell myself men aren't the be-all and end-all. I must live my own life. That's the important thing."

Roz said: "You're right."

"One thing that used to distract me was collecting the town myths about witches," Ms. Wardwell continued. Roz forced herself not to wince. "These days they don't seem so amusing. There's so much evil in the world."

Roz could see shadow demons slinking through the undergrowth, on both sides of the path.

She whispered, mouth dry: "Sometimes evil seems very close."

Ms. Wardwell nodded. "I try hard to believe there is good in the world too, and good matters."

She reached up a thin hand to touch a cross at her throat. Roz watched, amazed, as the shadow demons cringed and retreated.

"I have faith too," said Roz. "It comforts me."

Ms. Wardwell gave her a timid smile. "Would you like to come back to my house for tea—*is something wrong?*"

Roz had doubled over.

"No," Roz gasped as the cunning showed her what lay ahead, off the path. She straightened up now. "I just remembered something I have to do. Thank you so much, Ms. Wardwell! I hope everything works out for you!"

She wasn't sure it would. But she did understand now why Ms. Wardwell was Sabrina's favorite teacher. Roz hated to leave Ms. Wardwell alone on the path, and hated plunging into the dark woods on her own.

"Did magic really help her? Or you?" the bird whispered.

Because magic had brought Ms. Wardwell back, she'd been there to walk with Roz. The demons had stayed away from Ms. Wardwell, as though her goodness offered them protection.

It was nice to think of goodness having power.

"Go back to the path," sang the bird on her shoulder. *"Stay with that sweet woman. Make friends with that kind girl Lizzie instead of the devil's daughter. Make the right choice."*

She'd missed Sabrina so much when Sabrina ran off to witch school. At the same time, Roz understood the allure of having options. Like getting into multiple great colleges.

With her eyes healed, Roz could do so many things.

She could be a cheerleader. She could learn to drive. She could do a thousand fun, normal things the kids around her took for granted.

"You could have a different world," said the bird on her shoulder.

"You could have a different boyfriend, who would look only at you. All you must do is walk away from the witch and the quest."

She wanted a different world. But she didn't want to forsake her friends.

Between the trees were gathering shadows.

Roz shook her head and walked into the blinding dark. She choked, not on the smoke but on her own fear, as she saw a shape forming. High above Roz's head, neck arched, was the dark outline of a dragon. The creature was made of smoke, each scale a piece of insubstantial shadow, and its eyes burned.

"The great dragon was cast out, that serpent of old, called the Devil and Satan, who deceives the whole world," Roz quoted. "The great dragon was ... was cast out ..."

She plunged her hand into the seething breast of the smoke dragon and drew out a jewel. The gem fit in the hollow of her hand, red as a dragon's heart and glowing with inner fire.

Roz turned and ran out of the dark woods to Sabrina's door. To Roz's extreme relief, none of the freaky ghosts appeared. Nor did Sabrina's aunts, or the Academy students. Roz wanted only her best friend.

Roz's heart leaped at the sight of Sabrina's pale, tired face at the door.

"I got it," Roz said, breathless. She dropped the jewel into Sabrina's hand, and Sabrina gave a great sigh of relief. She drew Roz in toward her.

"Thanks, bestie," Sabrina whispered into Roz's shoulder.

Roz needed a break. They sat down on the split-level stairs of Sabrina's house with the jewel in Sabrina's lap. Sabrina turned the gem under her fingertips. The facets of the red jewel caught the light in strange ways, glinting sapphire blue, then silver, then black. The reflected gleams bathed Sabrina's intent face in an eerie glow.

Sabrina had the soul of a revolutionary. It was one of the things Roz loved best about her. There was so much about the world that needed changing, and someone needed to be an unstoppable force.

But it wasn't always comfortable, being best friends with an unstoppable force.

"I was glad to be able to do something for you," Roz murmured. "I know I owe you."

"For what?"

Roz blinked. "You've done so much for me."

"You don't owe me a thing." Sabrina sounded surprised. "I do things for the people I love because I love them. Doesn't everybody?"

Roz answered Sabrina with a kiss on the cheek. She leaned against her best friend, letting herself rest after the dragon and the woods, and she didn't say what she was thinking.

Forgive me, Sabrina. I don't want to go to hell.

In Sabrina's hands, the brilliant red jewel captured a ray of light streaming through the stained glass. It shone like a blood-stained sword.

HELL

LOVE RULES ME. —DANTE

N ormally when Nick opened a door to a pit full of demons, he said "Excuse me," and closed the door fast.

The demons had tried physical torture on Nick first. It hadn't worked, and they now seemed bored of trying, but Nick didn't have fond memories of the pit.

This time, Nick opened the door to a pit full of demons and plunged in. The hollowed-out cavern writhed with the seething oil-black and mold-green shapes of demons and rang with the screams of the damned. There were stalagmites carved in the shapes of agonized faces. Above them towered stone walls. There were jagged spikes projecting from rough stone, and ledges jutting out from a rock face.

On one of the highest ledges above the pit was Sabrina.

She was fighting demons with a sword in her hand.

Nick backhanded one demon, broke another's neck, stole a third demon's weapon and killed the creature with its own blade. By now, Nick was trained to leap to Sabrina's aid.

When Nick was first getting to know Sabrina, he had believed wooing her would be no problem.

There were many problems.

She was fierce and lovely, and he wanted her. He could tell she wanted him. And the Dark Lord commanded Nick to win over Sabrina. Nick was pleased. Everyone talked about dark devotions in hushed voices, but Nick got told to make time with a pretty girl. Nick felt his dark god had a firm grip on Nick's skill set.

But Sabrina kept talking about having a boyfriend, which was confusing. So what? Nick didn't understand why Sabrina thought having a dumbass mortal boyfriend precluded her from having an awesome warlock boyfriend, but Sabrina was used to mortal ways. She needed time to adjust. Nick would do whatever he must to accomplish Satan's will and be with her.

Bringing her forbidden books, offering her helpful advice— nothing worked. Every day Nick spent with her, it was clearer Sabrina was special. And Satan had chosen Nick for Sabrina. Satan meant them to be together.

It was the mortal's fault. *Why do bad things happen to good people?* mortals asked each other. (They didn't know it was because of Satan.) Nick wasn't a good person and the mortal wasn't a bad thing, but why did stupid mortals happen to brilliant witches? The mortal complicated everything.

"Kill him," suggested the Dark Lord in Nick's dreams, furnace-hot breath against Nick's neck.

The devil was tempting, and Nick was tempted. The mortal was getting in the way of what Nick wanted. The mortal was a witch-hunter.

Only...on the night after the summer festival when he first saw Sabrina from afar, Nick returned to the place where the festival had been. The wheel of light was dark, the striped tents packed away. The illumination and music, the boy talking about love and art, and the beautiful witch smiling in a world of mortals as if she belonged— they were gone. Nick was alone in a wasteland under the trees.

All that was mortal would soon be lost.

If the mortal died, Sabrina would miss him.

"If you command it, I'll kill him," Nick told Satan carelessly. "I'm arrogant enough to believe that's not necessary."

The Dark Lord laughed. He admired pride.

When Agatha and Dorcas collapsed a mine on the mortals, Sabrina's little mortal love would have died with the rest if Sabrina hadn't laid a protection charm upon him. Nick wondered if the Dark Lord had visited Agatha in her dreams when Nick resisted.

Sabrina decided to resurrect the mortal's brother, because she would do anything for those she loved.

Nick asked: "Can I watch?"

The Dark Lord wanted Nick to help Sabrina. Nick wanted to help her too. Everybody was getting what they wanted. There was no harm in it.

After the dark ritual was complete, Nick found out where the mortal lived. He went to the little green-painted farmhouse and heard the faltering voice of the mortal as he led his brother out onto the porch.

It was immediately obvious Sabrina's romantic gesture hadn't worked out as they'd hoped.

The mortal's brother was clearly still dead. The mortal's soft attempt at a childhood song broke apart in his throat as he stared at the revenant's empty eyes.

Nick murmured under his breath: "Back away slowly."

Instead, the mortal sat the *ravenous undead* in a chair and covered it with a blanket. The undead didn't need blankets!

"Gotta go to school. Wait for me here, okay?"

The mortal knelt down by the rocking chair so he could look tenderly up at the dead thing. Nick supposed the mortal was pretending to himself the creature could understand.

"I love you," the mortal told that vacant face. "So—so much. Tommy? I won't let you down. We'll get through this."

He drew the dead thing's head onto his shoulder. Nick saw the creature scent the mortal's skin with what would be hunger. Very soon.

The mortal had no idea.

I remember, Nick thought. *You want them not to be dead so badly, you can't see that they are. But they are.*

He was sympathetic at the time. This was before Nick got to know the mortal properly and realized the mortal had exclusively awful ideas. Embracing the undead was just the tip of the suicidal-notions iceberg.

The door of the mortal's house banged open so hard Nick

thought the frosted glass might break. An older mortal stormed onto the porch.

"Stop your pathetic bleating now!"

Witch-hunter, Nick thought coldly. *Worse.*

He saw the man move in a tight circle around Sabrina's mortal. The mortal flinched, then tried to range himself protectively in front of the zombie. This father was the kind of man who *caged*.

Best to murder everyone on that porch and get Sabrina's mortal away. Nick started forward, but the mortal said he was walking Sabrina to school.

"Hope the zombie eats you," Nick told the witch-hunter father, and followed.

Once the mortal was out of sight, he sat huddled among the leaves, apparently having trouble breathing.

Shhh, little mortal. It will be all right, Nick thought. *You're not alone like I was. She loves you. Get up. It's no good if you don't get up.*

The mortal did, after a while.

Nick teleported ahead to Sabrina's house. Sabrina was standing on her own porch, with her aunt Hilda calling her "my love." Sabrina's face was worried as it often was, because living among frail mortals was stressful. Usually Nick wanted to cheer up Sabrina when she looked like that, but the zombie situation had him concerned too.

When Sabrina saw the mortal make his way up the winding path to her house, she threw herself down the porch steps in his direction. The mortal caught her in his arms and spun her. Sabrina was beaming, her hand tracing the lapel of the mortal's dumb jacket.

"You're all right?" she asked him.

"Now I'm with you, I am."

Sabrina leaned her bright head down to his. "Same."

It gave Nick a strange feeling to see Sabrina and the mortal making each other happy even when they were miserable.

"I'd give all the witch orgies in the world," Nick told Sabrina later, "to have what you and the mortal have."

He meant it. But Sabrina wouldn't tell him what he had to do to deserve being with her.

The sorry business ended with the mortal putting his brother in the ground and Sabrina crying. Whenever Sabrina cried, Nick wanted to cry too.

Sabrina had indulged the mortal too much. He thought he could do any fool thing he wanted. The mortal stayed mad about the necromancy. Nick told him to forgive Sabrina, and hoped the mortal would see reason. The mortal never did. It was nothing but fuss, fuss, fuss. *I love crying and upsetting everybody, I love hurting Sabrina, I hate being protected, I hate magic, I hate you!*

The mortal was stupid. Nick was done trying. Satan could kill him, for all Nick cared.

Then the mortal made his stupidest decision yet. Nick persuaded Sabrina to come for coffee, and they saw the mortal with Sabrina's friend Roz. Sabrina called the mortal her *ex-boyfriend*.

If the mortal chose to fling love away, that was fantastic news for Nick. Sabrina said Nick might be her someone special. She took Nick to an adorable dance at her mortal school where they had funny paper decorations and no entrails hanging up anywhere. The mortal had lost his chance. Nick was the one who got to be with Sabrina.

Nick's only remaining problems were Satan and Sabrina's aunt Hilda.

Sabrina wished to follow many mortal customs. It was sweet. Nick liked dates. On their best date, Nick found many interesting books, and Sabrina said cute things like: "The store's closing! Do you want to get locked in overnight?"

"Wow," said Nick. "Yes, please."

Sabrina seemed worried. Maybe she thought he was asking her to sleep with him. Nick would be delighted, but he remembered the mortal rules about *consent, boundaries,* and people waiting until they were *in love.* Nick could wait.

Nick wanted Sabrina to feel safe with him. Even though she shouldn't.

"We can just sleep?" he offered. "Or stay up reading all night!"

Sabrina's mouth quirked. "And cuddle?"

Nick stared at Sabrina's beautiful hair in alarm. "We can go."

Sabrina helped Nick carry his many purchases, so he could still walk her home.

"I'd better not introduce you to the internet," she said as they went, laughing.

The internet sounded like a long, strange book. Apparently there were always new things to read on it.

"I want to have an internet one day," said Nick. "I will read the whole thing."

Sabrina took his hand. Nick wondered what he'd said to please her and how he could do it again.

On another day when he teleported into the Spellman house to pick Sabrina up for another date, Nick hoped they were going to the bookstore again. He remembered to teleport to the hall, since Sabrina got funny about him teleporting to her bedroom. He heard Hilda singing and followed the sound to their kitchen.

Nick stood listening and closed his eyes. It was nice in Sabrina's house.

When he opened his eyes, Hilda was staring daggers at him. Nick didn't step back. He offered Hilda an ingratiating smile.

"You again," Hilda muttered.

"Admit it," Nick wheedled. "You're getting to like me."

"You're the fling guy, not the forever guy. Fine. I can accept that." Hilda shook a spatula in Nick's direction. "Don't hurt my girl."

"No." Nick kept his smile in place. "I won't."

"I don't trust you. Look me in the face and tell me I should."

Nick's gaze dropped.

They were witches, made for sorcery, not honesty. What kind of witch was Hilda Spellman anyway?

What happened when the fling guy didn't want to be flung away?

He would prove himself. She'd love him. When she found out about Satan, by then she'd see it was for the best. Nick tried to do everything for Sabrina, without question.

Twice, he failed.

First Sabrina asked him to avoid the Weird Sisters.

"Don't you trust me?" Nick asked, wounded, then remembered with a guilty shock Sabrina was *right* not to trust him.

Nick stopped talking to the Weird Sisters.

He was always trying to make it up to her, and she didn't even know what he'd done. But Sabrina laughed more now that she was with him, as he'd hoped she would. Nick didn't know why Sabrina and the mortal had to take everything so seriously. You might as well have fun, even in a terrible world.

It was worth the constant worry if Sabrina was growing to love him. He'd told her he loved her. He thought she'd say it back, someday soon.

The second time he failed her, Nick and Sabrina had both been expelled for causing mischief. Nick forgot he owed Sabrina. Without the Academy, he didn't have a home. He had nowhere to go.

Sabrina did.

"Right back to your mortal school," Nick spat, when she found him in Dorian Gray's bar. "And your *mortal boyfriend*."

Being cruel was the only way Nick knew how to be unhappy. He snarled at Sabrina about being half mortal and saw her face turn white. She left. Nick knew where she was going.

He didn't blame Sabrina. If he'd had somewhere warm and bright, a place where someone might be kind to him, he would have gone.

But he didn't.

Nick stared into his glass, and then drained it. What he had was this.

When witch-hunters attacked, Nick realized he still had something to lose. He ran to Sabrina.

Someone else did too. Nick was forced to witness the mortal embrace Sabrina with tender concern.

Witch-hunters trapped their people in a reconsecrated church,

and only Sabrina could go in to save them. And the mortal—
what kind of witch-hunter was he!—said he wanted to help.

Sabrina said, very rightly, that the mortal couldn't go.

"You can't let her go alone," the mortal snapped at Nick.

"I don't *let her* do anything," Nick said.

Sabrina ran off by herself to fight the witch-hunters.

"If she's not back in five minutes," the mortal announced, "I'm
going after her."

Nick delivered a lecture to the mortal, explaining in detail all
the stupid things the mortal did and why he must stop doing them.
The mortal stood quietly, finally paying attention.

As soon as Nick turned his back, the mortal vanished.

Nick understood too late that when the mortal said *You can't let
her go alone*, the important word was *alone*.

The whole time Nick was talking, that fool wasn't even listening. He was counting. When the time was up, he went to Sabrina.

She wouldn't retreat from a fight. That mortal wouldn't leave
the church without Sabrina. They would both die behind church
doors Nick couldn't open.

Sabrina saved everyone, almost dying and displaying satanic
power to do it. The mortal returned at the head of the rescued
witches, Sabrina cradled in his arms.

At least the mortal looked as desperately worried for Sabrina
as Nick felt. It was a small comfort, not to be alone in that feeling.

When she woke, Sabrina told the mortal, "You're always there
to catch me."

Sabrina wanted only one love. The true love. Nick didn't
understand why. It wasn't like Sabrina only loved one of her

aunts, but he understood this: If Sabrina wanted the mortal, Nick was out in the cold.

"The mortal said you were like Dark Phoenix tonight," Nick said to Sabrina later. "I don't know her."

Sabrina, drying her hair, answered: "She's from a comic book."

"What is a comic book?"

"It's a book where the story is mostly told through pictures."

This was so much worse than Nick had believed. "Can he not *read*?"

Sabrina claimed the mortal could, but Nick had his suspicions. This was the man Sabrina believed would always catch her? He'd told Sabrina *he* wanted to be the one to catch her, and she kissed Nick, but she didn't tell him she loved him.

Sabrina said *always* to the mortal. She said *I love you* to the mortal. She never said anything like that to Nick.

The next day, everybody in school was talking about the stupid mortal helping to free them.

"When Sabrina dropped like a stone, I believed it was our end," Mania said at the next table. "But that witch-hunter untied me from the stake. He carried Sabrina like she was his infernal princess."

Elspeth nodded. "I now understand why Sabrina committed all that necromancy."

"Tall as a forbidden tree," sighed Mania. "Makes you want to go climbing."

Nick shoved his lunch tray violently away.

"I looked up at that witch-hunter and thought, who knows, maybe I want to do the will of heaven."

Mania and Elspeth giggled naughtily.

"Ladies, please!" said Nick. "There are ghost children present."

His voice made Sabrina look up from her book by Edward Spellman about the profound beauty of mortals. "What's that, guys?"

"Nothing, Sabrina!"

Nick eyed the book with hate. As Sabrina turned her water-creased page, Nick saw the words *Mortals have so much to teach us.*

Like what, how to be an idiot?

"I'm a supportive warlock boyfriend," announced Nick. "But I can't help feeling that this isn't your father's best work."

Sabrina gave him a red-lipped smile. "Complain on Amazon like mortals do."

"Teleport to the Amazon River and yell about bad books?" Nick frowned. "So crocodiles know not to read them?"

Sabrina laughed and kissed him. She had an adorable trick of touching his face and looking at him before they kissed. He'd been with many people and known that as far as they were concerned, Nick could be anyone. It mattered that he was hot or powerful. It didn't matter that he was *Nick.*

Imagine having it matter so much, that it was him, and it was her.

Sabrina might forgive him for lying, if she loved him. But if she didn't love him … If she loved someone else …

Between Satan and the mortal, Nick was having a hard time.

Sabrina could love people. If she didn't love Nick, it was because there was something wrong with him.

It emerged that Sabrina was Satan's daughter. Satan loved her about as much as Nick's parents had loved him, which was not at all. And Sabrina still didn't know what Nick had done.

Nick teleported to her bedroom one night and found Sabrina with her back to him, studying a drawing of the mortal's. He put his arm around her, teleporting them to her porch.

Sabrina turned, hands in fists, then relaxed and leaned against him. In the shadow of her porch, Nick saw the scarlet curve of her smile. She wore red lipstick more often these days. Nick let himself believe the lipstick was for him.

"I was passing on my wild way through the woods..." Nick began, then confessed: "I wanted to see you."

Sabrina made a purring contented sound, like her familiar. "And you wanted to teleport me to such exciting places as my front porch."

Nick dropped his face into the curve of her neck. He was tired, trying not to sleep. In his dreams, the Dark Lord would find him.

"Yeah," he sighed. "This is all I want. Sorry if I scared you."

"You didn't scare me," said his fearless girl. "I thought I'd have to fight. But I know you're on my side."

Nick nodded, grateful she couldn't see his face. He thought this was the worst he would ever feel. He went to hell to wipe away the guilt. To prove to her *he* was the true love.

Father Blackwood had forbidden them to read mortal books.

"Intellectual curiosity is a fine thing," he told Nick, "but there are limits."

To your intellect? Clearly, Nick thought.

He'd burned Nick's Shakespeare, but other mortals had

helpfully written books called *Crime and Punishment* and *The Demons*. Nick passed off those books as witch tomes.

There was a quote from a mortal book Nick repeated to himself when they tortured him. *Even if I cannot see the sun, I know that it exists.*

If Sabrina was safe, loving him, Nick could endure hell.

Now he was fighting through a pit of demons to get to her. She was in hell. How had she—? Why would she—?

Nick slew demon after demon. He wiped their dark blood from his eyes, and saw Sabrina killing and laughing on high.

It made Nick smile. He could never love a girl without a little she-wolf in her.

Too many demons came at them. Nick opened his mouth to warn Sabrina that she must escape.

Instead, she launched herself off the ledge and levitated over the pit. Wherever her burning gaze rested, there was fire. Demons writhed and exploded into ash.

Ever since the mortal described this, Nick had wanted to see it for himself. Now she was before him, robed in scarlet and shining.

Nick was, at last, the one to catch her. She tumbled through the air into his arms, then exclaimed: "Nick?"

Nick looked down into Sabrina's brilliant iridescent eyes, the color of dying stars. "Hey, gorgeous."

One of the remaining demons lunged toward her with a snarl. Nick turned, shielding her with his body, and knew nothing else.

He woke in a quiet chamber, emerald lights playing across his face. The air felt different, but not different enough to be another dimension. The smell of sulfur was faint, as though hell's fires still burned, but at a safer distance.

Nick lay in a soft bed wearing clean clothes. Green light was filtering through a vast mullioned window. Through the filmy curtains surrounding the bed, he saw Sabrina standing at the window, wearing a silver gown. Beyond the glass was an emerald city, towers shimmering with jade light against a strange sky. Smoky grass-green radiance caught in the snow-white curls of Sabrina's hair, lingering over the curve of her ruby-red lips. Her expression was faraway.

Nick shifted in the bed with a murmur, and Sabrina turned away from the window.

"Nick?" The way she said his name was so sweet.

Nick kept his eyes hooded as she hurried toward the bed. When she leaned anxiously over him, he clasped her slender silver waist in his hands and tumbled Sabrina down onto bed with him. She hovered over him with laughter in her dark eyes.

"You think you're so sneaky, Nick Scratch."

"What do you think, Spellman?"

Sabrina said: "I think you're a hero."

He leaned up and caught the crimson curve of her lips with his own. Sabrina smiled as she kissed him back, wrapped together against white pillows with her fingers stroking his hair. For a moment nothing hurt at all.

"I'm not," he murmured after a brief, breathless instant. "Sabrina, I'm *so* sorry. I know how you must have felt—tricked and—like nothing was real—"

"There's nothing to be sorry for," Sabrina said. "As soon as you made that sacrifice, I understood."

"That's why I did it," Nick told her eagerly. "Wait, no. It was for you."

Sabrina smiled at him. "It can be for us. We're a team, aren't we? You're on my side, and I'm on yours."

Nick nodded, a warm feeling unfurling in the center of his chest.

"You shouldn't be here, Sabrina," he whispered. "I hear him in my head all the time."

"I'll chase him out," Sabrina promised. "I'll keep you safe."

"I'm not worth it."

Sabrina framed his face in her hands. "You are to me," she said, with bright tenderness in her eyes. "You're everything to me."

He was so in love, he could hardly breathe.

"I'm sure your aunt Hilda doesn't agree."

"Aunt Hilda didn't want me to come," Sabrina admitted. "I still came. I don't care. You and I can get a house together."

Wasn't she upset? Nick thought with some disquiet. With a home like that, which she so dearly loved, where she was so dearly loved.

Sabrina bit her lip, uncertain in a way she never was with him. "Do you not want to?"

Nick had an inheritance, which he mostly used for books and travel. Being in a house by himself seemed hideous. A teacher had suggested he could get another familiar, and Nick was almost sick.

A house with Sabrina would be different. He thought of the

long-ago mortal girl, the light in her window. The light in Sabrina never went out. He wanted that light with him always.

"I do want to," he assured her.

"I'm so glad, Nick." Sabrina sat up, looking down at him fondly. "We might need two places? One on earth, and one in hell."

There was a pause.

"What's that, babe?" Nick asked.

"While I was intent on rescuing you," Sabrina explained, "I may have—accidentally!—become Queen of Hell."

Nick took a moment to process. He'd realized this might be a possibility, as Sabrina was technically next in line in the succession. His girlfriend was not an underachiever.

"You can't deny, this place needs to be better run," Sabrina continued. "I was thinking, we should try to save the souls of everybody in hell." Her face scrunched in a frown. "That might take time. And we should punish really evil souls. Anyway! I'll work it out."

Nick started to laugh. "I believe in you."

Sabrina watched as though she liked to see him happy. She leaned over and kissed him. Every inch of Nick's spine lit up, a line of radiance as joy and desire combined, the way that only ever happened with Sabrina. Nick nuzzled the long pale line of her neck, hiding there for a moment. Safe, even in hell, if he was with her. Sabrina began to undo the buttons of his shirt, and he let her do it rather than using magic. He wanted her to choose this, choose him.

He could believe in Sabrina as the Queen of Hell, or the Queen of Heaven. The queen of everything she wanted to be. If they were together, and she cared about the world and he cared about her, it was almost like Nick was good too.

There was a knock on the door.

Sabrina sighed. "Alas, my subjects await. Get the door, will you, honey?"

The door was incongruous in that green-and-gray room. It was a cage door.

Nick looked at the door, then back at Sabrina. The sight of her soothed away his fear.

"I love you so much, Nick," she told him.

"I love you too," Nick said, full of wonder. He'd never had the chance to say that before. *I love you too.* It was a different thing from *I love you.* He'd been afraid he was alone in *I love you.*

Sabrina smiled at him, marvelously. "I never really loved anyone else. I see that now."

Nick's whole body went cold. He tore his gaze away from Sabrina.

"That's not true," he told the glittering conquered city outside the window. "This isn't real. She wouldn't say that."

Everything turned to dust and crumbled away, the quiet bedroom and the shining city and the loving girl. Nick was left alone on the mountain again. He reached for Sabrina, far too late.

Nick shivered, on his knees as the snow fell. He wished he could hold her one more time. Even though she wasn't real.

Instead of the wolves, there was a woman waiting for him on the cold mountain. She had paper-white skin, black eyes with eerie green irises, and a golden crown. He didn't know her face, but there was something about the curl of her mouth.

"Lilith," Nick whispered.

She smiled thinly. "Clever boy. You always were. Thought yourself the prince of your school. Strutted around pretending to be on the women's side. All the time you were smugly doing your master's bidding. Not so smug now, are we, Nicholas?"

"Not to face-shame you," said Nick, "but I liked Mary Wardwell's face better."

Lilith waved her hand in a regal fashion. The pain made Nick double over. His skin sliced in four ragged lines across his chest, as though a she-wolf had tried to rip his heart out.

"Don't test me, pet. I've just had a trying interview with a demon prince. I'm in the mood to work out some frustrations, so you'd be wise to keep your pretty mouth shut."

Nick knew how to stay quiet and how to say what people wanted to hear. He'd done it a thousand times: for Amalia, for Father Blackwood, for Satan. For Sabrina.

"I imagine the prince was sorry he crossed you," said Nick. Lilith made a small satisfied noise. "What did he say?"

Lilith paced on the mountain. Frost glittered upon the velvet train of her gown, as though it was embroidered with silver.

"He claimed he hadn't noticed any unrest in Pandemonium. While literally standing on a burning ship."

"Vexing," murmured Nick.

She spared him an approving glance.

"Then he wanted to know about Princess Sabrina."

"About Sabrina!" Nick said sharply.

Lilith's next glance was not approving. She felt boys were meant to be shirtless on their knees in the snow and not heard; that was clear.

"Mmm. I suppose the prince wonders if the Morningstar princess might be like him." Lilith laughed. "Funny how the most irresistible thing in the world to a man is himself. He will never forgive a woman once he finds out she's more than a pretty mirror to watch himself in."

The winter wind dragged cold claws down his back. Nick shivered uncontrollably. He'd done this so the shadow of hell could be lifted from Sabrina. The idea of a new darkness on the hunt for her was appalling.

Lilith slapped Nick on the shoulder. Fresh blood dappled the snow.

"Not to worry, I'm sure she'll cherish fond memories of you. If you think about it, Lucifer did you two a favor. You will have the most perfect love story in any world, because you didn't have the chance to disappoint her."

Lilith's hand on him felt like the weight of chains.

"But what am I thinking," Lilith murmured. "You already betrayed her. After all, you'd known her five minutes."

"I'm *sorry*," said Nick.

He wasn't speaking to Lilith, but Lilith answered.

"Men always say they're sorry. But they keep hurting us. Don't hang your head. It's not about being men. It's about having *power*. In every world, the powerful hurt the weak, because they can. Everything luminous will be put out, everything sweet will be consumed. The only way not to be crushed is to be more powerful than everybody else. And Nicholas, you might have been top dog in school, but—what's the mortal phrase—you're playing in the big leagues now."

She laid her bloodred lips close to his ear. "Frankly, I think your time's up. There never was much to you, was there? And it's almost gone."

She rubbed her hands briskly together. His blood turned to red dust and drifted away in the wind. "This has been a delightful interlude, but I'm a busy woman. I'll leave you to the wolves."

"No," Nick begged.

Lilith was already gone, melting like a snowflake. He was alone.

Even if I cannot see the sun, thought Nick desperately, *I know that it exists.*

Sabrina was so far away.

GREENDALE

BE AS A TOWER. —DANTE

Y ou were at the lowest difficulty setting on our quest, and you had to overcome a smoke dragon." Theo surveyed the faces of his friends, sitting in a circle under the British flag. "Ohhh dear."

"Don't worry," murmured Harvey, looking worried.

Beside Harvey, Roz looked even more worried. She'd been quiet since she gave Sabrina the magic jewel last night. Theo had offered a high five because Roz had completed her quest, but Roz seemed in no mood for high fives.

"Are you okay, Theo?" Sabrina leaned forward. "Do you want me to... I could try to kill the Lady of the Lake?"

"Think that might be one of those solutions that only lead to more problems," said Theo. "Appreciate the offer, though."

He punched Sabrina's shoulder, to reassure her. Theo loved his friends, even when they were totally wilding. He loved them the same way they loved him: no matter what.

So on the regular occasions when the whites of Sabrina's eyes glowed and she announced she had a Plan, or the thankfully rare moments when Harvey's mouth went flat and he became determined, Theo was okay with it. It wasn't ideal, but life wasn't ideal. Sometimes his friends engaged in embarrassing romantic drama. Sometimes they got extra about the supernatural.

Theo'd known them for years. This was just like the time they were eleven when Sabrina lured them into the forbidden depths of the woods and Harvey found a baby bird.

Theo and Sabrina were climbing too-tall trees and laughing when Harvey's voice called them back to the earth. The baby bird in Harvey's hands was fuzzy and gray, with a weird long neck, too-sharp yellow beak, and too-big yellow claws.

"Sabrina!" pleaded Harvey, eyes huge in his thin kid face, tone effectively conveying he now loved this murder chicken.

Sabrina's face hardened into epic resolve.

"Something Must Be Done," she declared.

Roz was the normal one, who had friends outside their group because her dad made sure she ran with the church kids. Poor Roz fretted, "That bird is a vulture, and its wingspan will be..." but Theo said, "Guys, that is a messed-up-looking bird," then shrugged. He was pretty sure Harvey's grandpa secretly killed the bird later. If he hadn't, Harvey and Sabrina would've undoubtedly raised a vulture. And that was demented, but okay.

Stick with your friends and fight your enemies, that was

Theo's motto. The world was full of jerks. His friends were good people.

New guy Nick Scratch was Sabrina and Harvey's baby vulture now, and everybody had to deal. Theo wanted his friends to rely on him. He wanted people to think: *That Theo, what a guy.*

Still, Theo had to admit this was a freaky situation. Even for them. At least it was Saturday. Theo was thankful he didn't have to go to school on top of dealing with his hell quest.

Theo's dad owned guns, but he would've had questions if Theo started regularly carrying around a gun the way Harvey did. This morning, though, Theo woke and knew today he must find a cloak of feathers. He'd grabbed the key to the cabinet from what his dad imagined was a genius hiding place and had taken a gun. Better in trouble with his dad than eaten by demons.

Their latest meeting of the Fright Club concluded, they went downstairs. Theo remembered to shoulder his gun a moment after Harvey shouldered his. As they descended the split-level staircase of Sabrina's house, Theo heard the phone ring from their office under the stairs, then the crisp sound of Zelda Spellman's voice answering.

"You have a dead body?" Zelda snapped. "Congratulations! Do you want two? That can be arranged."

"Aunt *Z*!" Sabrina dashed down the steps. "Have you forgotten we run a funeral home?"

Sabrina's aunt Zelda seemed more on edge than usual, and she wasn't a relaxed lady at the best of times. Theo blamed her house-guests. Right now, three Academy students were standing in the hall looking up at them. Plus a ghost.

"Greetings, mortal," said Melvin.

"Hey, dude," said Theo.

Harvey swung the ghost up into his arms. Sometime in the last forty-eight hours, Harvey had adopted a creepy ghost child. Theo shook his head. Classic Harvey.

Creepy Ghost stared over Harvey's shoulder at Theo. When people thought Theo was a girl, they'd expected Theo to automatically think kids were cute. This kid wasn't. She looked like she'd been drowned, then dragged through a hedge backward. And left under the hedge for a hundred years.

The Academy students were as unraveled and disheveled as the ghost. Nobody had brought a change of clothes from the Academy of Unseen Arts. Theo supposed witches didn't go to the mall.

Theo used to make his own costumes for Christmas and Halloween. He could mend his own clothes, which was handy on a farm. He used to carry a sewing kit around with him everywhere. A few months ago, when everyone still called him by a girl's name, Theo would've offered to help out the witches. Now that he was openly Theo, he wasn't sure sewing was a Theo thing to do.

Plus, Theo didn't like the Academy kids. Apparently many witches pretended they were better than mortals. *Why*, Theo wondered, *could nobody accept people as they were?*

Elspeth sidled over to where Harvey stood. Agatha moved farther away from him, but she was watching Harvey too.

Certain witches were apparently devastated by Harvey. Since witches lived in opposite land, Theo guessed Harvey was the equivalent of a total bad boy who rolled in on a motorcycle while wearing a leather jacket, and maybe smoked. Theo sniggered. *Lock up your daughters, witch moms! Harvey might shyly ask her out for a milkshake!*

This explained a lot about Sabrina's attitude to Harvey over the years. And her aunt Zelda's.

"I'm heading out," Roz announced. "Lizzie asked if I wanted to go to the mall."

Roz hugged Theo at the front door, then made her way down the curving path into the woods.

Before he could close the door, a grinning demon swung from the lintel of the doorway and launched itself at Theo's face. Theo was knocked flat on his back, the creature's jagged teeth snapping an inch from his nose. Elspeth was screaming, Harvey was moving too fast, and Theo could hear the tap of Sabrina's shoes. Theo wrenched his gun desperately off his shoulder and shot the demon in the face.

The demon exploded into dust. Theo rolled over, coughing and choking. He saw Sabrina with shadows coiling around her white hair, and Harvey with his gun already aimed.

If Harvey hadn't been holding that ghost, he would've shot the demon. The Lady of the Lake said Theo was supposed to do this on his own.

Theo *should* be able to do this on his own.

Zelda Spellman burst out of the office, a terrifying vision in amethyst tweed. "Which of you miscreants summoned a demon!"

The Academy students cringed, far more scared of her than of demons. Theo felt slightly bad about getting the witch kids in trouble, but not that bad. The witch kids were jerks. He didn't know why Harvey was trying so hard with them.

What Theo knew was, he must get out of Sabrina's house.

"Off to shower demon dust out of my hair," he announced, and hugged Sabrina.

"I'll come with you!" said Harvey.

"Don't go, beautiful mortal," murmured Elspeth.

Maybe Harvey was the witch version of that Andrews boy from Riverdale. Last summer, Roz and Theo would go admire the construction site where Riverdale Guy built things. Shirtlessly.

Then one day last summer, Theo and Roz caught Harvey sneakily playing the guitar, and Theo saw Roz give him—*Harvey!*—the Riverdale Guy eyes. Even though Harvey was wearing a shirt. Actually, Harvey was wearing two.

Oh nooo, Theo thought, but decided Roz was smart. She'd get over it.

Last summer, life was simpler.

Theo felt better about life now, but the romantic drama was taxing.

He remembered the winter day Sabrina stunned Theo twice by announcing she was a witch, and Harvey'd broken up with her.

It was clear Harvey was melting down. Theo couldn't even think about what Harvey'd done—*shot his brother*—without feeling his own mind bend around the horror. But Harvey loved Sabrina so much, Theo was certain they'd get past this.

Only at the sweethearts' dance in February, Harvey told Theo he'd asked Roz out. And Sabrina showed up with an insanely hot stranger.

Theo seized Harvey's sleeve. "*Who is that?*"

"That's Nick Scratch."

Harvey intoned this as a farmer might say, "That's Hurricane Nick, come to destroy my crops."

Theo stumbled off to get air. When he went outside, he saw school bully Billy fumble to hide a cigarette.

"Billy, I'm not a teacher. I don't care if you smoke. It'll kill you, though; you're a dummy."

Theo was aware he got too angry when people were jerks. He was making an effort to be more chill, since Billy was trying to be less of a jerk. Theo strongly felt Greendale needed more chill.

"Hey ... Theo," Billy said awkwardly. Theo grinned.

"Don't mind me. Avoiding my friend situation."

Billy leaned forward on his crutches. "Yo, everybody knows your friends are crazy, but your friends are *crazy*. Is Kinkle going with Roz now? Aren't Roz and Sabrina best friends? If Carl stole my girl, I would be *pissed*."

Theo rolled his eyes. "Don't think that's super likely."

Carl was in the most obvious glass closet of all time, but Billy loved denial.

"Who's that guy Sabrina's with?" Billy demanded. "I've seen him around. Does he go to private school? Is Academy Guy aware of the *lunatic mess* he's walking into?"

"Anyone would be lucky to date my friends," Theo said sternly. "Not that I'd make out with any of them, ever, at any time. What a mess."

The mention of making out made Theo realize they were standing alone in the shadows. Maybe it was Theo's imagination, but he thought Billy was edging closer.

"Hey," said Theo. "I realize you find this confusing, but I'm a guy. If we made out, it'd be as gay as if you made out with Carl."

"I didn't ask to make out!" exclaimed Billy. "I wasn't gonna!"

Theo held up a hand. "Just wanna be clear."

He left Billy sputtering behind him and found that Sabrina and Roz had jetted off to the girls' bathroom to discuss romantic drama.

Nick Scratch was being swarmed by women. Also Carl. Theo didn't blame them. Theo might've seen Nick around, but he definitely hadn't seen Nick in a tux before. Jesus, well done, Sabrina. Roz and Sabrina had emerged from the bathroom and were trying to make their way to Nick through the rush. Harvey was standing off by himself. He looked thrilled to see Theo, then concerned.

"You okay?" Harvey asked. "Was Billy a jerk?"

"Surprisingly, no," said Theo. "Tell you later."

"We could go to the bathroom to talk," Harvey offered. "Like the girls do."

"Dudes don't do that, Harv."

Sometimes it was like Harvey had been raised in the woods by deer and little birds.

"Oh," said Harvey. "Well … do you wanna dance?"

Harvey, Roz, and Theo had been dancing together earlier, in a happy friend ring. That was different. Baxter High would definitely read arty Harvey dancing with recently demanding-to-be-called-Theo as romantic.

When Theo glanced up, Harvey was watching the interested spectators with a dark glint in his eye. Theo saw Harvey *did* understand how they'd be perceived and didn't care. Theo was almost tempted to say yes, but—Theo didn't want his first proper dance with a guy to be with Harvey. He wanted his first dance with a guy to mean something. To have some romance for his own.

"Nah." Theo shrugged. "You're a lousy dancer."

Harvey laughed. "I really am."

The sweethearts' dance was February. Now it was April. Theo still hadn't told anybody about liking guys, and he was psyching himself up for his solo quest.

Harvey followed him down the steps, past Sabrina's toad statues. "Let me drive you home."

"No, dude, I have to fight demons."

Sabrina was focused on saving Nick, the way she got super focused on projects. Theo should've realized Harvey would be the biggest problem. Still, surely Harvey didn't think Theo was chicken. The guys at school said *Harvey* was chicken. Since Harvey was willing to throw down with demons, Theo felt there was a high bar for guys.

Harvey paused. "... You could drive the truck."

Theo stopped in his tracks. "Oh, you wicked temptress."

Harvey never let Theo drive the truck. He was always like, blah blah blah Theo, you don't have a license. Whatever, Theo had been driving a tractor since he was twelve.

Theo grabbed the keys. Harvey climbed into the passenger seat and began conducting a driving lesson. Harvey thought Theo drove too fast, while Theo thought driving fast was fun.

"What if Sabrina and Roz were on the road right in front of us?"

Theo considered. "I'd hit Sabrina. She can do magic and stop the truck."

"No!" exclaimed Harvey. "*You* stop the truck. With the magical power of brakes!"

Another demon came slinking out from between the trees, a shadow with a ridged back and leathery wings. Theo ran over the demon and squashed it flat.

"Brakes?" Theo asked innocently. "What are they?"

As they drove down the winding road through the woods, Theo was still thinking about the sweethearts' dance. If demons killed him, Theo wouldn't have told anyone this truth about himself.

"Harvey will feel differently about you once you tell him," one of the creepy birds on Theo's shoulder whispered. Only one of Theo's birds seemed to have the job of undermining his confidence.

"He won't," Theo said firmly. "Don't be a moron, bird."

"Is one of your birds talking to you?" Harvey asked. "What did the bird say?"

Theo pulled over. "Moron bird stuff. Harv, I'm into guys. Definitely not you. Though I love you, dude, and I'm sure you're cute. To other people. I can't forgive that sleepover watching the movies with tiny hikers."

"The Lord of the Rings?"

"There was no need for extended editions! Those tiny hikers had already been hiking way too long."

Harvey was clearly charmed that Theo had said he loved Harvey. "I..." he began.

Theo patted his shoulder. "I know, Harv."

Theo gave the silver bird on his left shoulder a triumphant look. Yeah, that'd been real traumatic. In the end, telling the truth always made Theo feel better.

The bird hopped up and down on Theo's shoulder in a discomfited fashion, as if it weren't sure how to proceed.

Harvey said, in the tones of one who'd had a great idea, "Wanna talk about guys?"

Theo blinked. "With you?"

Harvey brightened, because Theo hadn't said his idea was dumb. Harvey always expected to be told off. Theo hated Harvey's dad.

"Yeah," Harvey said eagerly. "It's garbage to say guys can't tell if other guys are attractive. 'Course we can. And girls are trained to tell when other girls are attractive. Roz says it's just different forms of compulsive heteronormativity, and I don't like that."

"*Compulsory* heteronormativity."

"I don't like that either," said Harvey.

Harvey wasn't dumb, despite what Theo knew Harvey feared. But he *had* been basically raised by his brother and his friends, because his dad was a nightmare. And he was sometimes a big dope.

Theo grinned. "Not a fan myself. I kept thinking—guys are meant to like girls, so did I like guys because other people thought I was a girl? Might I start to like girls? When I did like guys, I thought: Is it because I want to be them, or be with them? Did I want to dress like them? I wasn't sure. So I kept it to myself until I was sure."

Occasionally Theo had looked at Roz, the most beautiful girl he knew, and wondered about finding her attractive. Probably for the best he didn't.

"So," Harvey said, hopeful. "So who?"

"I've had dark moments of weakness ... in which I found Billy attractive."

There was a pause. Harvey might've thrown up in his mouth.

Theo moved on quickly. "And I admit among the witches, one guy really stands out."

"I agree," said Harvey instantly.

Theo blinked. "You do?"

"He's so cool."

Theo nodded with enthusiasm. "I hoped we'd meet more witch guys like him. So I could ... maybe have someone like that for myself."

Harvey shook his head. "All other warlocks have been a huge disappointment."

"Melvin," murmured Theo. "Not the stuff of dreams."

Harvey checked a grin. Harvey worried about being mean, but Theo thought Melvin was a weasel and felt okay about judging him.

"So, my magic almost-crush isn't going anywhere either."

"I think you should go for it. Ask him out," Harvey urged.

Theo's mouth fell open. "Harvey! Do you *want* our friend group to explode in fire and drama? Do you wish to see Sabrina *kill me?*"

"Wow," said Harvey. "I'm sure Sabrina would like it."

"You are?" Theo asked faintly.

The witches must have brainwashed Harvey. Theo suspected Elspeth.

Harvey nodded. "You've gotta have more confidence, Theo. Sabrina would be stoked if you and her cousin hit it off."

There was a pause.

"Harvey. Do you think I'm talking about Ambrose Spellman?"

Harvey stared. "Obviously?"

"Ambrose is a handsome guy," Theo conceded. "But I noticed he seemed about twenty when we were six. Before we found out about everybody being immortal witches, I assumed Ambrose was forty with an awesome plastic surgeon. And I never thought about him that way."

He saw Harvey was in the midst of a terrible realization.

"So when you were talking about a cool witch guy, you meant…"

"Aw, I'm sorry, Harv," murmured Theo, while Harvey mouthed the name *Nick Scratch*.

"Well!" said Harvey. "Back to Billy!"

Theo snorted. "I'm not that hard up."

"When we get Nick back from hell, we can…go on triple dates. Me and Roz, you and Billy, Sabrina and Nick Scratch."

Harvey's face was that of a man anticipating being burned at the stake.

Theo slapped him on the arm. "You have only great ideas, Harv."

"Can't wait," said Harvey gloomily.

Theo murmured in a positive fashion, without actually agreeing to Harvey's loopy vision of the future.

"Everything going okay with you and Roz?"

Harvey hesitated. Theo's stomach swooped, dreading romantic catastrophe. "Roz wants me to…sing to her."

"Oh no," said Theo.

"If anyone's looking at me—my voice gets choked up in my throat."

"I know. Like the school play when you fainted."

"The school play when I *briefly* lost consciousness," muttered

Harvey. "The stage lights were hot. But Theo, I can't say that to Roz. I can't tell her I don't want her to look at me."

"Ooof," said Theo. "Sorry, bud. Don't know what to say. Hey, I won't tell you about crushing on people you hate anymore; we'll gossip like normal people. Let me show you a picture of my celebrity crush! He's in a Korean pop band."

He held out his phone for Harvey.

"His pink hair is awesome!" said Harvey, as expected. Harvey had seen a lady with a cool lavender mohawk at a festival this summer and talked about nothing else for weeks.

Theo thought about wanting to be with someone, or be like them, or even dress like them. Theo and Harvey dressed in approximately the same way, though Harvey had more nerd shirts than Theo. (Theo had some.) Flannel shirts, T-shirts beneath, and worn jeans: camouflage for guys trying to pass under the radar in Greendale. Theo'd always found comfort in dressing like Harvey. And Harvey dressed the way his dad did, the way his brother had, in the uniform of Greendale men. It'd never occurred to Theo before that Harvey, who loved art and all things avant-garde, might privately wish to wear rings or dye his hair.

"Do you wanna dress like Ambrose Spellman?" Theo asked.

"Maybe? I do think the way he dresses is cool and artistic. I definitely don't want to dress like a *Goth gigolo*." Harvey sounded revolted. "Learn what colors are, Nick, you monochrome jackass."

"If I dressed the way Ambrose does, with the velvet and the jewelry..." said Theo tactfully. "People would think it was girly."

"I'm sorry," Harvey told Theo at once. "You should dress however you want."

"Even if I wanna get a badass leather jacket and look like Nick Scratch?"

Harvey regarded Theo affectionately. "Get a badass leather jacket. You'd look way cooler than Nick."

"Thanks." Theo turned on the ignition.

He knew Harvey meant it, but Harvey thought anything Theo, Sabrina, or Roz did was brilliant and perfect. And Harvey would think so even if they wanted to dress up like giant chickens every day.

Theo had to work this out on his own. Still, he appreciated Harvey having his back. Theo's friends always did. Theo wanted to have theirs in return.

He kept remembering the time Roz collapsed screaming in class, and Theo had to get Harvey. Theo'd found Harvey in the boys' locker room.

Harvey ran, and Theo ran with him, but Theo didn't have the strength to carry Roz like Harvey did. Theo hadn't been able to help Roz. But Theo could help Sabrina.

"You know what?" Harvey said when they reached Harvey's house. "Keep the truck for today."

"So I can squish more demons beneath the wheels? Sweet."

Harvey didn't joke back. He sat there miserably quiet, until Theo gave him a hug. Harvey hugged back hard, hand curving protectively over Theo's growing-out hair.

"Be *safe*," Harvey begged in a fraught whisper.

Sometimes Theo noticed how worn and scared his best friend was, since the past cold winter. When magic got real, and Tommy died.

Theo drove home more carefully than he would've with Harvey in the truck, because Harvey was trusting him.

When he climbed out, a demon launched itself off the roof of the pickup. Theo leaped away and fired, and the demon crumbled to dust. The mark of the demon's claws still stung on his neck, beneath the collar of Theo's shirt, as he opened his front door.

Theo's dad was sitting at the kitchen table when Theo clattered in.

"Took one of the guns?"

"Um," said Theo.

"Out shooting cans with Harvey?" His dad's voice was mild. "Put it back."

"I will soon," promised Theo.

He edged closer to the table, trying to work out what he was seeing, even though it was simple enough. The table was piled high with flannel. His dad was sewing the buttons onto Theo's shirts.

"Noticed they were getting a little worn...son," Dad said.

"Oh, uh," said Theo. "Didn't realize you knew how to sew."

His dad gave Theo a look that reminded Theo of how Theo himself looked at his friends, loving but mocking too. "Who d'you think mends *my* shirts?"

Theo'd never really thought about it.

"Figured you made your hot secret mistress do it. Hey, remember when Sabrina and I were ten and tried to set you and her aunt Hilda up? You missed your chance."

"Hilda Spellman is a lovely lady," said Theo's dad, "but actually, her sister is more my style."

"Dad!"

"Fine-looking woman, Zelda Spellman." Dad kept peacefully stitching.

"Wow, Dad. I guess you live for danger." Theo took a seat at the table. "Speaking of dating... I'm interested in dating guys."

His dad was quiet for a while. Theo stared at his father's hands, work-scarred and growing more gnarled with age, plying the needle. His dad wasn't old, but farm work was hard on a body. Sometimes Theo was surprised, seeing his dad's hands. Thinking: *They got twisted somehow, when I wasn't looking.* Theo used to trot in his father's shadow from one side of the farm to the other. Theo was always small and his dad tall as a tower, but Theo wanted to be exactly like him.

"I remember when your uncle Jesse told our parents something similar," Dad remarked at last. "They weren't... real pleased."

"How about you, Dad?"

"You're your own person, Theo," said his dad. "You've always been that, thank God. But sometimes I think you're a chance for me to make up for a past I wish had gone differently. Some folks never get that chance. I'm lucky."

His dad had blue eyes like Theo, but paler and tired, as though time had washed the blue away. Even though his dad tried to be understanding, Theo kept thinking his dad's patience might get exhausted. Yet Theo couldn't stop pushing. If he had, he would've frozen in place, somewhere and someone he couldn't be.

Theo cleared his throat. "What do you say when people ask if you're ashamed of your... daughter?"

His dad said: "I tell them I'm real proud of my boy."

Theo leaned his cheek against his dad's shoulder while his dad kept painstakingly mending Theo's shirts. Then Theo said he had to see Sabrina. Before he went, Theo picked up the little sewing kit and put it in his pocket.

"He always pauses before he says son," said the bird on Theo's left shoulder.

"And he always says it," said Theo, and shut the door firmly. "C'mon, bird. You always tell the truth, but the truth isn't always lousy. You know that, right?"

After a moment, the bird cheeped assent.

Theo climbed into the pickup and drove through the night gathering among the trees.

"You love your father," said the bird. *"But you don't love this lost boy. Why go to all this effort?"*

Nick was a dreamboat, for one thing. More important, Theo now believed Nick was a decent guy. At first, he'd suspected Nick was a jerk.

The first time they actually hung out, Theo noted Nick watching Sabrina fondly in the diner as she ordered a milkshake. When it came to Sabrina, the guy was clearly Goth Harvey.

"Also a shaken milk for me," said Nick.

"Vanilla?" asked the waitress.

"Anything but."

Theo choked. Nick grinned. Then Nick caught Sabrina's eye and pointed to the jukebox, which magically started playing a song. That surprised a mischievous smile out of Sabrina.

Then Harvey came to the table, and everything got awkward.

Harvey called Nick *dude*. Nick smiled a sharply condescending smile, and called Harvey *Harry*.

"Nick," Sabrina scolded. "It's *Harvey*."

Theo eyed Nick coldly. If you were really into a girl, you didn't forget her ex's name. Nick was doing this to make Harvey feel small. Theo had no time for jerks.

On the day their gang rolled up to Sabrina's when the gates of hell were opening, Sabrina stepped forward and cried: "Harvey!"

Classic Sabrina, forever seeing him first.

Nick called: "Harry!"

Quit it, jerk, Theo thought. *Also, are Roz and I invisible?*

Theo was distracted when Sabrina explained about Satan coming to destroy them.

Then Theo saw Nick wince. "You're going to want to sit this one out, farm boy."

Harvey's eyes narrowed. "Yeah, I wasn't really talking to you, Nick!"

While Sabrina and Harvey made a truly, deeply Sabrina-and-Harvey scheme to blow up the gates of hell with dynamite, Nick visibly reconsidered his life choices.

Nick's gaze flicked from Harvey to Roz to Theo. He argued with Sabrina, though Theo could tell the guy hated doing it. "They're mortals..."

Nicholas, Theo wanted to tell him. *My guy. Trying to convince Harvey and Sabrina not to do stuff, that's baby vultures all the way down.*

Theo didn't plan on fighting his friends. He wanted to fight demons. The apocalypse was coming: It was time to empty the clip. But Theo liked Nick for his effort to shield them. From what Sabrina said, most witches were careless about mortal lives. Nick obviously cared.

In the truck, Theo said: "Does Nick Scratch think *you* live on a farm?"

Theo was the only farm boy around here.

"No," Harvey answered. "He just calls me *farm boy* sometimes."

"Uh, why?"

"Because he's *a jackass*," snarled Harvey, turning the wheel with a wrench.

Nick Scratch had a special joke name for Harvey but was pretending he'd forgotten Harvey's actual name. That made it such a weird and transparent pretense, Theo found Nick's behavior almost endearing. Nick wasn't doing this to make Harvey feel small: he was doing it because *he* felt small, for some reason Theo didn't understand. Okay, Theo decided, Nick Scratch wasn't a jerk. He'd just gone demented from romantic drama like everyone else. He was a big fake who must chill and introduce Theo to a hot magic guy.

Except Nick never got the chance. He was thrown in hell.

When Theo thought of hell, he remembered a blast of terrible heat and even more terrible light, when he thought the gates of hell would be flung wide. He'd run forward, trying to push them closed. Even getting that close had been too much.

Theo was driving more slowly.

"I like Nick," Theo told the bird who was questioning him. The other bird hadn't hassled him. Theo had no beef with the other bird. "And I love my friends."

"More than your father?"

Uncle Jesse was dead. Theo was all his dad had.

Sabrina'd explained to Roz and Theo that Satan had set up Nick and Sabrina without Sabrina's knowledge. Gross move on Satan's part, but Sabrina and Roz insisted it wasn't Nick's fault.

Nobody had explained the satanic setup to Harvey. When Harvey found out, there would be trouble. Theo didn't approve of what Nick had done himself.

"The boy stays in hell and makes up for what he did," suggested the bird. *"You stay with your father and find a love of your own."*

"What would my friends think of me?"

Up ahead, more winged demons gathered. He realized the whole road was blanketed with living darkness. Demons perched on the hood of the pickup. The arch of their wings blotted out the setting sun.

Theo revved the engine and drove into the cloud of demons. The demons shrieked. Theo drove with all the rage that made Theo fling himself at jerks in school, even though he knew he wouldn't win any fights. Theo had never run from a fight in his life.

"Left," said the bird on Theo's left shoulder.

Theo jerked the steering wheel left, hit another demon, and missed hitting a sleek black automobile.

The car halted. Zelda Spellman emerged, adjusting the tuft of lace on her jaunty hat, and shouted: *"Lux sit!"*

The demons around her burst into flame. Embers glowed in the air and burned out at her feet as Zelda walked over and rapped sharply on the truck window.

"Oh, hey, Miz S." Theo beamed at her innocently.

Zelda's eyes narrowed. "You haven't been—meddling with magic to change anything about yourself, have you?"

"I honestly haven't. I did think about it. When I didn't feel like me. But I don't know that changing myself would make me feel like me either. I'm okay as I am."

He'd imagined having a big muscular body would be great, and occasionally he still did, but—it was more complicated than that. He wanted to take his time, with his body and his mind, changing them when and if he felt it was right. They were *his*.

Zelda scrutinized him. At last, she nodded. "I'm glad to hear it."

"Sure. We have plenty going on without me summoning demons on the sly."

"It's not only that," Zelda told him. "I do occasionally listen when Sabrina talks about you mortals. One tries not to, but she has a piercing voice. I know you are harassed by lackwits groveling in their own ignorance for not fitting into the narrow boxes that are all their narrow minds can imagine."

Theo blinked. "You've got a real way with words."

"Two thousand years ago, people recognized six genders, but I suppose those imbecile children can't count to six. There are witches who want to fit people into narrow boxes as well." Zelda's mouth was a thin furious line for a moment. "A man recently tried to fit me into a box. Such a *pretty* little box, with flowers on it, placed a step behind him. A woman should be happy with such a box, he thought. No matter that I couldn't move in it. Never be confined by other people's expectations."

"What'd you do when the guy tried to shove you in a box?"

"When people have narrow minds..." mused Zelda. "The best thing to do is blast them wide open."

"Wow!" said Theo. "Did you explode his skull?"

Zelda gave Theo a startled glance. "I didn't. Though in the past, I have been known to—no matter. He believed he was made to lead, and I to follow, so I intend to be a greater leader than he could dream. You can be a better man than any who doubted you."

Theo considered Billy and his gang.

"You know, I really can."

Zelda nodded crisply. "Excellent. No summoning eldritch spirits, Theo, if you please. But excuse me, Hilda says I must visit a 'valued client' and apologize for 'making mock' of his 'bereavement.'"

It was something, the way Zelda Spellman could indicate finger quotes with a curl of her lip alone.

"By the way," Theo called out, "I wanna date guys!"

"Good for you," Zelda called back. "Personally, I'm thoroughly tired of men."

Zelda climbed into the back of her black car, and the car sped off. There was nobody at the wheel.

Genuinely, Theo wondered how it'd taken him so long to notice the Spellmans were witches.

Theo started the truck and made it almost to Sabrina's house when several demons hurtled right into his windshield. Theo jerked the wheel around and found himself tipping into a ditch. He immediately tried to back out. The wheels whirred, stuck in the soft earth. Theo jumped from the carriage and ran into the woods.

He texted Harvey as he went. *Drove ur truck off the road. Sorry!*

A demon flung itself at him. Theo dropped his phone, shot the demon, then blundered on.

Roz said she'd been in the woods after dark and had a vision. Theo was in the woods after dark, but he couldn't see anything. How was he meant to find some hidden cloak with the winged demons flying and falling around him? He couldn't. He was trapped in a storm of feathers.

Unless... Theo thought about Zelda Spellman, and Harvey, and his dad. Unless he wasn't trapped.

"A cloak of feathers," murmured the silver bird on Theo's left shoulder, who had been mean but then decided to help.

Everything Theo needed was right here.

Theo reached inside his flannel shirt for his sewing kit. The demons above him obscured the whole sky, but Theo kept his head down, intent as his dad. He collected jagged black demon feathers, and in every handful of darkness he found a few silver ones, delicate as lace and bright as the moon behind the clouds. Theo had to use every bit of thread from his kit, but the thread didn't break. The thread should've run out, the whole idea shouldn't have worked, but Theo kept stitching the different pieces together anyway. Feathers rained down in a cascade of mingled shadow and moonshine. The crisscrossing threads formed a rainbow tangle. The bird on Theo's left shoulder sang.

When Theo finally looked up from his stitching, there was a ring of the Lady's birds, flying in a protective circle over his head.

Feathers spilled from the sky like black snow. As Theo watched, the feathers formed shapes. A tower, and a boy. Theo thought he knew who the boy might be.

Before Theo could say Nick's name, the shapes disintegrated. The feathers blew away in a gust of wind that sent the Lady's silver birds tumbling. Demons launched themselves, shrieking, at Theo's head.

Theo snapped out the cloak of feathers, and the dark-and-bright garment turned pure dazzling silver. Like a stretch of water, transformed by something as simple as light.

He ran for Sabrina's house, toward the gables and the graves. The demons followed hard on his heels. And Theo saw Sabrina erupt from her front door, like a bullet out of a gun. White hair flung back from her grim face, hands uplifted, racing to Theo's aid.

Theo threw the cloak of feathers over his shoulders. He hurdled the fence between them and the gravestones in the Spellmans' yard, and found himself soaring, feathers catching a drift of wind and bearing him across. Theo fetched up on one knee, laying the cloak at Sabrina's feet as though Sabrina would walk across its silvery surface.

Sabrina seized the cloak in one hand and the back of Theo's flannel shirt in the other, drawing him to her in a tight hug.

"You did it," she whispered.

He'd done it. All on his own.

"No problem." Theo paused. "There were a few problems."

Sabrina held on to him fast. "Was it awful? Were you scared?"

While Roz was the best person Theo knew, and Harvey was Theo's best friend, Sabrina was Theo's partner in crime. Whenever Hilda and Theo's dad arranged a playdate for just the two of them, Theo and Sabrina would get up to so much mischief.

Theo didn't know why he'd been thinking of courage as a guy thing when Sabrina was the most fearless person he knew.

"Sabrina? Do you ever…doubt yourself? Like, is there a little voice in your head telling you that you shouldn't do something?"

"Yes," Sabrina whispered.

"Even for you, huh?"

Sabrina's mouth caught between a frown and a grin. "Even for me. I just don't listen to the little voice. Ever."

Theo reviewed their whole lives in his mind. "That makes sense."

Sabrina's voice went low. "I don't want anything to stop me. Especially now."

Theo nudged her. "I get it."

He'd always found Sabrina easy to understand. They grinned at each other, sitting shoulder to shoulder on the same gravestone, with the cloak of feathers held in both their hands.

"I worry all the time," Sabrina confided. "About whose daughter I am, what my family think of me, and—I want you guys with me but I don't want you to be in danger. Was it wrong to ask you to help?"

"Nah. It's a barn raising."

"A what?"

"It's a farming term, creepy funeral-home girl," said Theo. Sabrina grinned and kicked him in the ankle. "A whole community gets together to build a barn. One person can't do it on their own. They shouldn't feel like they have to."

Sabrina nodded thoughtfully. Their quiet in the moonlight was interrupted by Harvey, running up the curved path with his gun slung over his shoulder.

"Harvey!" Sabrina called out, as always.

Wow, his friends were an embarrassment. Sabrina and Harvey were genuinely terrible at not being in love with each other. They'd had no practice at it. Theo spoke quickly, before Harvey or Sabrina could say something dramatic.

"My man, just in time. I decided to help make clothes for the Academy students. Sketch me some ideas."

Harvey's expression softened from grim witch-hunter to dreamy artist. Sabrina grasped one of Harvey's sleeves and one of Theo's, towing them into her house.

Sabrina was a shrimp like Theo, and addicted to hair bands, but she wanted to protect everybody. It wasn't about being manly. It was just everybody being who they were. Nobody fit in boxes.

Theo acquired some old curtains and settled cross-legged in front of the fire, while Harvey leaned against him and drew sketches of a dress for Elspeth.

"I was thinking, if you do manage to sing with other people watching, what if we formed a band? Wouldn't that be cool?"

"*So* cool."

"Speaking of cool, I completed my quest," said Theo. "Gimme a high five for being a badass."

Harvey obliged. "You're always a badass."

Theo beamed. "You think so?"

"Everybody does." Harvey turned at the sound of the door opening and lit up. "Roz, who's the bravest guy we know?"

"Theo, of course," Roz answered promptly, stepping into the room. She looked much more cheerful after hanging with cheerleaders. "I remember how great you were when I collapsed in class," Roz added.

Theo blinked. "Was I?"

"You stormed right into the guys' locker rooms to get Harvey, in spite of how horrible they'd been to you!"

Harvey was nodding. "Then you ran forward and barred the gates to hell. You're . . . a more specific word than brave. Dauntless. You won't *let* yourself be daunted. That's you, Theo. I learn how to be the kind of guy I wanna be from you every day."

Theo regarded Harvey with dismay. Their tender flower already made a daily spectacle of himself over romance. Bromantic scenes weren't allowed.

"Too far, Harv."

Theo smacked Harvey on the back of his head. Harvey grinned down at Theo, and Theo loved the dude a lot. So it was whatever.

"What are you talking about?" Sabrina asked from the door.

"Theo being great," Harvey and Roz chorused.

Sabrina draped herself over Theo's shoulders, then enchanted the curtains, her spellwork combining with his stitching. Sabrina's aunt Hilda poked her head in to ask what they were up to.

Sabrina answered, arms around Theo's neck: "It's a barn raising."

Theo'd done what he wanted to do, and discovered he had nothing to prove. He sat in a circle with his friends, talking and laughing, well-known and well-loved and not one of them belonging in any box.

Maybe someone brand-new and exciting would come along

and take a shine to Theo, exactly as Theo was now, like Nick had to Sabrina. Theo could wait happily enough. Theo loved his life right now, loved the truth of it. He wanted to keep it.

Theo wished to be ride-or-die for his friends, but... he didn't want to actually die. He wanted to live in the light.

He didn't want to go down into hell.

ON THE ROAD

THE MARK OF THE LOVING HEART ... —DANTE

Ambrose spun down the Rue Crémieux at the golden hour of evening, the last and warmest sunshine splashing on each of the vibrantly colored houses in turn. Walking down this narrow cobbled street was like dancing along a string of colored glass beads, light infusing each color with brilliance so the beads transformed into a ruby, an emerald, a topaz, or a pink pearl.

The entrance of one house boasted a painting of a cat stalking birds, which made Ambrose imagine a hunting lioness. He cast a look over his shoulder at Prudence, ravishing in a black Audrey Hepburn–style dress and ornate earrings in the shape of guillotines.

Trompe l'oeil, he told her. "It means 'deceives the eye.' Art that uses perspective cleverly enough to give an illusion of reality. You almost expect the cat to move."

Prudence murmured under her breath. For a moment Ambrose believed she was admiring the sight.

Then the artistic illusion of the cat leaped up and consumed a fluttering bird in one bite. A spray of red paint on the cat's whiskers was all that remained.

Prudence stalked away down the street.

Ambrose was beginning to get the feeling Prudence might be annoyed with him.

"Prudence, can I make something clear about our last night in Florence?"

Prudence was adjusting her black lace gloves and didn't spare him a look. "I have something to say about that night as well." She spoke with perfect sangfroid. Prudence already had an air of belonging in Paris, as though her arch loveliness granted her automatic citizenship. "Thank you."

There wasn't much gratitude in her tone.

"Ah, yes, you're welcome." Ambrose directed a quizzical look at a lamppost. "For...?"

"As a daughter of the Church of Night, I do disport with dark carnality, ruin men for anyone else, cause them to die wasting away with longing for another glance from my brilliant eyes, and so on." Prudence waved her gloved hand. "You know, the usual."

"I do know the usual," said Ambrose. "I thank all the tiny imps in hell for dark carnality."

"This isn't the time for it." Prudence spoke with finality on carnality. "What was that absurd poem you were reciting?"

Ambrose brightened. "You'd like to hear the poem again?"

"I wouldn't," Prudence declared. "*'The lioness, you may move her, to give o'er her prey.'* Nothing moves me. I must dedicate myself, body and soul, to my revenge mission."

"Would it be inappropriate to say that's very hot?" Ambrose asked.

Prudence sighed, exasperated, in the direction of Versailles. "I don't wish to be distracted by irrelevant nonsense. You may be a romantic fool, but I'm not. Frankly, given your lurid family history, I'm concerned you might become fond of me. I can't imagine anything more inconvenient or unwelcome."

She shook her head with the expression of a woman who wished to hold her nose but was trying to conceal her distaste.

Ambrose murmured: "Wouldn't want that."

He was dispirited for the length of several streets. Then he reminded himself that the idea of softer feelings must be strange and new to Prudence. Still, they were in the City of Lights. Paris might open her eyes to new possibilities.

The Marche d'Ailleurs meant the Market Besides, magical stalls existing side by side with the markets of mortals. Hung about with illusion, this market wove around the other markets like a crimson silk thread through white wool. There were goblin fruits of pearl and scarlet on golden dishes, nestled among stalls of humble mortal tomatoes and carrots. Skirting around a Frenchwoman with a woven straw bag went a shadow with a long rat's tail. An unwary mortal might stumble across these wares and buy dancing shoes to make them dance a thousand years.

"No need for such a lovely lady as yourself to come buy,"

whispered a man with a cat's face and hairy human hands. "Try a bite. The nectar of this fruit is more luscious than wine."

"I really wouldn't, Prudence," Ambrose warned.

Prudence selected a golden fruit and took an enormous bite. Nectar gushed down her chin.

"The goblins' fruit removes inhibitions," Ambrose said anxiously.

"So it does, *ma belle*." The goblin fastened a hand around Prudence's wrist. "Is your head whirling? Is your blood racing? It grows dangerous in these streets so quickly."

Prudence unsheathed her swords. An instant later the goblin's cat-faced head, removed from his shoulders, was rolling among the cabbages in a nearby stall striped with white and green. The mortals screamed.

"Very dangerous," murmured Prudence.

Between a stall selling round white cheeses and another selling truffles, Ambrose saw purple and pink blossoms waving. Clary sage, for clear sight.

"Adore your enthusiasm for decapitation, but I think we've found Urbain Grandier."

Prudence cast the goblin fruit aside and strolled through the curtain of flowers. The cloying, bewildering scent of the blossoms surrounded them until the petals fell from Ambrose's sight and they stood in a wine cellar with stone walls. Almost a cave, if not for bustling Paris without and the dusty wine bottles within.

A thin-faced, dark-haired warlock in a white tunic was lolling in a golden chair, apparently asleep. Ambrose coughed.

"Ambrose Spellman and Prudence Blackwood." The warlock

Grandier didn't open his eyes. "Come to my city on a mission of revenge. This market offers every treat, including dishes best served cold. You two are the most attractive guests I have received in many a year."

"I get that all the time," said Ambrose.

Prudence advanced, her sword at the ready, blade slick with goblin blood. "You can't even see us."

Urbain Grandier's eyes snapped open. They were black, with whirling stars in their depths.

"My dear. I'm a Grandier, the blood of oracles. We saw the light of witch burnings a century before they happened. I saw you coming."

Quick as lightning in a little black dress, Prudence laid her sword against his throat.

"Have you seen my father?"

Urbain Grandier arched an eyebrow. "Like me, he saw you coming. He put himself outside time and space to hide from you, child. Time's never on your side, is it? Time's never on anyone's side."

"He couldn't enchant time on his own," Prudence spat. "Who's helping him?"

"Clever as she is beautiful, isn't she?" Urbain asked Ambrose.

"That's how I like them," said Ambrose. "Clever, beautiful, and bloodthirsty. They named her Prudence, not Patience, so I urge you not to be enigmatic. Blackwood kept in touch with several of his past pupils. Which one is it?"

Urbain righted his chair. "You're no slouch yourself, are you?"

Ambrose grinned. "Clever as the devil, and five times as pretty."

"Funny you should mention the devil," said Urbain. "You and

your family will have the devil to pay soon enough. First, I'll want payment myself."

Prudence purred: "Does sparing your life count?"

"Forgive Prudence," said Ambrose. "She ate goblin fruit recently. She'd normally wait, oh, a good five minutes before threatening to cut your throat. What's your price?"

"An oracle gets so lonely, waiting in his cave, just him and the truth. I've been looking forward to a delightful hour with an alluring companion."

Ah, Paris. Ambrose leaned against Prudence and smiled. "Which of us?"

"You," said Grandier. "She's a little terrifying with her swords."

"Isn't she, though," murmured Ambrose, proud.

He winked at Grandier, then turned to give Prudence a kiss. Prudence's mouth was unyielding under his, but she allowed the display to show Ambrose had a partner he intended to return to.

They'd agreed to pass themselves off as a young magic couple romancing and ensorceling their way across the world. It wasn't true. Not yet. But Ambrose could hope. Unlike most things, hope was free.

"Amuse yourself at the market, my little cabbage," said Ambrose. "I'll be ..."

"A rather exciting forty-six minutes," supplied Urbain Grandier.

"Forty-six minutes. Go buy me some sparkly jewelry. Think of me while we're apart."

"I most certainly will not."

Prudence disappeared through the curtain of flowers. Ambrose turned back to Grandier with a lazy shrug.

"*L'amour*," he remarked. "*La belle dame,* totally *sans merci.* What can you do? Anyway, carnal delights in exchange for information? Or were you simply hoping to get the less dangerous one alone so you could kill me, because you're actually in Blackwood's pay?"

Urbain Grandier blinked. Ambrose had moved quickly.

"Here's the thing," Ambrose continued. "I also have a sword? My aunties had me anoint the hilt with red verbena to hide it from those with foresight. They're strict about these little precautions because they love me."

He gave Grandier another saucy wink. Grandier swallowed, throat moving against the blade he hadn't seen coming.

"Being less dangerous than Prudence means I'm still pretty dangerous," Ambrose informed him. "We could've had a nice afternoon! But no, everything has to be dark treachery. It leaves so little time for dark delights. Information, please."

Seeing the future taught you to be philosophical.

"Mercy," drawled Grandier, lifting his hands in surrender, and gave Ambrose the information.

"*Merci* to you as well," said Ambrose, and headed off to find Prudence.

She was easily described to the denizens of the Marche d'Ailleurs. Even in Paris, very few were like Prudence. Ambrose made his way deeper into the market, past pied pipers piping and a large aquarium in which seven mermaids were milking a sea cow. The milk-mermaids wore cute seaweed aprons.

There was a stall called Icarus's Emporium, draped with long golden feathers instead of ribbons. Ambrose selected a mauve quill made from a phoenix feather with a corona of flame at the feather's tip. He dipped the quill into shimmering purple ink and wrote, on the inside of his own arm, a brief, pointless message for his cousin.

Witches could write to each other with enchanted implements. He'd taught Sabrina the spell before he left. Perhaps it was a foolish impulse to reach out to her.

He'd be a fool, then. It wouldn't be the first time.

Beside the feather emporium and across from the milk-mermaid aquarium, Ambrose saw a stall with a shimmering canopy made from the pink mist of youthful fantasies and glittering with the sparkling jewels of tears. This was a seller of dreams.

Surely Prudence wouldn't go anywhere *near* such a place. Yet Ambrose found himself drawing closer. The purple ribbons in the entryway stroked his arms as he passed, and he heard Prudence's unmistakable voice.

"Dreams are for children. I only care about vengeance!" Prudence declared.

"That's nice," said the witch. "Did you want to buy a love potion? Dreams of love are the most popular. A knot of nine to make his heart thine, an enchanted bee to set your name buzzing in his ear? Can't go wrong with a standard love philter."

Prudence was silent. Ambrose was about to tell Prudence if she did want a love philter, his auntie Hilda was a dab hand with them.

Only then an idea struck, falling into Ambrose's mind naturally as an apple of knowledge into a witch's hand. He'd sulked to Aunt Hilda that he liked Luke, and Luke didn't want a second date.

Oh, you didn't, Auntie Hilda. Did you?

To make her boy happy, she might. It all fit. Luke's sudden ardent attention, when he'd disappeared after their first date. The way Luke, focused on tracking down evil witch-hunters and being Father Blackwood's perfect pupil, readily became entangled with a warlock criminal. Ambrose's heart sank, remembering. Luke was right to fear witch-hunters. They'd killed him. He'd followed Father Blackwood, thinking that would keep him safe, and he'd loved Ambrose, thinking love was real. The poor boy had died under a delusion. Ambrose had *known* something was off.

He'd wanted to believe he could be loved. As if he were so irresistible. As if he might win over even Prudence.

Ambrose smiled bitterly, and toyed with a curling ribbon. He didn't need to buy dreams here. He'd always had too many.

"I have a secret." Prudence's voice was slightly slurred.

"You've been at the goblin fruit, haven't you?" asked the seller of dreams.

"It's a humiliating, obscene secret. It makes me burn with shame to think of it."

"Oh well," murmured the seller. "Go on."

"I have a charnel pit where a heart should be," said Prudence. "Nothing soft survives between the cold stone walls of the Academy. I could never love anyone."

"But?" supplied the seller of dreams.

"I liked a boy, once," said Prudence. "He didn't...really notice me."

Silence followed. The ribbons curved around Ambrose like leaves furling with the evening.

"With a face like yours, dear heart, I find that hard to believe."

"Oh, we indulged in many lustful activities, obviously," said Prudence. "But I wasn't... *special* to him. And—oh, I sicken myself!—I did want to be. He was different from anyone I'd ever met. *Trust no man. Every man is out for himself.* I learned those lessons by heart. I taught them to my sisters. But he proved everything I knew wrong. He sacrificed himself for us."

Ambrose drew in a deep breath as he understood.

"I don't understand how such a revolting thing happened to me. What more could a girl want than dark delights and even darker desires? Only I wanted..."

"What did you want?" The dream seller's voice was intent, scenting the possibility of a sale.

"I wanted him to *smile* at me." Prudence sounded despairing. "Why would I want something like that? A smile's pointless. Only he walked through the dark halls of the Academy, and his smile let in more light than a window. I never imagined anybody having a smile like that. I never dreamed of someone on the Path of Night walking in so much light."

"Ah," said the seller of dreams. "So you want a love potion for this charmer."

"I want," Prudence snapped, "to stop being a fool. There's someone I must hunt down."

"This smiling man?"

"Someone very different," said Prudence. "One is the best kind of man, and the other the worst. The man I'm hunting is wretched and twisted, and I will drink every drop of his dark blood and spit it out. I must make him pay for what he did to me and mine. I can't afford to be distracted! I *must* save my little brother and sister."

There was a clink, glass on metal, of potion bottles and shifting stoppers. Ambrose moved forward, away from the clinging ribbons, to her side.

Prudence's head was in her hands. "He has Judas and Leticia. I don't know what he's doing to them."

"Aha," said the seller of dreams. "So what you need is—"

Ambrose coughed to cut off the sales pitch. Prudence's spine went sword-straight, dark eyes blasting startled disdain upon him.

"That certainly wasn't forty-six minutes!"

"He had a case of premature expectation—the expectation being that I was an easy mark. So I got the name and a location out of him at swordpoint. Shall we go?"

The seller of dreams looked miffed to be balked of her sale. Ambrose gave her a charming grin as he escorted Prudence outside and away from the Marche d'Ailleurs.

"Your father went to school with, and recently paid a large sum of money to, Nicolas Frochot," Ambrose told Prudence, "who lives in the Paris catacombs, where anything can be hidden behind the walls of the dead. Father Blackwood may be with Frochot yet."

Prudence lifted her chin, a huntress catching the scent of her prey at last. Her loping stride lengthened.

Ambrose kept up, staying by her side so close their hands brushed. When they did, Prudence glared venomously and yanked her hand away.

Ambrose and Prudence made their way to the catacombs through the Parc Montsouris, past ivy-draped houses and fervently blooming rosebushes in an enchanted square. Petals tumbled through the air as though there were always a parade in this twisting cobblestone lane. Rich perfume made his senses reel.

He felt he'd made many discoveries in the market.

He'd believed Prudence only cared for her sisters and thought it beautiful she could love them after the Church of Night had tried to crush the heart out of her. Once again, he'd failed to see all of her.

There was room in Prudence's heart for a boy.

Someone at the Academy. Someone she'd been intimate with. Someone who'd *sacrificed himself.* The answer was obvious.

Prudence had cared about Nick Scratch. Longed for him, desperately wanted him to smile for her. And Nick cast Prudence off. He chose Sabrina.

No wonder Prudence didn't even want to hold Ambrose's hand. She'd been thrown aside by the only boy she'd ever wanted, then viciously betrayed by her father. Ambrose was surprised she'd let him come with her on this quest. She must be sick of men.

"Prudence," Ambrose said as they moved from the roses and toward the dead. "I know how scared you are for Judas and Leticia."

Prudence eyed him in disbelief. "Fear's not a feeling I'm familiar with. And I don't intend to get acquainted."

"If it was Sabrina," Ambrose persisted, "I'd be sick with terror."

Prudence's lip curled. "No doubt. You Spellmans indulge in all sorts of pointless emotions."

"That's us." Ambrose smiled.

Prudence turned her face away, toward the shadowy entrance of the catacombs.

"I only want you to know, I won't rest until you have your brother and sister back," Ambrose promised. "You don't have to trust me. But you *can* trust me. I won't leave your side or break my word. I'm with you until the end."

He paused before stepping into the shadows with her.

"Coming?" Prudence asked. "I don't care if you're with me. I only care if you delay me."

They descended the spiral staircase into the ossuary together.

Above the door, in French, was graven the words STOP. THIS IS THE EMPIRE OF THE DEAD.

Centuries ago, the cemeteries of this city had teemed with bodies. Floods sent corpses erupting from their graves and into the streets. Millions of long-dead Parisians were dug up from their graves and their bones thrown in the quarries beneath the city. The warlock Nicolas Frochot seized his chance to have the bones arranged in mystically significant patterns and built himself a charming magic-infused home in the depths of this empire of death.

Fragmented skeletons were the walls of these chambers, their skulls the wainscoting. Ambrose and Prudence passed down several galleries lined with bones. Where light struck, the walls of bones were deep somber yellow. All the rest was dark as the shadows in a skull's eye sockets. In one wall there were skulls set in the pattern of a heart. Ambrose was about to point out this romantic sight, but it might make Prudence think of Nick Scratch in hell.

Poor brave Prudence, and the broken heart she'd been hiding.

Ambrose had never particularly noticed Nick Scratch's smile, which Prudence was so enthusiastic about. He guessed Nick's smile was fine. Seemed a little fake to Ambrose, but he hadn't taken much note of the details of Nick until the end. When Prudence showed up in Ambrose's room with her friends, Ambrose thought: *Some guy. He's hot! Good for him!* Then he'd seen the way Nick scrambled up to greet Sabrina, nervous in a way Nick wasn't in a tangle of the Weird Sisters.

Ambrose realized, *Oh, that's for Sabrina, then*, and hid a smile. Ambrose loved Sabrina to have nice things. He fully supported Nick persuading Sabrina to follow the Path of Night, where Ambrose hoped Sabrina would be immortal and powerful and happy. The way Nick looked when Sabrina came down the stairs of Ambrose's home in a beautiful bloodred dress... that wasn't fake.

But Ambrose didn't like to think of anyone hurting Prudence.

He recalled Prudence's uncharacteristically soft voice, describing Nick. He wondered what it would be like, to see Prudence smitten.

Prudence ran her fingernails over a vast circular pillar made of tibia and skulls, her spell summoning dark things out of hiding. *"My power came from the Morningstar. So come out, come out, wherever you are..."*

Ambrose joined his power to hers, making sure they didn't touch but their shadows did.

The skulls whirled in the walls, empty eyes pointing the way through the labyrinth. The problem with mystical configurations was that any witch could use them.

They saw the flicker of a robe, no more than the edge of a fleeing shadow. Prudence gave chase with a bloodthirsty howl. Ambrose listened to the echoing footsteps and worked out what direction they were headed.

He teleported to the shadows beside the Fountain of Lethe, where ghostly fish swam through silver waters. When Nicolas Frochot ran past, Ambrose tripped him up.

Prudence threw herself on the man, straddling him. Ambrose didn't see why evildoers got so lucky.

Nicolas Frochot was pale with the soft, disturbing pallor of a creature who never saw the sun. After centuries in the dark, his eyes were almost gone, tiny dots of darkness gleaming in eye sockets veiled with flesh. He wriggled beneath Prudence like a bug found under a rock.

"Faustus Blackwood!" Prudence snarled. "Where is that coven-murdering traitor, and what did you help him do?"

"He…bought some of my bones, to use for a spell to tear a hole through time and space," Frochot stammered. "He went to New Orleans, to buy the last ingredient he needed. P-please, I didn't know anything about him harming his coven, I just wanted the blood—"

"*What blood?*" Prudence demanded.

Frochot's sluglike tongue touched his lips. "The best spells are made from blood and bone. It gets so dry here down among my bones, but Faustus had two children with him. He let me have some of the girl child's blood. Not the boy's, since he's worth more…"

Prudence brought her sword down in a killing arc.

"Prudence, *no!*" Ambrose shouted, but she'd already buried her blade in Frochot's chest to the hilt.

"I hope my sister's blood was worth *this*," she snarled.

The bones around the fountain opened up, an earthquake of corpses creating a chasm to swallow them.

Ambrose and Prudence tumbled fathoms down, onto broken bones. Ambrose rolled on his back to see where they'd landed. In the darkness he made out towering walls and, far too high above them, a circle of faint ghostly light. This was a charnel pit, the walls skulls, the floor made of bones shattered so many times they seemed coarse sand.

"Frochot used the catacombs to power protection spells," Ambrose said breathlessly. "That's why he never left the shelter provided by his bones. He believed nobody would dare kill him down here."

Prudence sat up, her little black dress covered in white bone dust.

"You might have mentioned that before!"

"I didn't think you were going to murder him within three minutes," said Ambrose. "In retrospect, that was foolish of me."

He cast a spell to levitate them. There was no result. Prudence's eyes narrowed, and she cast a different spell to blast them out. The quiet of the catacombs was their only answer.

There was a reason nobody had slain the warlock of the catacombs before.

In this pit of bones, their magic didn't work. They exchanged a look as that sank in.

"Who lurks in underground cities populated only by the dead

and builds booby traps?" Ambrose demanded. "Prudence, people don't trust one another anymore. It's shocking."

For a time, Prudence didn't answer. When she spoke, her voice was very calm. "You don't have to keep making light of the situation."

Ambrose shrugged. "It's my way."

"I know that," said Prudence. "But I killed Frochot. I left you with the oracle at the market. I've made too many mistakes. I deserve whatever punishment you wish to inflict upon me."

It took him a moment, in the quiet, to absorb the full impact of what she'd said. Ambrose was really looking forward to hunting down Faustus Blackwood.

"Your own father tried to kill our coven and abducted your baby brother and sister," he said. "You're frantic with worry, and furious with him. If you make a few mistakes, I understand."

"I told you before," Prudence hissed. "I do not. Have. Feelings!"

"Come on, Prudence. Yes, you do. I heard what you said to the seller of dreams. About the boy you liked."

A different silence followed this statement. It was a trembling silence, as if Ambrose had plucked too carelessly at a string on a musical instrument. Now they waited in the hush following a discordant note to see if the string might break.

"Did you," Prudence said at last.

"Maybe," Ambrose suggested gently, "your feelings wouldn't get in your way as much if you acknowledge you have them. That's how it worked for me. You don't need to limit yourself. You don't need any limits at all. You're allowed to hate your awful father. You're allowed to fancy a boy. If I'd known how you felt—"

"I don't need your *pity*," Prudence spat.

"—how you felt about him, I would never have mentioned Nick Scratch."

"*Nick Scratch!*" exclaimed Prudence, as though the name was wrenched out of her.

Ambrose nodded. "It must be hard for you to know he went to hell for someone else when you feel about him the way you do."

"Feel the way I do," Prudence repeated, voice hollow as a skull's eye socket. "About Nick Scratch."

"Someone from the Academy who sacrificed himself," said Ambrose. "Who else could it be?"

"You have discovered my secret," said Prudence. "I was enamored of Nicholas Scratch. I enjoyed the way he ditched me and my sisters for Sabrina. Not to mention, his deeply attractive and not at all obsessive interest in mortal trivia. How he kept piles of books around his bed and I would almost break my neck tripping over them. How Nicky insisted on giving five-hour presentations in one-hour classes. Also, his occasionally terrible hair."

"When you lose someone, you miss even the little things about them," Ambrose murmured sympathetically.

"Yes," Prudence said. "I miss. All that."

Her voice was very flat. Ambrose supposed admitting these feelings was difficult.

"Especially the whining about sexy illusion spells," Prudence added.

"Whatever you're into," said Ambrose doubtfully. "Why didn't Nick like illusion spells? They're so sexy."

"I know, right?" Prudence demanded. "What a whiner. Who I had romantic feelings for. Sweet lady Medusa, I cannot wait for my epitaph. It will read 'She Died in a Pit in Paris, Never Got the Bloody Revenge She Deserved, and Was Accused of Having Feelings.' I expect you sorely regret coming with me."

Prudence was braver than Ambrose in the end, because she was the one who admitted what could happen.

They might die in this maze of bones, far from home. His aunts and Sabrina would never know what had happened to him. Ambrose was suddenly glad he'd sent his silly message to Sabrina. He wanted Sabrina to know.

Ambrose reached out a hand, feeling blindly among the bones until he found Prudence's. There was something else he wanted. He didn't want Prudence to be alone.

"I'm glad I came. I said 'with you until the end.' I know you had no reason to believe me, but I meant it."

She sighed and leaned her head against his shoulder. Perhaps it was easier for her to do in the dark.

Softly, as though it was the most shameful confession she could imagine, Prudence whispered: "I believed you."

GREENDALE

I watched Dorcas spinning around the kitchen in curtains Theo'd made into clothes. I didn't think any of the witches had thanked Theo.

I didn't know how to thank Theo enough. He'd driven Harvey's truck off the road to avoid demons. He or Roz could've been killed.

Theo and Roz had left together, Roz conferring with Theo in a low voice I wasn't meant to hear.

They were safe now, I told myself.

"Now it's Harvey's turn," whispered the silver bird with the blue eyes.

Harvey had stayed with me to go through the books on hell I'd collected from the library at the Academy of Unseen Arts. I wondered if he was scared.

"'Brina." Harvey's voice was low as he leaned across the table. "Are you all right?"

I was scared.

I remembered the day the mines collapsed, when I felt helpless as any mortal, terrified Harvey had been killed. I'd hurled myself at him, my whole soul a prayer in his arms. *Thank you, thank you, thank you.* In that moment, his life was all I wanted.

"But you're greedy," chirped another of my silver birds, perched on a chair.

"I'm all right!" I told Harvey.

I glared at the bird, then realized Dorcas thought I was glaring at her. She sniffed and stalked off.

"Should I eat these birds?" Salem proposed, sitting on a book with his tail curled around his paws. He saw everything I saw.

"No, Salem, they're for our quest! Aren't you worried about Nick?"

"When I'm worried, I eat," Salem claimed.

I shook my head. Salem turned his back on me and nudged Harvey's hand with a meow.

"Pick me up and walk around the house, mortal. I will sit upon your shoulder and survey the lesser beings like a king!"

Harvey stroked Salem absently, worried eyes on me. "You sure you're all right? 'Brina, you look—"

I laughed. "Terrible?"

"Like you hardly ever sleep."

I had to work out configurations to open the gates of hell. I had to accomplish this quest. I couldn't rest while Nick was suffering. I couldn't stand to lie down and listen to my thoughts.

"You're guilty," chorused the birds. *"Greedy. Guilty."*

I pitched my voice low. "Worry about yourself, Harvey. You're next."

I thought of Roz shaking against me, of Theo fleeing from demons. The worst shadow of danger was on Harvey now. I wanted to call off the whole quest.

That would be abandoning Nick. How could I, when I'd let Roz and Theo suffer? What would Harvey think if I said: I can't bear it, if it's you?

"That you're still in love with him," said the bird. *"Your best friend's boyfriend."*

I wasn't. I was in love with Nick, and I needed to get him back.

"I'm happy," said Harvey, "to help. That was the worst thing for me, Sabrina, when you seemed so far away. You never told me what was going on. I know you thought I was useless, compared to—"

"Harvey, no!" I exclaimed.

"Harvey, yes. Like the time you and Nick shoved me out of your witch school—"

"We wanted to protect you! We couldn't let the other witches see you."

Harvey rolled his eyes. "No more garbage about protecting me. I'm a witch-hunter who broke into their desecrated church, right in front of the coven. Pretty sure the witches *already noticed me.*"

"We did." Elspeth whisked in to fetch herself a snack. "Everybody in the Academy was talking about it."

"You and Nick could've just said you wanted to be alone," said Harvey.

It never occurred to me he'd see it that way. I truly had wanted Harvey out of danger. I hadn't wanted him to go at all. When I kissed his cheek and thanked Harvey for always being there to catch me, I wished I could cling to him.

But I couldn't. Not then, and not now. I'd made out on my bed with Nick that night, Nick whispering that he wanted to be the one to catch me. It would feel disloyal to correct Harvey.

He was shaking his head. "All I meant was, it's great to have the Fright Club. I want to be useful." He sighed. "Even if it means reading books about hell. They're messed up. Mind you, so's the Bible."

I pursed my lips. "Since when have you read the Bible?"

"Since last month when Nick sneered at me for not having read the Bible. It's got some nice stuff, but 'Brina, I have several issues—"

"When Nick did what?"

Harvey sighed. "Sorry, when Nick tried, in his friendly and sympathetic way, to protect me ... from being ill-read—"

I seized a book titled *The Next Person You Meet in Hell.* "You don't understand Nick."

"He can't," sang out a silver bird. *"Harvey's honest. Nick's a liar."*

I murmured an excuse and ran upstairs. I looked in my chest of drawers at the jewel and the cloak my friends had brought me. Then I drew the sketch of Nick from under my pillow and smiled.

I'd been so miserable about Harvey and the heartbreaking mess with his brother. I believed being in love meant doing anything for each other, but Harvey couldn't forgive me. Then Nick rushed to make me laugh. Nick understood about being a witch. It was such a relief to be happy, to dance away from my problems on the Path of Night with the ideal partner.

Nick did everything I asked. I thought, *this must be love.*

Once, kissing on this bed, I'd whispered to him: "I wish our first kiss hadn't been during a school play. I wish it'd been real."

Nick's eyes were hooded as he whispered back: "I'm just glad we kissed, Spellman."

"He was acting on your father's orders," said the bird perched on my wrought-iron bedstead. *"None of his kisses were real."*

I stopped smiling. Nick had disobeyed Father Blackwood for me, been an ally before he was anything else. I'd trusted him, but the whole time Nick was serving a higher authority than Father Blackwood. My father, the Father of Lies.

Some ally.

"No," I whispered. "It doesn't matter. Enough was real."

Theo said the birds helped him when he told the truth. But the birds seemed like my enemies.

"Because your father is the Prince of Lies," said the bird. *"And you are the Princess of Lies. You and your boyfriend have a lot in common."*

My gaze dropped to the drawing of Nick on my pillow. We'd lain twined together on this bed, his kisses long and deep and hot, and I'd thought, *maybe—*

I'd almost slept with Nick. I could've trusted him that way, when he was a spy for Satan.

"Oh, but it doesn't matter," sang the bird mockingly.

Then a demon loomed from behind my chest of drawers, where the quest objects were hidden. The demon was a shadow, as Roz had described, but with ridged wings like Theo'd said.

"Attack is vain, be cleaved in twain!" I shouted, and watched the demon slice slowly in half, as though I'd ripped a piece of paper apart.

I stood breathing hard, then watched as both halves of the winged shadow twitched horribly, rose, and lunged.

I picked up my lamp and threw it. One half of the demon hurdled my bed, and I heaved the bed up as I ran behind it, knocking over my nightstand. The other half of the demon circled around the bed, giving a low, torn moan.

Footsteps thundered up the stairs. My door rattled and stuck. My nightstand was jammed against it.

"'Brina!" Harvey shouted.

"No!" I yelled. "You can't help me!"

I seized the star-patterned bedspread and caught one lurching demon in a net, then leaped on the blanket-clad demon.

"Nihil," I hissed. The blanket collapsed in on itself just as the other demon half pounced on my back, claws shredding the black satin of my blouse.

The door burst open. Salem bounded in, his leaping shadow on the wall far bigger than a cat's. He seized the demon and shook it in his jaws like a rat. Harvey ran to me, even as I searched frantically through the chest of drawers to be sure the quest objects were still there.

"Salem," I said after a moment. "Are you eating the demon?"

"*When I'm angry, I eat,*" said Salem, slightly muffled.

"What are you two *doing?*" demanded Aunt Zelda.

Harvey and I spun around. I had the magic jewel in my hands. Harvey had his gun.

"I can explain, Aunt Z!"

"Seems obvious," commented Elspeth, peeping over Zelda's shoulder. "Clearly, they're playing valiant home defender and sexy jewel thief."

Harvey and I exchanged a glance. I surveyed the wreckage of my room, including the overturned bed and shredded tangle of blankets.

Aunt Zelda, already wearing a black-and-gold negligee, raised a single shoulder in a shrug. "If that's all. Do whatever cheers you, Sabrina! Keep it down, though. I need rest to run the coven with maximum terrifying efficiency."

She began to close the door, then paused. My blood ran cold.

"You enjoy the sexy jewel thief game?" Aunt Zelda asked. "*You*, Harvey? Seems advanced."

"It's super fun so far," said Harvey in a strangled voice.

"Probably Nick taught Sabrina and now Sabrina can guide the mortal through it," Elspeth remarked. "Sweet Satan, Nick was a great sexy jewel thief."

"Jewel thieves need privacy!" I yelped.

Aunt Zelda snorted and closed the door. Harvey and I leaped apart.

My hands flew to my mouth. "I'm so sorry!"

"It's...fine," Harvey muttered. "Are you...okay..."

His voice trailed off. My eyes followed his gaze, and I hastily pulled the shredded remnants of my blouse up over my shoulder. It wasn't anything Harvey hadn't seen before, but I'd bought more black lace since I started dating Nick.

"I'm gonna go back to researching hell while you get cleaned up!" Harvey announced, negotiating his way around the debris of my possessions.

Then he stopped. There was an open jewelry box at his feet. Inside shone the gold of the necklace he'd given me the first time he told me that he loved me.

"Oh," Harvey said, sounding lost. "I—thought you'd thrown that away."

I dived for the box, desperate to shut it up.

"No," I whispered. "Why would I?"

With a visible effort, he smiled. "You're right. Doesn't matter."

He shut the door. I threw the box into a drawer. I set my room to rights with my own hands, not spells, then spun around so I was wearing pants and a black cowl-necked sweater. I restored Nick's picture to pride of place on my pillow.

"Sorry about the commotion, sweetheart," I whispered, then grinned. "Kind of funny, right?"

It was always fun to get up to mischief with Nick, tricking Father Blackwood or Dorcas. I never thought he'd trick *me*.

"Why not you, like everyone else?"

"Because Nick would never hurt me!" I snapped. "He told me—"

"He lied," piped all the birds in chorus.

I ran out of my room. As I descended the stairs, I heard a different song. I crept slowly toward the kitchen, pushing the door open. The lights were low, making our turquoise cabinets gleam.

Aunt Hilda's cooking was simmering on the stove. Elspeth was sleeping at the kitchen table with her head in her arms, and Lavinia was peering at what Harvey was reading. Harvey sang a soft song to the ghost child, giving her a butterfly kiss as he turned a page. I leaned against the doorway, the choked feeling in my throat easing.

Harvey was only wearing a gray T-shirt, because he'd covered Elspeth with his flannel shirt. He was singing to a ghost, with my aunt stirring her cauldron in time. *This* was the guy who could never understand my magical world?

Elspeth shifted and yawned. Harvey glanced at her, then over his shoulder at Aunt Hilda, melody dying on his lips.

I cleared my throat and picked up the thread of the song. Harvey's head turned. When he saw me, he smiled. I danced into the kitchen, still singing, waving my hands about.

Harvey's teeth skated over his lower lip, not quite biting, then his voice hesitantly joined mine. Elspeth waved her hands around, imitating me. Aunt Hilda was already spinning around the kitchen floor with her wooden spoon. I joined Aunt Hilda, dancing as we used to when I was happy and Ambrose was here. Lavinia peered shyly from behind Harvey's legs. Harvey took her little hand and twirled her. Harvey and I were singing together properly now, heads thrown back. He shuffled, always awkward about dancing, which I'd always found impossibly endearing. He twirled Aunt Hilda, and Aunt Hilda whooped with glee. He reached out for me and I moved toward him, into the circle of his arm, my face tipped up to his.

Harvey went pale. He stopped singing.

"I …" he said. "I'd better go."

He bolted out of the house without a backward glance. I walked slowly to my room.

I'd forgotten, after the misery of Tommy's death, how happy Harvey used to make me. I'd forgotten that when Harvey said he loved me, I danced all the way up my stairs.

The daughter of the devil and a mortal woman seduced by magic. I was a battlefield of two worlds. I was hell and earth, with not a bit of heaven in me.

But there was heaven in him.

"You turned your back on heaven," said the bird wheeling around my head. *"For what? Because you were hot for a little hell?"*

"Stop. That isn't what Nick was. Nick loved me. He proved it."

"He loved you, and suffered," said another bird. *"Your mortal boy loved you, and suffered. Don't you see what a monster you are? You use them like toys. If the mortal's heartbroken, you pick up with the warlock. If the warlock's damned to hell, the mortal might be amusing again. It's not about which boy you love. You can't love anyone. You only ruin them."*

I ran, not downstairs but to Ambrose's room. I always went to my cousin when I was in trouble. I threw myself down on Ambrose's bed and buried my face in his pillow.

"If you ever cared about anybody," sang the birds, *"save the mortals. Give up your quest. Or everyone will see you are your father's daughter. We will know where you belong."*

Suddenly my arm burned, and I remembered the communication spell Ambrose had taught me before he left. I sobbed as I slid my sleeve up, waiting to see what new disaster had occurred. My cousin might be in trouble.

My sob caught in my throat.

Across seas and miles, across my skin in purple script, Ambrose wrote: *Hey, cousin. I love you.*

I started to smile as I traced the words. Salem purred.

"I *am* where I belong," I told the silver flock. "I'm Sabrina Spellman. And I never give up on anyone I love."

GREENDALE

A FEARFUL THING
TO LOVE, TO HOPE, TO DREAM, TO BE . . .
AND OH, TO LOSE.
A THING FOR FOOLS, THIS,
AND A HOLY THING. —JUDAH HALEVI

Harvey could sing at his brother's grave. Nobody was watching him there. He sang the lullaby their mother used to sing, hoping their mother's song would help Tommy rest in peace. Tommy had been disturbed enough.

His song dying away in the dawn air, he told Tommy about the past few days.

"I guess I ran out of Sabrina's house because I was embarrassed," he confided, tracing his brother's name on the stone. "I can't really dance, not the way . . . some people can.

And ... I can't do anything I wouldn't want Roz to see."

He wanted to do his best for Roz always. So he'd sing, with the weight of her eyes on him. Somehow.

Harvey leaned against the gravestone as he used to lean on his brother.

"Bye, Tommy. I'll come back soon. I still love you. And I'm still sorry."

When he left the churchyard, he found the little ghost waiting outside the gate. He hadn't realized they could wander so far from the Spellman house.

"You were singing to someone dead," she whispered as he swung her up into his arms.

"Yeah," said Harvey. "My brother."

Lavinia sighed. "He must be glad of you."

"How ... do you know?"

If she could talk to Tommy, if Tommy could talk to her. If he could only tell his brother how sorry he was. Harvey's heart beat too hard at the thought, in hope and terror.

"I'm dead, and I'm glad of you."

Harvey kissed her curly hair. "Thanks, my small sweetheart."

Now that Harvey was used to the ghost, he thought she was really cute. He'd been stupid to be scared.

He dropped Lavinia off in front of the Spellman house, deciding not to go inside. He'd visited a lot lately and didn't want to intrude.

As he passed the curve in the road, he saw a flicker of movement among the trees. It was the pale flutter of a girl's gown.

"Lavinia?"

"Carry me!"

Harvey smiled. He carried her back to the Spellmans', set her down, and retraced his steps.

Every time he reached the curve in the road, she was there, lifting her arms imperiously. Kids enjoyed playing games. He carried her back more than a dozen times.

Finally she wasn't there. He rounded the curve in the road and saw the demons. They lay in heaps, not smoky like Roz's demons or winged like Theo's. These were misshapen lumps covered in eyes. Even their elbows had eyeballs set in the curves. The only place the awful creatures didn't have eyeballs were in the gaping wounds. Something had ripped all these demons' throats out. Or someone.

Harvey ran back to the Spellmans', kneeling on the porch where the child waited. She yawned with bloodstained teeth. "I'm tired now."

"Thank you," Harvey whispered. "Why are you helping us?"

She touched his hair. "You could have got cross and said you wouldn't carry me." Her voice was fainter than wind. "But you didn't."

She dissolved before he could say of course he hadn't. It wasn't much, to carry someone.

After Nick made his sacrifice, Harvey had carried Nick down to the gates of hell. It wasn't easy like carrying Lavinia. It was very rough going. Nick wasn't as tall as Harvey, but he wasn't short either. Harvey was badly worried he might drop Nick. At certain moments, Harvey thought with exasperation that it'd help if Nick Scratch worked out less.

Harvey was grateful he had to concentrate on holding on to Nick, so he wouldn't think about where they were going. Sabrina was at the head of their group, shining like a golden torch. He fixed his eyes on her, and followed.

Nick's dark head lolled against his shoulder. Harvey'd stopped several times, to carefully adjust position so Nick would be protected. It probably wouldn't matter if Nick's head hit the wall, not where he was going—but Harvey didn't want Nick to get hurt. He felt responsible.

At the gates of hell, the demon Lilith turned and swept Nick away.

Harvey let Nick go. Sabrina obviously regretted letting Lilith take him, but this wasn't only Sabrina's burden to bear. If it was wrong to hand Nick over, Harvey did it too.

But they could make it right.

He wanted to. He wasn't scared. One thing about hell Harvey was certain of: Tommy wasn't there.

As Harvey passed his neighbor's house, he saw her struggling hanging up the laundry and helped. Mrs. Link invited him in for a cola.

"Haven't seen much of you lately."

"I'm planning a trip with some friends."

Harvey hoped she wouldn't ask if they were going somewhere nice.

"Is your friend Nick going?"

"My what?" Harvey asked. "You must mean Sabrina's boyfriend."

"Oh dear, that has to hurt."

"Nope," Harvey said defiantly. "Not anymore. I'm with Roz now."

Mrs. Link put a wrinkled hand on his shoulder. "Still, you were with Sabrina a long time. It must be hard knowing you were her gateway crush."

Harvey blinked. "Her what?"

"Girls need training wheels. Someone sexually unthreatening," Mrs. Link clarified. Harvey choked on his cola. "Like the pop stars in skinny jeans who look twelve. Girls practice until they're ready to find a real man."

"You're pathetic. You long to keep people safe," whispered the birds, *"when everyone wants danger."*

Harvey washed his glass and left. After that, he couldn't face his dad, so he went back to Sabrina's house. It was okay to go. He wasn't being a nuisance.

He hoped he was helping Sabrina feel better. He probably wasn't.

Hilda Spellman said to go to Sabrina's room, so Harvey did. From outside, he heard Elspeth's voice.

Elspeth, his potential new friend, always looked pleased to see him. She was more shaken by the attack on the Academy than she let on, so she pretended to be sicker than she was. If Elspeth liked being looked after, that was fine with Harvey.

He opened the door and was instantly punished.

Elspeth and Melvin were making out on Sabrina's bed. There weren't many clothes involved.

"Sweet Jesus!"

Elspeth and Melvin hissed: "Stop *swearing!*"

Harvey shielded his eyes. "I'm so sorry. I'll go."

Elspeth murmured: "Or..."

Harvey shut the door. Then he opened it, eyes still covered. "Get out of Sabrina's room!"

He found Sabrina curled asleep on Ambrose's bed beside her cat, the drawing of Nick clutched close and tears glittering in her lashes. Seeing her miserable made everything go wrong in Harvey's chest, scrambling and desperate to fix this for her.

Salem meowed. Sabrina said he was talking when he did that.

"Hey, buddy," Harvey murmured. "I see you're looking after her. Thanks."

He felt he and Salem basically understood each other. He stole away from Ambrose's room. He shouldn't just hang around, but he could make Zelda coffee.

He didn't try approaching the other witches. Most wanted nothing to do with mortals. Agatha, the meanest witch, had refused to let Harvey carry her even when she was too weak to walk.

To Harvey's surprise, Melvin joined him at the kitchen table.

"Mortal, could I have a word?"

"Sure," said Harvey. "Sorry about...interrupting. I didn't know you and Elspeth were dating. I thought you were dating the redhead. Guess I got that wrong."

Melvin blinked. "You didn't. Dorcas and I have been together since the glorious occasion of my deflowering, on Lupercalia."

A thin, startled sound escaped Harvey, as if he were a scandalized kettle.

Melvin bristled. "It's not so unusual for warlocks to be chaste!"

Harvey leaped to reassure him. "Of course not. You want to wait for it to be right. Hey, actually, me too."

Maybe this was great. Melvin was one of the more

approachable witches, and Harvey had questions. He'd never been able to talk about this with his friends. Roz had come home from summer camp with important news. Harvey thought he knew what it'd been, but everybody stared until he slunk away. Even though he wanted to hear too. Now it seemed sometimes like Roz wanted to move things further, but he wasn't sure. He'd been wrong about how Sabrina felt.

Harvey didn't like being touched when he didn't want to be. He felt unwelcome in his own home. He couldn't imagine anything worse than getting this wrong.

Harvey asked his first question. "What is Lupercalia?"

"It's a witch festival. How to explain? Perhaps I should mention the anointing with blood? No, perhaps I should describe the wolf costumes?"

"Blood and wolf costumes," Harvey murmured, in terror.

Roz *couldn't* be expecting blood and wolf costumes.

"Dorcas wanted to be with Nick Scratch for Lupercalia, but I didn't take that personally. Obviously anybody would prefer Nick."

"Guess who's mortal and tired of talking about Nick Scratch! This guy."

Not a day went by without someone mentioning Nick was a satanic sex god. Harvey would've been plenty intimidated if Sabrina's new boyfriend had a cool car. Nick's whole deal was ridiculous overkill.

"Dorcas was one of Nick's girlfriends, back when he had three," Melvin explained.

"Back when he had—? Sure. Fine. Jesus."

Melvin gave Harvey a sad look for swearing. The universe cackled at Harvey.

"Sometimes one wants variety. You were seeing Satan's daughter. Now you're seeing a"—Melvin made a face—"priest of the false god's daughter. You don't have a type."

Harvey thought of Sabrina radiant as moonlight, Roz glowing like the sun. Harvey's type was people who were great and beautiful.

"Don't mention I was messing around with Elspeth," added Melvin. "Dorcas knows she could do better than me, so she can disport with whomever she pleases, but she'd be insulted if I was faithless."

"That's awful!"

"Sabrina got to be with Nick Scratch and you. Is it different because you didn't know?"

"That didn't happen."

"It definitely did."

"No, it *didn't*," snapped Harvey. "You should be ashamed of deceiving your girlfriend."

He took deep breaths and tried not to hate witches. He had to keep trying, to make up for misunderstanding Nick.

There'd been so many lies. But he didn't believe Sabrina would do that.

It didn't matter now.

Harvey'd always believed waiting for it to be right would mean him and Sabrina choosing each other. In the November woods, Sabrina'd asked him to search her for witch marks. He'd thought she might be sending him a signal.

It never happened again. Harvey had worked out when Sabrina started witch school. After Sabrina met Nick Scratch, she stopped taking off her clothes and telling Harvey she was sure about him. She wasn't sure anymore.

In December, Sabrina tried to bring Tommy back, and Harvey needed a break. He kept imagining the cold weight of the gun in his hands. He was afraid he'd be cruel to Sabrina if he was around her, and ruin everything between them. Harvey thought he could take some time. They loved each other. He believed that, even if everything else was a lie.

Then Nick Scratch showed up on his doorstep, obviously interested in Sabrina, and Harvey knew he was doomed.

He'd fought the realization.

It was February when he last kissed Sabrina. That was the last kiss.

On the day she finally returned from witch school they ended up kissing, falling backward onto his bed, whispering they'd missed each other. This time, Harvey told himself, he didn't mind being dumb and wrong, he was deliriously glad. Magic didn't matter, Nick Scratch didn't matter. She loved *him*.

Then Sabrina chose the witches. She recoiled from him, babbling about protecting him and going too fast. Harvey felt a lurch of horror. He watched Sabrina leave him for another world, and a realization came.

If he saw Sabrina turn away from him one more time, he would die.

He told her it was the last time. She walked out. Then Harvey asked Roz to the sweethearts' dance, and Sabrina took Nick Scratch.

Harvey wasn't surprised. He'd seen the writing on the wall all along.

What he hadn't expected was for Roz to start reacting when he touched her, as if she cared. That felt like being rescued, at the exact moment he was certain he'd drown.

He couldn't be without Sabrina. But they could be friends, as they had been since they were kids. Sabrina would be with the witches like she wanted, and Harvey wouldn't be entirely alone. Nick Scratch didn't seem too bad. He clearly thought a lot of Sabrina.

Maybe, Harvey told himself, everything could be okay.

Then he and Nick had a talk at the sweethearts' dance.

Sabrina, Roz, and Theo had disappeared. Harvey would personally have felt tempted to hide behind a curtain if left alone in a room of strangers who knew each other. Nick stood around looking smug in his tuxedo while girls threw themselves at him. Right in front of their dates.

Natalie Garside—shame on you, Natalie!—told Nick about the after party and her hot tub.

"I'm with Sabrina Spellman," Nick answered politely. "I'll be going where she's going."

Harvey nodded. Correct response, well done.

"If you want to have fun with me," Nick continued, "you have to ask Sa—"

Harvey, at the snacks table, dropped his plate and made urgent eye contact. When Nick's dark gaze flickered questioningly, Harvey made a throat-cutting gesture. So Nick would cut it out.

"I'm making a mortal joke," Nick told Natalie. "Excuse me."

"So handsome," Natalie murmured in his wake. "So home-schooled, but so handsome."

Nick appeared by Harvey while Harvey was contemplating the wreckage of his crackers. Harvey dropped his last cracker.

Nick seemed indifferent to mortal snacks. "Which part of that was wrong?"

"Maybe don't talk about, uh, having fun with anybody when you attend mortal functions."

"That can't be right," argued Nick. "How do mortals ever have any idea what's going on?"

"God, I don't know! We'd rather not have any idea what's going on than risk getting embarrassed. The human race still manages to continue."

Nick made a face when Harvey said "God," but seemed to think over the rest.

"I don't want to embarrass Sabrina," Nick admitted.

"The first thing you said was good."

Nick nodded as if committing this advice to memory. Harvey figured this interaction with Sabrina's new guy was going well.

Then Nick said: "What's a hot tub? What do mortals do in them?"

It would be so nice, Harvey thought wistfully, *if the ceiling crashed down and killed them.*

"That girl told me I wouldn't need a bathing suit," Nick added.

"*Natalie*," murmured Harvey, aghast. "Um. I don't know! I don't go to parties with hot tubs. Our group usually plays games."

"Games, sure." Nick nodded. "Like seven minutes in hell?"

"What's that?"

"You fit as many people in a closet—or a crypt—as you can, and for seven minutes—"

"Dude!" said Harvey in a panic. "Please stop talking!"

Nick regarded Harvey with an offended air, as if it was Harvey's fault witches were so alarming.

"Wow," said Harvey. "No. We play Dungeons & Dragons."

"You play with *dragons?*"

"I don't..."

"You must not do that."

"They're pretend dragons," Harvey said desperately. "And there's, like, a Dungeon Master."

Nick did something upsetting with his eyebrows. "Who is the Dungeon Master?"

"Well..." said Harvey. "I am."

Honestly, it was tough convincing the others to play at all.

"Oh, *this* is appropriate to talk about in public," Nick muttered darkly. "Mortals make no sense."

Suits were uncomfortable, so was this situation, and Harvey's tie was coming undone. Natalie hovered on the edge of his peripheral vision. Harvey glared. Nick batted at a red paper streamer as though it was a cat toy.

"Hey, you're not meant to touch the decorations."

"Oh?"

Nick's attitude remained nonchalant, but Harvey would've felt bad if *he'd* been somewhere unfamiliar, doing the wrong thing.

"It's fine," Harvey said gently. "You didn't know. Listen, I was thinking"—Nick arched a skeptical eyebrow, which Harvey ignored—"Roz and Sabrina are friends. 'Brina and *I* are friends. We don't have much in common, but we can put up with each other, right?"

He saw Nick's face change. Subtly, but enough that Harvey knew Sabrina had walked in.

He couldn't look. He'd caught a few glimpses out of the corner of his eye. She was wearing a bright red dress—how much had Harvey been holding her *back*—and she and Nick both really knew how to dance. It was all unbearable.

Harvey could look at Roz. She was always lovely, but it was different tonight, when perhaps some part of her golden loveliness was meant for him.

Roz was already looking at him. He shot her a shy, delighted smile.

Then he realized Nick Scratch was giving him the evil eye. The evil eye from a warlock was dreadful.

"I don't foresee us ever getting along, Harry," drawled Nick.

"That's not my name!"

Nick made a mock-surprised face. "Sorry, farm boy. Guess I forgot. Doubt it'll matter. Sabrina and I are walking the Path of Night. You'll be left far behind. See you. Or not."

"The path of what?"

Nick was already arrowing toward Sabrina.

Did witches have any non-ominous names for stuff, or was it all Path of Night, Curtains of Disquiet, Toilet Bowl of Eldritch Horror? Also, Nick Scratch was a *jackass*.

He called Harvey *Harry* several times. Harvey was almost a hundred percent sure Nick was doing it on purpose. Nick disliked Harvey as most cool guys did, but with an additional mean edge. Because Nick Scratch was a horrible person. Harvey could hate Nick as much as he wanted.

Then Nick Scratch turned out to be a hero.

Harvey sighed, laying his coffee cup down on a stack of paper. Then he lifted the cup. Sabrina's aunt Zelda read newspapers in fifteen different languages. Zelda was a scary person, but she was smart and awesome.

It was nice in Sabrina's house.

If he'd left a coffee ring on one of Zelda's newspapers, however, he was fleeing the country.

The stack wasn't newspapers.

Harvey glanced at the top page.

The buxom witch leaned into her saucy demonic lover's embrace. "I should return to my unfeeling and ungrateful sister's side, but I crave your touch."

"I must have you!" declared the passionate incubus, cleaving her luxurious curves to his body. She felt his heart—among other things—pounding. "My manly fires cannot be denied!"

She flung back her head. He strained against his chains that they might be more fully one, united by the pure light of love and the urgent crimson cloud of lust that none, magical or infernal, can withstand...

"Holy God," Harvey whispered.

"My love, the Academy students are sensitive about your language," said Hilda Spellman from the doorway.

"Sorry, Miz Spellman."

Her sky-blue eyes were fixed on the papers.

"Sweet Harvey, did you read any of that?"

Harvey coughed so hard he felt he might be strangling. Hilda walked over and noted the page he'd read. "Not sure that's my best work."

"Oh! You *wrote* this?"

Hilda made a dismissive gesture that ended in hand-wringing.

"Wow," said Harvey. "You must be really clever. I mean—I knew that, but I've never met a proper author before."

Hilda's hand performed a circle, then patted her hair. "Thanks, my love. With the Academy fuss, Zelda's awful husband, and poor Nick, I wanted to write about happiness and love. This hasn't been printed yet. Could you be a darling and keep it hush-hush? I don't want Zelda stifling my creative expression."

"'Course." Harvey grinned.

"It's our secret." She held a finger to her lips. He had a secret with Sabrina's aunt Hilda. And such a cool secret.

Harvey risked another look at the pages. He'd gotten a shock at first—but the story was about joy and love. Hilda was the kindest, wisest woman he knew. He didn't want to ask awful Melvin questions. Perhaps he could ask her.

"Miz Spellman," Harvey began. "You've always been so nice to me..."

"Well, Harvey, I love you," said Hilda. "You know that."

Harvey went still. "I, uh. I didn't, I—"

He sounded every bit the dumb kid he felt. She must mean it like saying you loved dessert. That was already so nice. She didn't have to *mean* it.

Hilda slid her arms around his neck, resting her chin on top of his head. "I love you. I never intended to. I loved Diana, you see. Sabrina's mother was *wonderful*—"

Harvey thought of Sabrina. "She must have been."

"When she died, I told myself...loving mortals hurts too much. Many witches do. But you followed Sabrina home, and oh, your eyes. Like a ghost child's who died starving. Still, you poured love on her. There are people who can only give the love they get, but others invent love from first principles. No matter what cruelty they breathe in, they breathe out love. They walk in love, every day of their lives."

"Like you." Harvey fought self-consciousness, desperate to get it out. "I—I love you too."

He felt Hilda's smile pressed against the top of his head. The most kindhearted woman in Greendale—probably the world. And she loved *him*.

"So I loved you. Now I love Dr. C. I'm not a proper kind of witch at all."

"You're the best kind of witch."

Hilda hummed. "I wanted Sabrina to always have—what I saw when she brought you home that first day. And I didn't trust Nick Scratch. Our Dark Lord is the Prince of Lies. Witches' tongues wrap around deceit as easy as enchantment. I thought she'd be fooled. I was frightened for her, and I failed to see he was just a boy. He loved her the best way he knew how. I wish I'd been kinder now."

"Me too," mumbled Harvey. "I never liked him. I didn't even try." Hilda sank into the chair beside him. Harvey reached out and squeezed her hand. He wished he could tell Hilda, *We're going to get him back.*

Hilda would be glad.

"Do you know what the name 'Hilda' means?" she asked. "*Battle*. And do you know what the name 'Harvey' means?"

Harvey shook his head.

"*Battle ready*. We're both fighters in our own way, my love. We'll get through these dark times. Want to stay for lunch?"

"Oh, no! But thanks." He stood, then stooped and gave Hilda a kiss on the cheek. *Thanks for loving me*.

He walked out of the Spellman house, taking the steps two at a time.

"She loves me," he murmured. He slung his gun over his shoulder, lifting his face to the spring sunlight and smiling.

He'd always loved five people: Tommy, Sabrina, Roz, Theo, and his dad. Now it was six. Maybe someday, he'd have too many people to count on both hands.

He sang quietly, practicing for Roz. A couple demons came at him, so he shot them. The singing wavered when he imagined Roz listening.

Billy Marlin's truck rolled up right after he shot a demon.

"Dude, are you *shooting up the woods?*"

"No offense, Billy..." said Harvey. "I hate you. Get lost."

"Why are you people like this?" Billy drove off.

Theo could do better, Harvey reflected as he entered the woods.

Why were people such *fakes?* Melvin, deceiving girls. His dad and Billy, pretending to be tough. Also, Satan.

Harvey understood why Sabrina had put on a masquerade to trap Lucifer. The guy shone the way Sabrina did, but there was nothing behind it. Whatever fires had burned in him, they were ashes now. Satan was ultimate evil and all, but he was so fake.

Nick Scratch had struck Harvey as fake too, but he'd gotten Nick wrong. Nick had been real when he said, *I love you, Spellman. You taught me how to love*, and sacrificed himself.

That was super romantic. Harvey wasn't sure why Nick called Sabrina by her surname, but he assumed for cool witch reasons. Nick and Sabrina were a cool witch couple who did cool witch things and had an epic love. Probably Nick didn't mind not hearing *I love you* back. He must've heard it frequently.

The first time Harvey could remember saying *I love you* to anyone was Sabrina, right before Halloween. He'd practiced before, but like singing, on your own didn't count. He didn't know what he would have done if she hadn't said it back.

When Tommy died, Harvey couldn't remember if he'd ever said he loved him. They'd said fake guy stuff instead of important things. Harvey wished he could tell Roz, Sabrina, and Theo every day.

He couldn't tell Sabrina, because he used to mean it one way and had to mean it another way now. Sabrina'd never really loved Harvey. He'd been training wheels.

Harvey worried, while distracted by demons, that Roz might find an awful boyfriend too.

Then he recalled *he* was Roz's boyfriend, and smiled.

Unless Roz dumped him. She kept saying, *I want to see...*

What else could she mean? *I want to see other people. I was confused like Sabrina.*

She'd asked him to sing to her. He should be able to. No wonder Roz wanted to break up.

Maybe Roz had only liked him when she was sick, and Sabrina was at witch school. Harvey'd been lonely then too.

He'd understood Sabrina not wanting him now that she had someone better, but he couldn't understand her abandoning Roz and Theo. They were irreplaceable. He got mad every time he thought about it. When Sabrina returned, he got mad at her.

Then Sabrina helped Roz when Harvey couldn't. They were the Fright Club now and could help people as a team. If Harvey didn't mess up.

When the demons landed on the road, it sounded like a thousand falling grapes. The jelly-like substance of their eyes wobbled. When they landed on him, he felt the gelatinous coating as their many eyeballs slid against his skin. That was worse than teeth. He rolled into the undergrowth, hurling a demon into a tree.

Harvey shot his rifle and plunged through the woods with the viscous shreds of demons squishing beneath his boots. He wished Roz wanted him to kill demons for her. It seemed easier than performing in public.

The Lady of the Lake called him a knight. He was coming around to the idea. Knights bravely fought evil. Being a knight would make sense of the desperate urge in his chest to help Sabrina. She'd be his queen, Roz his lady love, Theo his comrade in arms, and he'd be loyal to them all.

What would Nick Scratch be, once they got him back? Harvey made a face. Not a king.

"Hello, beautiful mortal." Elspeth appeared from behind a tree.

"Please don't jump out at me, okay? I have ... worryingly good reflexes."

Harvey put a protective arm around Elspeth's shoulders.

"I had a dream about you last night. We were dancing. You'll never guess where your hands were." Elspeth paused. "On my *waist*. Because you respected me!"

"That's where they would be," Harvey said absently.

Elspeth sighed. "Sometimes I worry I'm a dreadful deviant."

Harvey wasn't really listening. "There's a word for being with a queen, but not a king, right? Prince con...something."

"Prince concubine?"

"*Not that*." Harvey researched on his phone. "Prince consort!"

He also looked up Lancelot, who was supposed to be a good knight. When he read the things Lancelot got up to with his queen, Harvey put his phone away.

Forget being knights. They could be a superhero team.

"Hey, I don't think Melvin respects you."

"I don't respect him either," Elspeth said brightly. "Ungracious Satan, I don't care. Witches don't care about much. That's the witch way."

It wasn't Sabrina's way. Sabrina helped people.

When witch-hunters came for the witches, Sabrina went to rescue the others alone and got hurt. Harvey helped untie the witches and carried Sabrina out, but he couldn't do much.

Sabrina was the hero who saved everybody.

"People have to help one another. Or nobody gets saved. Could *I* get some magic help?"

The many-eyed demons were creeping close. They seemed to be in a forest of eyes.

Elspeth surveyed the demons. "Sorry, no." She teleported away.

Elspeth wasn't going to be his friend, then. Harvey sighed. He'd got things wrong again.

Harvey was alone in the woods, and scared. Roz and Theo had been alone too. Thank God they were out of danger. Thank God it was him.

Nick was alone in hell. Sabrina was a savior, and she was in love with Nick. She wanted to save him more than anything.

Harvey sometimes thought about asking Sabrina, so she'd tell him she loved Nick. That would—feel like the end, of everything that was already over.

There were more eyes in the dark than stars. Harvey had to reload, and he knew it would take too long.

A demon knocked him down. Claws raked his face, blood in his eyes.

"*Venturis ventis!*" shouted a girl.

Harvey's hair was blasted back by wind that sent the demons scattering. He turned in amazement to see Agatha, black hair streaming like a mourning flag. A demon launched itself at Agatha, so Harvey spun her out of danger.

He set Agatha down, reloaded, and fired. Together, they beat the demons back.

Harvey wiped his forehead with his sleeve and panted, "Why'd you do that?"

Agatha fixed him with a cold stare. "Why did you run to save us from witch-hunters?"

"I ... couldn't do anything else."

"I was sure you were a threat," she murmured. "You and your family. It doesn't matter. You don't matter. But I was so sure."

"We're even now."

A smile touched Agatha's mouth. "I don't think so."

That was fair. She'd helped him more than he'd helped her. But maybe they could keep helping each other.

"I'd kill anyone who hurt my sisters," Agatha added.

Another witch who cared about people. Harvey smiled back, with sudden hope.

"Don't even look at me," sneered Agatha. "Are you close to home?"

Not a friend, then.

"Yeah. You can go."

She vanished in a sigh of wind. The claw marks on Harvey's face ached. Blood and the wind made his eyes sting. He went home to get more ammo.

His dad came in as Harvey was washing his face. Harvey started, hitting his head on the tap.

He didn't think his dad would hit him again, but once you got hurt enough, it was hard to remember feeling safe.

Sometimes Harvey imagined feeling safer at home than anywhere else. One day, someone might welcome Harvey home. Sabrina, he used to dream, but now he focused his mind on Roz's face.

"This is all you get, forever," whispered the bird.

Theo had said the birds helped him. Theo was brave enough to make a friend of the truth, but not Harvey. The truth had hurt Harvey too much. The only thing worse were lies.

"How was work, Dad?"

"Fine. Wanna take on another shift?" His dad cleared his throat. "No pressure."

His dad remembered to say that, now that they got along

better. *Enjoy sports. Work in the mines that terrify you. Be someone different. No pressure.* Harvey could feel the pressure crushing him, but his dad meant well.

"Sure. Gotta go."

"You're spending a lotta time away from home. You could … bring Roz here."

Harvey'd never been able to have his friends over, because Dad might be drunk. But his dad didn't get drunk anymore. Last night, Harvey'd had a look around the garage.

"Could I have my friends over for practice? We were thinking of starting a band."

His dad shrugged. Harvey was allowed to clean up the garage, then, for the band. He beamed.

"Thanks, Dad."

Dad grunted. Dad got embarrassed whenever Harvey showed he was happy. "You'll be … home more, then?"

Harvey asked, shocked: "Do you *want* me to be?"

"Kid, I don't care."

Maybe Dad did, Harvey thought as he ran down the porch steps.

It was okay Dad didn't like Harvey. Ambrose didn't like Harvey either, but Ambrose was never mean. His dad was letting him have the band.

"It's not you he wants," the bird whispered.

Harvey said: "I know."

Harvey understood his dad wished Harvey had died instead of Tommy. Harvey wished that too.

He'd come home more, if Dad was lonely.

He put on headphones as he plunged into the woods. Headphones were useful. He could tell when there was an actual threat, and if people at school were mean, he'd rather not hear.

Harvey sang softly as he went. *Wait, Rosalind.* Everybody called Roz by her nickname, so Harvey called her Rosalind, to show she was special to him.

"Give up. You won't ever be who you want to be." The birds' whisper condemned him. *"You're always going to be who you are."*

Night fell, eyes gleaming through the leaves. He preferred night to day, but in tonight's dark his awareness of a threat was acute.

The wind rose, leaves dancing with darkness. There was a sound like racing paws on the earth. An animal. A pack.

On the rising wind, Harvey heard a howl.

Jesus, wolves. Thanks, magic!

Wolf howls sounded in the night air. Coiling around branches were the smoke demons that had chased Roz. And everywhere there were glaring, staring eyes. He couldn't put them out fast enough. He would be eaten before an audience of demons, the noise of his own shots ringing in his ears.

Beneath wolf howls, the crack of bullets and the hiss of flames came a low voice.

A voice he knew.

"Nick?" Harvey cried. "Nick! Where are you?"

He ran toward the sound of Nick's voice, saying—marble? Surely not...

Tree roots and stones crumbled away. Suddenly Harvey was falling.

He landed hard on rocky ground, rolled, and got his gun up.

He was in a quarry, surrounded by eyes. He felt like a frog boiling to death in a stone cauldron, with merciless witches watching from above.

Shadows simmered all around. He was lost in a dark where the only light was eyes. Watching and judging, finding him wanting. Every instinct told Harvey to run.

The thing he hated most was feeling helpless. He wished he were better, but he could at least try.

Harvey reached out in the dark.

The branch lit without burning. It shone, radiant and clear. Like the light of Sabrina's eyes when she burned the witch-hunters.

Her father had been an angel once. The light was like that.

Harvey'd wondered how he would know if a branch was sacred. Turned out it was like meeting Sabrina, Roz, and Theo. You found them and knew.

He broke the branch off a tree, holding it up high. He left a trail of poison for the demons following him. A witch who loved him had told him about lashardia seeds.

Harvey walked through the woods toward Sabrina's house alight with victory. He peered in the kitchen window, and saw Sabrina, Theo, Elspeth, and Lavinia sitting at the table. Sabrina's face was pinched, and Harvey's heart clenched.

He hid the sacred bough, to surprise 'Brina.

He walked into the kitchen, startled when everybody stood. "Anything wrong?"

Sabrina threw herself at him. "Harvey!"

Harvey's arms went around her as he understood. Oh. She'd been worried.

"If anything happened to you, I would burn down the world!"

He smiled down at her snow-white head. She was so little and cute, and fearsome.

"Guys, take it down a notch." Theo gave Harvey a sideways hug. Harvey got his arms around both of them.

"Sorry I left you to die!" said Elspeth. "Mortals don't matter as much as witches. We live longer."

"I wonder if *you* will," murmured Lavinia, in her most blood-chilling voice.

Harvey said: "Lavinia, be nice."

Sabrina whirled on Elspeth. "You left Harvey to what?"

"Sabrina," Harvey said, before she burned Elspeth to ash, "I heard Nick."

Sabrina turned so fast she wobbled, her face alight with love and hope.

"Nick?"

Harvey's throat closed up as he nodded. *Yes. Be happy.*

"Roz and Theo saw him, and you heard him," Sabrina murmured. "Are you sure it was him?"

Harvey cleared his throat. "Yeah. First I heard wolves—"

"Nick's familiar was a werewolf!"

"That's cool," Harvey muttered unhappily. Nick's familiar couldn't be a weasel?

Sabrina frowned. "It wasn't really cool. But you heard *him*. What did he say?"

"It doesn't make much sense. I think he said Mabel."

"Probably a sex demon," Elspeth announced.

Harvey frowned. "A sex demon called ... Mabel?"

Magic kept letting him down. Nick was apparently letting *Sabrina* down.

"It's okay!" Sabrina said. "He doesn't know if he'll ever see me again. Whatever he's doing is fine. I forgive him for everything! He's not in trouble."

"He's in *huge trouble*," snapped Harvey.

"You don't understand how witches do things!"

Harvey didn't. But he knew *her*. He saw the trouble in her eyes as she twisted her reddened mouth into a blasé witch's smile. It was one thing if Nick had shown her a wonderful new world of festivals and costumes. It was another if Nick was hurting her.

"You can't understand, beautiful mortal," murmured Elspeth. "But if you—"

"Mortal," Harvey repeated.

"Not Mabel." The joy in Sabrina's voice made Harvey smile. "*Mortal.*"

"Me. He... knew I was there."

Harvey felt bad for thinking Nick would betray Sabrina. He muttered: "Misunderstandings about sex demons wouldn't happen if Nick *called* people by their *names*."

"We can't judge him for temporarily forgetting people's names while he's suffering in hell!" Sabrina exclaimed.

Personally, Harvey could. Then he remembered the sound of Nick's voice. He'd sounded scared. Nick Scratch, so cool and untouchable.

"Oh, Nick," Sabrina murmured, so quietly only Harvey could hear. "We're coming."

Harvey nodded, pressing the hand he was still holding. Then he let her go.

"Your concern's understandable, Sabrina," Elspeth said chattily. "Nick did only date you on Satan's orders. You must wonder if anything he ever said to you was true."

There was a silence. Theo and Sabrina exchanged a guilty look. Harvey thought, shock echoing through him: *They both knew.*

Harvey said, voice distant in his own ears, "Nick did *what?*"

"It's not as bad as it sounds," Sabrina whispered.

Lies had wrecked Harvey, left him in pieces he was still trying to put back together. He loved Sabrina. He couldn't bear the idea of her being broken.

Sabrina loved Nick so much she didn't even care about the lies. If Nick was Sabrina's true love, he should *be* true.

Roz and Theo had put themselves in danger for that fake. Nick wasn't worth it.

Harvey loved Sabrina enough to follow her to hell, but she shouldn't go. As far as Harvey was concerned, Nick could stay in hell. Where liars belonged.

PEACE TO YOUR HUNGRY SOUL. —DANTE

Lilith hadn't tortured Nick today. He'd acquired a shirt, a sword, and the illusion of control. He was hanging on by a burning thread, but in hell, this meant he was doing fine.

Until Nick turned a corner in the stone maze. He was watching the sparks above as though they were red stars, and he almost walked right into the stupid mortal.

"Nick?" The mortal was wide-eyed with surprise.

"*You?* No." Nick turned aside and shouted upward at the flying sparks. "I have never been so insulted in all my life, *Lucifer.*"

The mortal frowned as though he had serious concerns about Nick's mental well-being. Nick felt even more personally insulted by Satan.

"Why are you yelling at the sky?" the mortal asked in a pained voice. "Get a grip, we have to find the others."

"What others?"

"My friends. Sabrina got us to come rescue you." The mortal scowled. "Believe me, it wasn't my idea."

"Shut up," Nick said flatly. "You're not real. Lucifer is rifling through my memories and creating hallucinations in order to break my mind. But—do you hear me, *Satan*—you're scraping *the bottom of the barrel* with this one. It isn't going to work!"

The mortal stood there as if this was one more Nick-related horror he was forced to endure. He was wearing his stupid fleece-lined jacket, *in hell*.

He gave Nick his usual look, as though Nick were a particularly unpleasant magical toad. Because Nick had Sabrina, and the mortal was jealous. Sad for him. Nick didn't personally know what jealousy felt like.

"Why would you hallucinate me?"

"I wouldn't!" Nick snarled. "Why would I? I don't even know your name!"

"Okay," said the mortal. "So the logical inference would be you're *not* hallucinating. Come on, I can deliver you to Sabrina, and not deal with"—he made a small gesture, full of distaste, toward Nick—"any of this."

He reached for Nick's arm. Nick jolted back, remembering Lilith.

"*Don't* touch me."

The mortal retreated. "I won't. Listen..."

"I will not. You're not here!"

"I wish I wasn't," the mortal snapped. "I couldn't let Sabrina go alone, but I didn't want to come. You're not worth hell. I know what you did."

There was a hissing silence. Nick had known the mortal would look at him like this once he found out.

"Don't stop. Tell me how contemptible you think I am."

The mortal's lip curled. "Beneath contempt. Actually. And you always pretended you were so much better than me."

"Oh, I'm sorry. Sometimes I act superior...around people who are inferior to me."

The mortal looked down his nose at Nick. "Forget it. If you don't want to be rescued, you don't have to be. I'll tell Sabrina you like it here, and you're gonna stay." The mortal nodded. "I feel great about that. Bye."

He headed back the way he'd come. The ground was uneven, dropping and rising, ledges and loose earth. Nick watched as the mortal disappeared from sight.

He wasn't real. They hadn't come for him.

If they had, Nick mentally rehearsed a future conversation with Sabrina. *Yes, I let him go off alone and a demon ate him, but in my defense...*

"Bitter merciless Satan, what I have to put up with," Nick muttered. He ran after the mortal, scrambling down rocks. "Wait up, Harry!"

The mortal threw an unimpressed look over his shoulder. "Decided to come along, did you?"

"I'm not buying any of this," Nick snapped. "But whatever. I'll amuse myself by insulting you."

"How long were you planning to keep insulting me?"

"Until you die!" Nick responded promptly.

The mortal stared.

Nick grinned. "Why not? I have five minutes."

"Oh Jesus," muttered the mortal.

Nick waited for the walls to collapse and the ground to give way. "You *cannot* talk like that in hell!"

"Thought I wasn't real? I can do whatever I want."

One of the heaven-sent, wandering through hell. Surely Nick's mind wouldn't have come up with this. Nick was too smart.

No, he wouldn't be fooled.

"Has it ever occurred to you," Nick said conversationally, "I don't have to endure your mortal insolence? I could rip your throat out. Anytime I wanted."

Said throat was about eye level. Nick glared. He could do it. Any wolf could.

"*Listen*, Scratch—"

"*Look*, Kinkle—"

"You know my last name but not my first name? Seems likely!"

Nick maintained calm. "I only remember your last name because it's funny."

The mortal frowned. "Why's it funny?"

Nick brightened. "I'm glad you asked."

"Wait, I don't wanna know."

"Too bad," said Nick, "because—"

The mortal wasn't listening. His face lit up in the way it did for only three people in the world. Nick turned, heart hammering in his ears, the frantic beating of a winged thing sensing the sky.

Sabrina, Nick thought, *please*—

It wasn't Sabrina, or even Roz. It was Theo.

Roz was Nick's favorite mortal. The mortal was his least favorite by miles. Roz was Sabrina's best friend, which meant Sabrina also thought Roz was the best one. Roz believed in Sabrina and was charmed by Nick. He appreciated Roz distracting the mortal so he came up with fewer suicidal ideas.

Theo was different. Sabrina had told Nick about Theo, and when they met, Nick saw Theo thought Nick was hot, though not in a serious way. Nick figured it would be easy to get Theo on his side.

Then Theo gave Nick a very clear-eyed look, as though Theo could see through Nick like a windowpane.

Nick understood Theo had picked the mortal's side.

One thing Nick did for Sabrina's sake was make sure her mortals were all right. Sabrina would be devastated if anything happened to the mortal. So Nick checked in occasionally, to ascertain he hadn't gotten his fool head eaten by a wild goblin. Usually the mortal was relatively safe in his house, wearing overly large headphones and singing gross mortal songs, and drawing pictures. Sometimes he wandered outside—into the woods full of witches and familiars, the idiot. Sometimes he did so in company.

Nick had seen Theo and the mortal out shooting cans on fences. They did a weird handshake together. Sometimes they hugged. Nick had heard the mortal tell Theo he *loved* him. It was sickening.

Theo's attitude was the mortal's fault. Now they'd gang up on Nick in hell.

"You found Nick!" Theo said brightly. "This is great."

Nick sneered: "I don't believe in you either."

Theo gave the mortal a questioning look.

"He keeps saying we're hallucinations from Satan and none of this is happening," reported the mortal wearily.

"None of this *is* happening," Nick insisted. "Sabrina wouldn't come to hell dragging a pack of mortals. That would be reckless and ridiculous."

"Um," said Theo. "Have you ... met Sabrina?"

The mortal exclaimed: "Theo!"

"Just saying."

Nick couldn't agree with Theo, because that would be insulting Sabrina, and he couldn't agree with the mortal, because he'd rather die. He walked ahead. They were on an uphill slope, the maze turning split-level, so Nick could see over one wall to the dark passage below.

When Nick looked up, he found Theo's blue gaze on him. Seeing a little too much.

"You've been having hallucinations from Satan? That doesn't sound good."

This apparently hadn't occurred to the mortal and seemed to disturb him. Now they both looked at Nick, Theo's gaze bright and knowing, the mortal's soft and dark.

The mortal feeling sorry for him would be the last indignity.

"Nick," murmured the mortal. "What has hell been like?"

"*Awesome*," Nick snapped.

"I heard somewhere," the mortal offered, "hell is other people?"

"If those other people are you," Nick said, "could be!"

From below came the sound of feet marching in unison. *Not the rabble of random demons*, Nick thought. *A cadre of soldiers, sent to apprehend the intruders.*

The mortal shouldered Nick aside so the mortal was in front, moving toward the low stone wall.

"Theo," said the mortal, "on my mark."

They fired. The ranks fell and scattered, some fleeing, a few heading toward them. Theo and the mortal ducked behind the wall to reload.

Nick drew his sword and headed toward the demons. The mortal motioned for Nick to stay back. Nick made his own gesture indicating *Buzz off, you bother me*, and swung. Both the demon's head and his sword dropped in the dust.

Two slashed throats later, there was only one soldier left. Nick followed him over the wall, but as he did, the demon pulled Nick down. Nick landed on the rubble with the demon's slimy tusks an inch from his face. The demon snarled, Nick snarled in return, and the demon collapsed with a sword in its back.

Nick stared over the dead demon's shoulder at the mortals, peering at him over the wall. The stupid mortal was squinting in a slightly uncertain fashion. Theo, the sane one, seemed horrified.

"Harv!" Theo exclaimed. "You can't throw swords!"

"Sometimes I just do things," mumbled the mortal.

"I'm so deeply aware of that!" Nick threw the demon's corpse off and sat up in a rage.

"I was trying to help—"

"Help by staying in your home!"

The sword had gone through the demon and cut Nick, but his shirt was dark and the mortal would get upset. He twitched the torn material aside. Theo's eye caught the movement.

Theo tugged on the mortal's sleeve. "I think Nick's hurt."

The mortal mysteriously stopped being angry. "Oh no. Did you hit your head? How many fingers am I holding up?"

"Can you not *count?*" Nick climbed back over the wall. "It's fine. I heal almost immediately, no matter what they do to me. I think it's because of Satan."

Satan, lurking beneath his skin. Lucifer, whispering low. Typically, the mortal ignored Satan to focus on useless things.

"What are they doing to you?"

Nick wrenched his mind away from memories of the pit, and Lilith.

"What do you care? You don't like me."

The mortal snorted. "What's there to like about you?"

Not much. But Nick didn't want people to *see* that.

Nick plunged on. "And this is what I deserve. Right?"

He knew it. The mortal knew it. He'd known the mortal would think so.

"No," the mortal said.

"What?" Nick asked, after a split second's hesitation.

"No," said the mortal. "Nobody deserves this."

Nick scoffed. "Doesn't matter."

"It does," the mortal insisted.

Nick took a step toward him, eyes narrowing. "You're the only one who believes that. There's no use talking about justice, and respect, and boundaries, and consent. Did Sabrina want to sign the Book, did I want to do what the Dark Lord said? As if it matters what people feel about what's happening to them. I—I didn't want *any* of this. The world doesn't care what anybody wants."

"I care," said the mortal.

"That," Nick hissed between his teeth, "is because you are *stupid.*"

The mortal's face underwent a silent revolution of frustration.

"Guys!" exclaimed Theo. "This is a fun philosophical conversation we're having among piles of demon corpses, but what do you say we find Sabrina and Roz, then get the hell out of hell?"

The mortal's attention shifted entirely to Theo as they resumed negotiating the maze. If beloved Theo didn't want to be around demon corpses, the mortal would make it so.

"Whose bad idea was it to split up in the first place?" Nick fell into step with Theo and jerked his head in the mortal's direction. "His?"

Theo cleared his throat. "Maybe you could ease up on Harv a bit."

There was a pause.

"You keep calling him that," said Nick. "Is it short for something?"

Up ahead, the mortal kicked a rock into a wall.

"I get that you two are bestest friends," Nick continued scornfully, "but reconsider going along with his terrible plans. Also reconsider the friendship. Given his attachment issues, once Roz runs for the hills, *you're* up next to date him."

Theo looked dismayed.

"When that happens, get ready for his weird fetish."

The mortal wheeled around, voice cracking. "My *what?*"

"You know," said Nick. "Where you want people to tell you the truth all the time."

"Honesty is not a fetish."

"You demand it in a romantic partner!"

Outrage and embarrassment struggled for supremacy on the mortal's face. "That's totally normal."

"Everybody thinks that about their fetish," said Nick triumphantly.

The mortal rolled his eyes and resumed walking. He did that with people he didn't like, became increasingly silent, hunching his shoulders and praying for the offensive presence to depart so he could be alone with his precious friends.

"You mortals are lucky I'm here," Nick announced. "As a warlock, I'm more intelligent and experienced, so I'll be leading this misguided group."

The mortal stopped dead. "Wanna be the leader, Theo?"

"I want no part of this," Theo murmured.

"You can't be the leader," the mortal informed Nick. "We're rescuing you, and you can't lead your own rescue mission."

Nick raised an eyebrow. "That's narrow-minded."

For a moment, Nick wondered if he was going to get punched.

"I try to be patient," the mortal bit out. "But I've had enough. It doesn't matter how awful you pretend to be. You're getting rescued and delivered to Sabrina. Shut your annoying mouth. *Do as you're told.*"

Nick blinked. "All right. There's no need to get nasty."

The mortal raised his eyes, peering above the sparks, trying to find heaven. Then he gestured at them to follow and went on. He wasn't walking as far ahead of them as before. After a while, they drew level.

"Congrats on making Harv lose his temper," Theo muttered.

"Thank you."

"Do you *want* to get witch-hunted?" asked Theo. "Don't you think you have enough problems?"

Nick genuinely hated being ignored. Possibly it brought out the worst in him.

That was why Nick disliked illusion spells, which made you feel nothing was real. And more recently memory charms, which made people look indifferently through you, as though you weren't there.

"That was cool, with the sword-fighting," added Theo.

Even when it was Father Blackwood, a man Nick actively despised, he hadn't been able to stop the instinctive grin at being praised.

"Thanks, tiny mortal."

"Have you been doing much slaying of the vicious and remorseless hordes of hell?" Theo continued.

The mortal was tilting his head toward them, as though possibly he also found sword-fighting cool.

"I used to partner with Prudence in fencing class," said Nick. "Talk about vicious and remorseless."

He caught the mortal smiling, head ducked to hide it. That was another senseless thing the mortal did. There was no *point* smiling just for yourself. Smiles were useful. You could charm people into giving you things.

"Could I learn how to sword-fight?" asked Theo.

"Sure. I'll teach you. There are interesting books about the history of magical swordsmanship you should read. The best is *Dueling with Excalibur.* Let me quickly sum up an incident from the fourteenth century."

Neither mortal tried to stop him, though the Weird Sisters knew to stop Nick before he said, "Let me sum up."

"Hey, nerd," said the mortal at last, and Nick went still. "This bit of the maze is a dead end. Let's rest here. We've got a ways to go, and you look tired."

The mortal insisted he'd take first watch. He removed his jacket and folded it so Theo could use it as a pillow.

In dreams, Satan was so close. Satan was *Nick*, or perhaps there was no Nick anymore. Nick was being blotted out. Lucifer was all that remained. Nick woke shuddering to find the mortal studying him with concern.

"Get *back*." Nick recoiled. "I'm not *safe*."

The mortal came closer. Nick didn't know what he'd expected. He let his head drop, too exhausted to lift it.

"Why did you come here, farm boy?" Nick asked, so weary his voice was a whisper. "I—I wanted to be the hero. We can't both be the hero."

"She's the hero, Nick," the mortal murmured, patient after all, and laid a hand on Nick's back. "We'll get you to her. Sleep."

There were gray stone walls all around and restless red sparks overhead, but the mortal was standing guard. When Theo murmured in his sleep, the mortal patted Theo's shoulder and sang as he did when he thought nobody could hear. A lullaby for fools, promising a kinder world. Nick rested his head in his arms and pretended it was meant for him, too.

Nick woke with a start, realizing there was an emergency. The mortal was giving Theo romantic advice.

"Don't listen to a word!"

Theo looked up at Nick with obvious relief. The mortal began to complain.

"Hush, little mortal." Nick patted his head. "Stop misleading poor Theo."

"Get off me," the mortal muttered. "I'm supporting—"

"You are like a tiny stupid baby." Nick turned to Theo. "Who do you think has more expertise?"

"Well, you," admitted Theo.

"Pick out someone good. Be useful!" said Nick. "Do what they want. Be sexy. You'll do fine."

Theo grinned. Nick felt Theo would soon understand that Nick was a much better friend to have than the mortal.

"Dude, you're not helping," the mortal scolded. "It's not about being useful!"

"You think that because you're useless."

They started to march again. The mortal offered Nick gross mortal bars in packets to eat, and Nick waved them away.

"You're probably a hallucination sent to trick me into eating things in hell. Which I've been trying not to do, unless Lilith made me."

The mortal got upset. "I won't make you do anything! Because of boundaries."

"Oh," said Nick. "Do I get boundaries?"

Theo was nodding, so this wasn't the mortal being wrong as usual. Nick considered boundaries he wished for.

"Why must you be unnecessarily tall, Harry?"

"I can't help that."

"I don't blame you—"

"Big of you," said the mortal, not without irony.

"—but there's a spell," Nick continued.

"No!"

"This is why I don't like you," said Nick. "Or why I wouldn't like you, if I ever gave you any thought, which I never do. You are so stubborn, even when totally reasonable suggestions are made to you."

"I don't think I am stubborn," said the idiot, stubbornly. "But nobody ever makes reasonable suggestions to me. Your boundaries should be about you."

Nick had feared this was the case. He didn't think the mortal understood it was difficult to admit you felt bad about what you couldn't stop.

"I *could have* boundaries. Anytime I wanted."

"Okay," said the mortal. "When you work them out, tell me what they are."

"See, guys, that was really good," Theo said encouragingly.

Maybe, Nick thought with tentative hope, *the mortal could be made less unintelligent?* Maybe if he was given a reading list.

There were no reading lists possible in hell, which was one of the many things Nick disliked about hell. There *were* mists in hell, fits of darkness that rose and curled around you. Gloom came over the walls now, mist slinking around their ankles like gray cats, and Nick tensed. But no horrors followed. Not yet.

The mortal was hanging behind Theo and Nick. When Nick glanced over his shoulder, the mortal seemed pleased by the mist. Of course. People couldn't look at him in the mist. Nick understood shyness was one of the many mortal emotions. Sabrina didn't suffer from this one, so Nick didn't need to put up with it.

The mortal began to sing a song to himself.

"It's funny how many mortal songs are about love," Nick remarked.

The mortal went reproachfully silent about Nick ruining the illusion nobody could hear.

"What are witch songs about?" asked Theo.

Nick shrugged. "In choir we sing about damnation, lust, and entrails."

Through the mist, Nick saw Theo go green. Maybe Theo didn't enjoy entrails. Mortals ate strangely, though Nick liked what he'd tried of mortal food. He liked mortal songs too. Nick didn't mind that the songs were about love. It was new to him; that was all.

"In choir?" asked the mortal, sounding surprised.

The mortal seemed to believe witches exclusively did wicked things that upset him. Nick nodded.

The mortal drew nearer. "So—you sing?"

Nick said: "Not alone."

There was a pause.

"That's not how choirs work?" Nick pointed out. "You're tragically dim-witted."

The mortal's irritated silence was deafening.

"I know…" Nick offered, "a few mortal songs."

He tried singing a line, and waited.

The mortal cleared his throat, as if he really might join in, but only silence followed. When Nick glanced back, all he saw was mist.

"Mortal?"

In the dark there came a shriek of rising wind, and worse. Like the sound of a coming storm, the worst storm Nick knew. The thunder of swift paws on snow. *Not the wolves*, Nick thought. *Not with the mortals here.*

These mortals would try to fight. They'd die so quickly.

"Mortal!" Nick shouted.

Nick grabbed Theo's collar and shoved Theo behind him. Everything was howling darkness, wind cold as snow, falling leaves, and the coming of the wolves.

"*Nick?*" the mortal called through the dark. "Nick! Where are you?"

Nick went quiet. The sound of the mortal's call was strange. It was Nick's name, but it didn't seem like that voice could be for him.

Then the mortal blundered out of the mist.

Nick blinked. "You sounded farther away."

"What?" asked the mortal. "Hell plays tricks on you."

"Oh," said Nick, "it does."

The mortal took hold of Theo's shirt, not grabbing. It was strange, how easy gentleness came to him. The mortal pulled Theo in. "You all right?"

Theo hugged him back. "Yeah."

Nick leaned against the stone wall, cold as a wall of ice. The mortal turned to him.

"Nick, you all right?"

"Obviously," snapped Nick. "We have to get out of here. The wolves...I know mortals don't matter. But—"

"*Why* do mortals not matter?" the mortal demanded.

"If mortals matter," Nick said, low, "it will be awful when you die."

"It should be awful when people die."

Maybe it was easy for mortals to accept death. They had no other choice, but Nick did. Life was awful enough.

When Sabrina talked about becoming mortal, Nick was terrified. He'd decided long ago that would be the ultimate horror. What, get some sweet, softhearted mortal to love you and make you a home and make you happy, then home *dies*?

No, thank you. Nick had home die on him once already.

It was the test the mortal failed, not being able to accept Sabrina's magic. Nick would fail if he couldn't accept Sabrina's mortal side. He was still terrified. He didn't want anything to hurt her.

So he'd done what he'd done. Now Sabrina and the mortals had thrown themselves into danger *again*. Terror was exhausting. Nick wanted it to stop.

"If we get over this wall," the mortal said, "the wolves can't follow. Let's get Theo over first."

Theo, by far the smallest and lightest, was the only one they *could* get over. Before the mortal would let Theo go, he insisted on embracing him again.

"I love you," he said into Theo's shoulder.

"Is now the time?" Nick demanded.

He helped the mortal boost Theo over the wall and watched Theo scramble to make it.

The mortal urged: "Let's find a door. Sabrina's really close. Here, help me."

Nick reached out, in the dark and mist, and his fingers curled around the bars of a door.

"Come on," said the mortal. "I know the right thing to do."

Nick took a step back. "How nice for you."

"You can't let Sabrina down again."

The mortal's eyes narrowed, judging Nick. He didn't understand anything.

"*You* let her down first!" Nick shouted. "You were supposed to love Sabrina and you dumped her for no reason. She cried, and now I'm supposed to be the one who loves her, and I'm trying but I betrayed her. I don't know how to love anybody. Where was I supposed to learn? From the witches? From the *wolves*?"

"The wolves?"

Nick shook his head, speechless with misery.

"Nick," the mortal said softly. "Are you crying?"

"I don't do that!"

"Do you"—the mortal hesitated—"want a hug?"

"How dare you?" Nick snarled.

The mortal, the worst fool to be found in any possible world, moved forward.

"I get you're mad at me," he murmured. "But you know, I did you a favor. Sabrina wouldn't be with you if I hadn't left her. You wanted to be with her, right?"

"I did," said Nick. "But I didn't understand what to do. I tried to please my parents and Amalia and the whole Academy and the Dark Lord and Sabrina. How was I supposed to do any of that by telling the *truth?*"

The mortal's face crumpled. "You know I wouldn't lie, right?"

"I'm not you," snapped Nick.

"You don't have to be. Listen. Sabrina loves *you* now. We all came for you. I wanted to. What you did was really brave, and we couldn't let you stay down here. Trust me."

"I *can't*," Nick said savagely. "I'm almost sure you're not real."

The mortal gathered Nick carefully in toward him, the way he did with Theo and Sabrina, to keep them safe.

"Hey," said the mortal, in the tender way that would get him eviscerated at the Academy. "Nick. You had a really hard time, didn't you? But it's okay now. I'm sorry for everything. You can come in out of the cold. All you have to do is open the door."

"Oh no," Nick whispered.

Nick put his head down on the mortal's shoulder for a minute. Just a minute. He couldn't let himself cry.

Then Nick lifted his head.

"This isn't real," he said. "That wasn't for me."

The mist and the mortal faded away. Nick was back on the mountain. The snow was falling, and the cold went deeper than his bones.

GREENDALE

**BUT OUR LOVE IT WAS STRONGER BY FAR THAN
THE LOVE OF THOSE WHO WERE OLDER THAN WE—
OF MANY FAR WISER THAN WE—
—EDGAR ALLAN POE**

The warmth seemed to drain out of my kitchen as I looked into Harvey's furious face. There was light in him I'd always loved, but now the light was cold. "It doesn't matter if Nick approached me on Satan's orders."

"Do you hear yourself?" Harvey demanded. "I get you've lost your mind over this guy, but 'Brina, this is horrible. If everything was a lie from the start, how could you ever trust him?"

"Wow," murmured Theo. "This is so bad. Gotta go."

Harvey grabbed for Theo, but Theo evaded him.

"Where are you going?" I asked desperately. We could explain to Harvey together.

"I'm gonna see my other friends!" claimed Theo.

"What other friends?" Harvey demanded.

"I won't let you meet them, because you guys embarrass me," said Theo. "Work this out! Leaving now."

Theo darted off, Elspeth following. Even the ghost child vanished.

Harvey and I stood alone together. His face was cold as the sculpture of an angel. Like the witch-hunters in the church, come to pass judgment on my kind.

"Nick was so good to me, in so many ways—"

"Because he felt guilty for being a sleaze, like a guy cheating on his wife and bringing her flowers?"

"It wasn't like that!"

Harvey didn't understand witches. My aunts and my cousin had performed their own dark devotions. When you walked the Path of Night, darkness entered your heart. Someone with no darkness in his heart couldn't imagine that, and perhaps could never forgive it.

"He'd do anything for me."

"Except tell the *truth*?"

Harvey was shaking his head, refusal in every line of his body. If he thought Nick was so horrible for lying, maybe he hadn't really forgiven *me* for lying about what I was. Maybe he secretly thought I was horrible too.

I burst out: "You can't understand."

"Because I'm just a mortal?"

Harvey turned away. I caught up with him in the hall and grasped his sleeve. "Harvey, please. You can't go."

"Why not? Only you're allowed to leave. Is that it, Sabrina?"

"What? No," I faltered. "But you promised to help me."

"Right," Harvey sighed. "All you care about is Nick. How can you be this sure of him?"

"She wasn't. She asked Nick not to talk to us," Agatha's voice rang accusingly from the stairs. "And he obeyed."

The students and ghosts of the Academy were lined up on the stairs watching. I realized how upset Harvey must be when he glanced over and scarcely seemed to care there was an audience.

"Sabrina wouldn't ask her boyfriend not to talk to people."

Harvey looked to me for confirmation. My gaze dropped. "I had to—"

"If you couldn't trust him, you shouldn't have been dating him!" Harvey's mouth twisted. "But you *couldn't* trust him. He wasn't worth trusting. When we were dating, you didn't ask me not to talk to Roz and Theo!"

My hands clenched into fists. "Considering what happened with you and Roz," I said in a small cold voice, "maybe I should have."

Harvey's eyes went dark with shock. My heart seemed to sink to the bottom of a lake, tumbling too deep ever to get back.

Aunt Zelda's voice rang from above.

"Sweet starving Medea, are we now enacting teenage drama in the hall with an audience choking up my stairs? Hells below, I hope somebody brought popcorn!"

She stormed down the steps, Academy students and ghosts

retreating from her with speed. Quentin dematerialized right through the banisters.

Aunt Zelda's gaze, flying sparks like a comet, traveled over the hall and fastened on me. I didn't know what she saw in my face, but under her bronze tea dress her shoulders bunched like a tiger's. I thought she might lunge down the stairs at Harvey.

"I may be forced to entertain the pestilential children of my coven. I may be invaded by ghosts. I will *no longer endure* mortals distressing my niece! Why are you always *here?*"

Every one of us saw Harvey flinch. Even Aunt Zelda bit her ruby lip. I reached out, but Harvey started back as if he thought I'd hurt him.

"I was just leaving."

"Harvey, no—"

"I'm going, 'Brina!" Harvey turned, almost tripped over Lavinia and Quentin, then closed his eyes for a frustrated instant, as if resigning himself to feeling ridiculous. "And I'm taking the ghost children with me. Not because I'm ghost kidnapping them. They follow me around."

The slam of the door echoed through my head.

"*Begone*," Aunt Zelda told the Academy students.

"Where?" Melvin asked.

"Follow Nicholas Scratch to hell, for all I care," snapped Aunt Zelda, and I put my head in my hands. I heard the confident stride of my aunt's heels on the stairs, and felt her arms come around me.

"Sabrina," she murmured. "Don't weep. I'll make his blood into a nourishing soup for you."

I buried my head in her shoulder. "Don't do that!"

Aunt Zelda rocked me. "I know this is a trying time. Hilda and I have been occupied holding together the shattered fragments of our coven. And you're used to having your cousin at home to hatch absurd plots with."

"You miss Ambrose too."

"Well." Aunt Zelda stroked my hair. "I know you must be troubled with the revelation of who your father is, but you can always come to me. You're not alone."

"It doesn't change anything, who my father is," I whispered. "I won't let it. You made me. He didn't."

Aunt Zelda held me. She'd held me on the night Harvey put Tommy down and broke both our hearts. She'd held me on the first day of the new year. I knew she'd hold me every day for all the years to come.

"I know I'm not alone," I said. "But—Nick is."

If I was trapped in hell, my family would come for me. But nobody was coming for Nick. He only had me.

"Ah, you're weeping about another boy. I suppose when you're sixteen, it's always true love," Aunt Zelda murmured, with a touch of scorn.

Stung, I jerked back.

"Why not?" I demanded. "How did marrying for power work out for you, Aunt Z?"

Outraged silence was Aunt Zelda's answer. She stood, her shadow falling over me.

"What's wrong with wanting to love people?" I asked. "What's wrong with wanting to trust them?"

"Nothing," answered Aunt Zelda. "If you can trust them. Can you?"

Nick lied. Harvey slammed the door on witches and their wicked ways.

"You say you want to save people, not hurt them," whispered the silver birds. *"So why is there devastation all around you?"*

I jumped up and fled to my room. I scrambled onto my bed, sobbing, reaching blindly under my pillow for Harvey's drawing.

No, the picture of *Nick*.

Only it was both. I stared at the paper in my lap, the lines of Nick's face blurring as tears rose and spilled down my face. Fury burned as hot as hell inside me. I ripped the drawing into a dozen pieces, devastation all around me as usual. I cried, homesick for the past, when Edward Spellman was my father, when Ambrose was always here, when I would only ever have one love and that love would be true.

"'Brina?" Harvey whispered from the door.

I scrubbed at my face with both fists, like a little kid. Harvey stood on my threshold outlined by light. In his hands was a slender branch infused with silvery radiance. The sacred bough.

"Harvey?" I faltered. "You came back."

Harvey shrugged awkwardly. "I had to give you this."

I nodded, swallowing a sob. Harvey walked into my room. He didn't sit beside me. He knelt, laying the luminous bough at my feet and gazing up into my face. Despite his flannel shirt and battered jacket, he seemed like a knight in shining armor to me. He caught hold of my hand, and I clung.

"Don't cry," Harvey murmured. "I—I can't bear it. I don't like what he did, but I'll go anywhere. I'll do anything. As long as you don't cry."

I wiped away my tears with my free hand, trying to stop as soon as he asked. Harvey bit his lip.

"What you said before, about Roz…"

"I'm sorry!"

"You know when I was dating you, I never looked at anyone else," Harvey said earnestly. "I never thought of anyone else. You believe me, right?"

"I believe in you." I twisted my hands together. I didn't want to lie. "I…did have thoughts, about Nick. But I would never have done anything to hurt you. I adore you."

Harvey's mouth trembled into wounded crookedness as I spoke, but as I finished speaking, the ends of his mouth curved upward. Only slightly, but it made all the difference.

"I adore you," he said, then cleared his throat. "As a friend."

I nodded vigorously. "We'll always be friends."

"Always," Harvey echoed. "But just to let you know, if Nick calls me Harry after you get him back from hell? I will punch him in the face."

My throat was clogged with tears, so the laugh stuttered, but laughter felt good. "Who's Nick? Names are really hard to remember."

Harvey laughed too. He was kneeling at my feet, his whole clean heart in his eyes. I could reach out and touch the lapel of his jacket, the ends of his hair, with infinite tenderness. The way I used to.

He noticed when trouble touched my face. "What is it, 'Brina?"

"Everything's so difficult and complicated now," I said in a low voice.

"Yeah," said Harvey quietly. "But if we love each other as much as we can, if we try as hard as we can... surely there's a chance everything will work out. Don't you think?"

There were tears in my eyes, and his. I let my back bow under the weight of my burdens, rested my cheek in the crook of his neck and shoulder, and whispered: "Harvey, I do."

His hand stroked my hair, once. Then he scrambled away.

"I'd better go. If your aunt Zelda sees me in this house after she banished me, she'll turn me into a frog."

"She would never..." I stopped. "I would never let her do that."

"Thanks."

"I know the quest was tough, but it's almost over. Tomorrow morning, when dawn remakes the day, I go to the Lake and the Lady. I find the grail, give her our gifts, and get the weapon we need."

"I'll be with you." Harvey hesitated, then leaned down and kissed my cheek. "Sleep well, 'Brina."

I nodded mutely, sitting among my tangled blankets and the torn fragments of paper, as the door closed. My hands were still lifted, fingers half-curled, to hold on to him. I listened to his steps on the stairs, and the sound of my front door closing.

Then I was off the bed, hurtling down the stairs after him. I raced out into the shadows of the porch and saw his retreating back and opened my mouth to call his name.

Around the curve of my road, under the moon and past trees gone black in the night, my best friend came running.

"Harvey!" Roz called. "I was worried. I went to your house, and then ... I knew you'd be here."

Harvey dived toward her, wrapping her up in his arms.

"Rosalind," he said into her hair. "You came for me. Thank you, thank you, thank you."

I stopped with my hand resting on the toad statue guarding my porch steps. Roz was one of my touchstones for goodness and warmth, for the best of mortality. And I was a wicked witch. I'd hurt Harvey too much. I couldn't be in love with him anymore. Harvey and Roz were in love with each other. I was in love with Nick.

And as a wicked witch, I had the power to get Nick back.

A demon rushed at me through the night, a dragon with huge eyes, razor-blade wings, and something satanic about its leering face. I lifted a hand and burned it to ash and walked through the falling ashes to my door without a glance behind me.

Once in my room, I laid the sacred bough down in my drawer with the magic jewel and the cloak of feathers, the gifts my friends had brought me. I gloated over them like a dragon over its treasure.

In my mirror ringed with white roses, I saw the light of the holy bough catch my eyes and turn them suddenly to silver to match my hair. Magic made me shine like moonlight on snow, burning as pale as a morning star. I was ready to embrace any power to save him.

I smiled for the glass, as I always smiled for Nick.

My friends came with the dawn. I crept out of my house to join them.

Elspeth stirred from her nest of blankets in the hall and saw me, my arms filled with feathers, the jewel, and the bough.

"Are you going to commit naughty deeds in the woods?" she asked. "With props?"

"That's…exactly what I'm doing," I answered. "You can't come."

Harvey, Roz, and Theo were standing at the foot of my steps. I beamed at the sight of them.

"Harvey!" I said. "Guys! Let's do this thing."

The silver birds flew around us like attendants, the rays of the rising sun catching their wings. As we headed into the trees, another demon hurtled toward me. I raised my eyebrow and watched the demon crumble into ash and smoke.

"You seem cheerful today, Sabrina," said Theo. "Which is great! Though confusing."

"I'm really happy," I told Theo. "You all got glimpses of Nick, or heard him." I nodded toward Harvey. "And Nick heard Harvey too!"

"Wow, did he?" asked Roz.

"Who knows," said Harvey.

"The veil between us and hell is growing thin, like the Lady said," I continued. "Today is my turn. Today I might see Nick!"

"Oh, joy," muttered Harvey.

Roz hit him on the arm. Harvey rubbed his bicep, making a mock-reproachful face, then grinned down at her.

"Surely he'll see me too," I went on. "Nick said once he and I have a connection."

"Smooth," said Theo. "Uh, but I'm sure he meant it."

"You have more of one than he and I do, since we don't have one," said Harvey. "And I'd honestly prefer if Roz didn't have one with him either."

"Not my type," murmured Roz.

"Thank God," said Harvey.

Another demon flew at us. Harvey reached for his gun, but I transferred my bundle of quest objects to the crook of my arm and waved airily. The demon collapsed with a slow, sad moan, as though it had always been a hollow thing.

"Your eyes have a silver sheen to them," Theo told me. "They're cool, but they're not contact lenses, are they?"

I shook my head.

"She's doing her Dark Phoenix thing," Harvey said.

Theo, better acquainted with comics than I, though not a full nerd like Harvey, frowned. "Gaining incredible power until she gets stabbed by a dude with claws that come out of his hands? Or, uh, sacrifices herself?"

Roz and I exchanged a doubtful glance.

"That's the made-up bit," said Harvey. "In stories, people come up with reasons why they have to cut down a girl with power. Why hurting her is a good thing to do. Like that's how the story always has to be."

"These patterns reinforce the inherent misogyny of the system," said Roz.

"Right," murmured Theo. "What Roz said, yes."

Harvey sent me a sweet little smile. "So we help the girl with power instead."

"I just love you guys," I sighed, and burned five more demons to cinders, turning my face up to the sun as it rose and flooded the woods with warmth.

We reached the hollow of light by the dark river, and I spoke the words to summon the Lady.

The pool of light spread, as before. The light changed to water and rose. I waited, holding my breath.

Roz gave a cry, her eyes flickering the way they did when she had her cunning visions. "Everybody, *run*!"

We knew better than to ignore Roz's warnings.

We scattered, racing wildly back from the pool of light, into the trees. We moved just in time. Light and water coalesced into a flood. The cracking earth collapsed with a groan like a dying man and fell away. Trees toppled. The ground beneath us shuddered, tipping us over as we shouted warnings and ran as hard as we could. I clutched my quest objects to my chest, seized Roz around the middle, and threw a web of magic onto a nearby bush. Both of us landed safe in shimmering lines and leaves, magic our safety net.

"'Brina!" Harvey shouted. "Roz!"

"We're okay!" Roz called back. "Sabrina has me!"

"Did the earth move for you guys?" Theo yelled.

The earth had stopped moving. Roz and I scrambled out of the bush, and Theo and Harvey let go of the tree they were holding, everybody windblown and scratched. Half the terrain was now pointing at the air, as though we stood on the deck of a huge ship broken in half.

The silver birds flew over the edge of a white precipice, leading down to a huge dark lake. The piece of ground on which we stood, a clearing of a few bushes and trees, had been cut out from the surrounding woods and lifted high as a tower. On every side was a sudden terrible drop. The silver birds circled like seagulls waiting to be fed. I had a bad feeling we were on the menu.

"Oh, a huge cliff," gasped Harvey. "*Why*, magic? These look like the Cliffs of—"

"Dover?" said Roz.

"I was gonna say the Cliffs of Insanity," said Harvey. "From a movie."

"I wish I had a broomstick," I murmured.

"*You're* a cliff of insanity," Theo said, affectionately head-butting me in the arm.

We peered over the edge. It was a long way down. Depending where we jumped, we would either hit the ground or the lake.

Even from a distance, I could feel the chill emanating from the water. My aunt Zelda had told me a tale about the coldest lake in the world. Bodies were thrown into that lake, froze as they sank, and were never found. The lake lay like a cold black stone far past our feet.

"This is the last stage of the quest," I said. "Mine is meant to be the hardest part. I need to find the grail. Roz, you said you had faith and found the jewel. Theo, you said you got the birds to help you by telling the truth. Harvey, what did you do?"

"Just...my best," said Harvey.

"I'm going to jump," I announced. "I believe in myself. I can make the birds believe in me too."

"And make the birds believe in you in midair?" asked Theo. "What happens if it doesn't work?"

"I'll decide what to do on the way down."

I shook out the cloak, each feather blade shimmering in the dawn light. I placed the magic jewel on the fork at the top of the sacred bough. The facets of the jewel reflected the bough's glow, turning them into a scepter I could wield. The wind ruffled the cloak on my shoulders. Currents of air lifted the cloak and me with it.

I'd tangled with a river spirit at summer's end, and researched protection charms in the dead of winter. On the edge of spring, I reached into the pocket of my witchy little black dress and produced a pearl.

"No fire, no sun, no moon shall burn me,
No water, no loch, no sea shall drown me."

I swallowed the pearl and stepped to the edge of the earth.

"I don't know about this, Sabrina," murmured my best friend, her eyes full of visions.

"Have faith, Roz!"

"I do."

"I know. That's why I love you."

I smiled for her, and leaped.

The winds caught the ends of my feather cloak and the jewel in my scepter caught the light. Below me stretched my woods and the Lady's waters, turned to gold by dawn.

Having stepped off the high mountain, it seemed I saw all the kingdoms of the world and their glory. For a shining moment, I hung suspended as a morning star. I felt I could fly into the heart of the sun.

Then I plummeted down into the dark.

STEP BY STEP, DROVE ME BACK DOWN . . .
—DANTE

Nick dragged himself along, hand against a cavern wall. He wasn't able to walk without support, wasn't sure where he was going or why he was trying. When he looked back, he saw he'd left a trail of blood, not bread crumbs.

When he looked ahead, he saw Prudence stepping out of the shadows. Her cropped hair and her scimitar of a smile caught the red lights of hell.

That surprised a weary laugh out of Nick. "I suppose you're here to rescue me?"

"Yes, Nicky, I'm on a selfless mission to liberate your soul from hell," purred Prudence. "Like I care enough to bring you a glass of water from the next room, let alone hurl myself into the abyss. No, the real me is somewhere indulging in glorious wickedness with either my sisters or Ambrose Spellman. This is a hallucination. But you knew that."

Nick nodded, too tired to speak.

Prudence lifted one shoulder in a shrug. "Took you long enough to catch on."

Even though she wasn't real, it was a comfort to have her near. Her façade had always been that crucial bit better than his. Nick trailed behind Prudence as they entered another cavern, this one smaller and darker. There was faint luminosity on one wall, by turns sharp rippling silver and murky green. Nick couldn't tell where the light came from.

Prudence sat with her back to the uneven curve of the stone wall, facing the strange light. Nick slid to the floor beside her.

"What are you doing?"

"Darling Nicky, I'm the messenger."

Nick scoffed. "You know they shoot those, right?"

Prudence's black-cherry mouth curved. "Not before they get the message."

The light projected against the cave wall shuddered. Nick had seen movies in mortal movie theaters several times, so he was basically an expert. Movies amused Sabrina, and she had insightful thoughts about symbolism in horror and the feminine grotesque. The mortal tried to hide behind shoulders during violent bits, which made Nick worry the mortal was too stupid to know movies weren't real. Nick had tried superhero movies and felt the magic didn't bear logical examination. In Nick's opinion, movies weren't as good as books, but everyone else seemed enthusiastic.

This was similar to mortal movies, but not entirely the same. The image against the irregular rock face of the cavern flickered and wavered, resolving into clarity. There was a depth to the sight, a pitch to the sound, more vivid and real than hell. Nick blinked to make sure he was seeing right.

It was the mortal. And it *was* him, not a hallucination made up of the bits and pieces of Nick's memories.

"You're going to show me that idiot mortal until I give in? They truly do torture you in hell. Is there a hot poker shortage?"

"Watch," said Prudence.

"I demand hot pokers! I know my rights," muttered Nick.

There were new leaves on the trees in Greendale. A ghost stood at the curve of the road, her leer pitiless as a shark's in a china doll face. The mortal—oh no—lifted her up in his arms. A sinister revenant, and because it was small, this fool thought it was a baby.

"Idiot-plated *idiot*!" said Nick. "That moron would try to carry Satan around."

"I already know you think he's stupid, Nick," drawled Prudence. "You've told me before."

"Of course I have. I tell everyone."

"Are you sure it's true?" asked Prudence.

"*Yes*," snarled Nick. "He broke up with Sabrina!"

"You can't imagine being so wounded you might do that?" murmured Prudence. "Even now?"

"No," Nick lied.

He'd spent months, in hell and Greendale, wanting nothing more than to be with her. But with Lucifer's whispers echoing in his mind, with every drop of blood in his veins burning like the fires of hell… perhaps Nick understood better how it might be, to crave a space where you could be alone and heal.

The mortal was still stupid.

The mortal called the ghost *sweetheart*, the worst pet name Nick had ever heard. Was he trying to remind the ghost that hearts were delicious? Over the mortal's shoulder, the ghost unlatched its jaw, exposing rows of glittering teeth. Demons moved in the trees. Every shadow circling him was a threat.

The ghost hissed and the demons fell back. Nick blinked. The ghost was guarding the mortal.

"You *cannot* keep escaping danger because dark supernatural forces fall in love with you," Nick told the mortal. "I'm astonished by your current success rate!"

"You made yourself into a hamster ball for the Dark Lord," Prudence reminded Nick. "You're a fool now too."

"That was an emergency!" snapped Nick.

"With Satan's spawn, there will always be another emergency."

Prudence's voice was amused. The image on the wall flickered and became Sabrina's best friend Roz, running down a long hall as a shadow demon chased her. As Roz stumbled and fell, the image dissolved away.

"Wait," said Nick. "Is she—"

Theo was in the mortal's death trap of a truck, blanketed by winged demons. The truck swerved off the road, and the cave wall went dark as the windshield.

"Are they…" Nick whispered.

There was the mortal again, walking too near the woods with blood on his face.

"An evil supernatural creature is going to *kill you*," Nick snapped at the mortal. "I hope it's me."

"It's not going to be you," said Prudence. "You're going to die down here. And he's going to die up there."

There were demons covered in staring eyes—oh, the mortal would hate that—on every branch in the nearby trees. The moon was blotted out by a shadow. The mortal's eyes narrowed as he took aim and fired, again and again.

"What's going *on?*" Nick demanded. "He doesn't fight like this for himself. Is Sabrina in trouble?"

"Considering who we're talking about . . . what do you think?"

"Have you noticed those panic attacks have stopped, now he's hunting?" Nick asked.

Nick had worked it out. The heaven-sent one, who grew up with the devil's daughter. Every instinct must have told the mortal there was something wrong. He'd turned that inward, hurting himself, which was just like him.

Those instincts were meant for witch-burning.

"I don't notice mortals," said Prudence. "But I know witch-hunters are dangerous. He'll die, but perhaps he'll kill her first."

Nick shook his head.

Prudence laughed. "With witch-hunters, you can't ever be sure."

Nick decided to ignore her. "Harry, don't go into the woods."

The mortal headed into the woods.

"I can't watch this," Nick said, watching it. "He should be put in a box."

Prudence smirked. "Like a coffin? He will be."

"A box in which he's alive!"

"A cage," said Prudence.

"*No!*" said Nick.

"It's allowed if it's a mortal, right?" Prudence asked. "They don't matter."

Nick was silent.

The image of the mortal alone in the dark woods faded away. Instead, there was light. The mortal was somewhere safe.

The image expanded, to show a table littered with books and a witch sleeping at the table. Nick squinted at her. It was Elspeth, from the class below his. As Nick watched, the mortal took off his flannel shirt and covered Elspeth with it. So she'd be warm.

Why was the mortal doing that? Nick had never found Elspeth particularly appealing. Did the mortal love her now? He was exhausting. And he was touching books that belonged to *Nick*.

The ghost child appeared at the mortal's elbow, and the mortal gave her a hug. The ghost child poofed away, then reappeared at his elbow so the mortal would hug her again. The ghost child was looking up at the mortal as though she'd never seen anything like him before.

Naturally, she hadn't. The ghost child was used to the Academy, where they educated people properly.

Nick made an irritable gesture. "Fine, I surrender to the whims of hell. Make this go away."

Prudence shrugged. "This is hell, not a restaurant. You don't get to order your torments off a menu."

"If I'm being shown the world, why can't I see the best part?" Nick demanded. "Bring me *Sabrina*."

He had reason to believe this demand might be fulfilled.

He knew the hellebore-patterned wallpaper. He knew the turquoise cabinets. And he knew the books spread out on the table. They were from the Academy library, and Nick thought of every book in that library as his. There was a witch student sleeping at the table and a ghost child drifting over the floor. There was Hilda Spellman, eyes not crystal-hard with judgment but soft blue like summer skies over the mountain. He was looking at Sabrina's house and their school, both at once.

The mortal dipped his head and rubbed his nose against the ghost child's—was this an attempt to get his face eaten?—then began to sing a song. Nick gave it two minutes before he realized Hilda was watching. Right on cue, the mortal faltered.

Except then came a voice that gleamed true gold even in the darkest places. The voice Nick had fallen in love with.

Sabrina stood in the doorway of her kitchen, her face shining with love. The mortal caught the thread of her song as his eyes caught the light of her face, and they moved toward each other.

Nick couldn't watch any more. His throat was closing up. He was speechless with longing. He wanted to go *home*, please, please.

But there was no mercy in hell.

She was there, and he wanted to be there too. But he wasn't. The mortal was there instead.

Nick knew what the moment before a kiss looked like.

When Nick raised his head, the mortal was walking away from the Spellman house, his face uplifted to the sun.

The mortal said, so happy: "She loves me."

"Tell me something I don't know," Nick snarled, wretched.

The images on the wall flickered again. Nick saw Sabrina in her room, furniture flying, demons attacking. He should be there to protect her, and he wasn't.

The next instant, Sabrina was sitting on her bed surrounded by torn fragments of paper, crying her fierce heart out. She only cried like that for one person, and there he was, walking through Sabrina's bedroom toward her.

"What did you *do?*" Nick snapped, but the mortal couldn't hear. He was looking at Sabrina.

"I adore you," Sabrina told the mortal, in her clear voice.

"I adore you," the mortal assured her, so gentle.

Sabrina's drying tears caught the lamplight in her room, diamond bright, as she smiled.

The mortal murmured: "If we love each other as much as we can, if we try as hard as we can ... surely there's a chance everything will work out. Don't you think?"

"*Can* you think?" Nick demanded, in a subdued voice.

Perhaps this was all right. What had Nick thought would happen, in the end? It hurt to watch, but he didn't wish Sabrina unhappy forever. He wanted her surrounded by love and warmth, light and tenderness, and all good things.

He'd chosen to sacrifice himself for her. He wanted to make the sacrifice with a little grace.

"Who's Nick?" Sabrina asked the mortal, laughing.

Her mouth was open, bubbles floating from her lips in green and gold. She raised her scepter again.

The mortal caught her wrist. He was flailing underwater, flannel shirt billowing, but he held on to Sabrina fast.

"I've *had* it with you," Nick snapped.

The mortal's eyes went to him, widened slightly, then returned to Sabrina. The mortal was pulling her away, and Nick didn't want her to go.

Sabrina's gaze went to the mortal and stayed there. She took him in her arms. They clung together, in the hazy green light, in the shifting shadows. Sabrina's white hair flared like a halo around them. She was buoyant in the water, the mortal sinking lower, but she bent her face down until her lips found his. Nick saw the mortal's eyelashes fall dark against his cheeks as his eyes shut, and his hands clasped at the small of Sabrina's back.

Sabrina and the mortal were kissing. Caught in the swaying current, with no space between them for either dark or light. Then they began to swim away. Sabrina looked over her shoulder once, her lips moving. Nick couldn't make out the word she was saying.

That was the last Nick saw of them. The water receded. He was left alone listening to the fires of hell.

"She doesn't love you," Prudence murmured. "You think you can buy love through sacrifice? Nicky, you always prided yourself on your ability to learn. You know better. Being loved isn't about what you do. It's about who you are. You have to be someone else. And you know who."

Nick leaned his head back against the stone. "I have no idea who you're talking about."

"Always lying, Nick. Isn't it time to stop? Aren't you tired?"

Nick was so tired, he felt he was burning slowly to cinders. To nothing at all. Prudence's face was very close to his. Red flames danced in her dark eyes.

"You wanted love. But there's no way for love to exist without cages," said Prudence. "You know that."

Nick cleared his throat. "I've always known."

"So you chose to be caged, instead of her?"

"Yes," Nick answered.

Prudence's smile was stunningly cruel. "How do you like it in the cage, Nick? Was love worth it?"

Was anything worth this? And yet, Sabrina's hands touching his face, her eyes on his. That had been something. More than he'd ever had before. Slowly, Nick nodded.

"A liar to the end," said Prudence. "Are you sure you even love her? Or is it that Lucifer directed you toward her, and you were desperate? Desperately guilty. Desperate for a touch of light from the mortal world. Don't forget, I'm inside your head. She had a home, not you. She had a family, not you. She had mortal friends, not you. Is that what you loved? Is that why?"

Home. Family. Friends. Nothing a witch should want. Even though Prudence was a hallucination, Nick was so embarrassed.

Sabrina's love for her home, and her family, and her friends was part of what drew him to her, like a moth to a flame. Now he was burning.

"Why does anyone love a girl?" Nick grated. "I can love her if I want. You don't get to say how I feel."

"It doesn't *matter* how you feel, Nick," Prudence whispered.

"That's the message. You thought you were winning, because you can tell we weren't real. You missed the crucial part. Nick, you're not real. Have you ever truly believed in yourself? When have you ever been enough?"

Nick swallowed.

"You can't remember your mother's face. She was always turning away from you. She never loved you."

"I know," said Nick.

Prudence trapped his face between her fingers. Her nails cut like claws.

"And the real me. Nothing you did was good enough, and then Ambrose Spellman won me with a smile. You thought witches can't feel, but we can. It was never me. It was you. There's something badly wrong with you."

"I know," said Nick.

"Sabrina's aunt recognized you were poison."

"I know," said Nick.

"None of those mortals will ever be your friends."

"I know," said Nick.

"And your darling Sabrina." Her voice curled in a growl around the name. "She's a sheltered child, so you managed to trick her. She wanted you, that was all. It wasn't enough. She's already forgotten you. Nobody loves you. Nobody ever will."

"I know," said Nick.

Prudence smiled by the red light of hell, and she wasn't Prudence. She was Lilith, crowned with flames.

Then her pitiless face changed, snout lengthening and fur crawling from her pores, teeth growing huge.

"*Only I could love you,*" said Amalia. "*And I died, because you had to chase after a girl.*"

He shivered, alone on the mountain as the snow fell. He should have known it was the wolf.

"*Nobody's coming for you. Nobody cares that you're here. You will die alone. There will be nothing left, no sign in any world that you ever existed. Not a drop of scarlet blood seen on the snow, not a child's cry heard on the wind, not a whisper, not a tear. You'll be nothing.*"

Amalia bared her teeth.

"*Or you can come with me.*"

"Please," Nick said. "Anything but that."

"*Anything?*" said the other, darker voice. "*You were never good enough. But you could be evil enough for anybody.*"

There was an escape from being nothing. All he had to do was listen to the voice of his own worst impulses, the urge to cruelty he'd been born with. Under the blood moon, the chosen of the wolf, close enough for Satan to whisper in his ear, and it was inevitable that he'd do something terrible. Why fight it?

Let Lucifer have his way. Everything Nick had ever faked could be made true.

In the heart of hell, Nick tried for grace and found it out of reach.

Only one thing was in reach. Nick put out his hand, and his trembling fingers curled around the bars of the cage door.

He shoved the door wide open.

GREENDALE

**THE SHINING STRENGTHENED ME AGAINST THE FRIGHT
WHOSE AGONY HAD WRACKED THE LAKE OF MY HEART.
—DANTE**

The birds surrounded me in a flock of silver whispers. I was airborne, and then the water had me. Icy shock enveloped me. I nearly dropped the scepter, almost panicked. I'd come close to drowning once before.

All the times I'd almost died taught me I could survive. I hung suspended in the water, breathing through the pearl in my throat. My eyes adjusted, shapes materializing in the shadows. From black and gray, the waters changed to dark green shot through with sunlight. The birds were with me, needlepoints in the dark, silver gleams suspended in the gold rays piercing the water.

A monster loomed at me out of the darkness. A ghost-pale

shark, sleek white skin and bared hungry teeth. Behind the teeth was a waiting abyss. I turned it to ash in the water and swam down. I was in deep, and I'd go as deep as I needed to.

"All this for a liar," the birds said. *"It's not too late to turn back."*

Theo said I could make a friend of the birds if I made a friend of the truth.

I let out a deep breath. Silver ripples moved the birds, like watching the currents change.

I'd lied to my mortal friends all my life. I'd even lied to Nick sometimes. It wasn't the same as Nick's lies for Satan, but I'd felt so guilty, and I knew I'd hurt them. I tried to make up for it, yet sometimes trying to make up for lies made the truth worse. My friends still loved me.

My aunts and my cousin had performed dark devotions for the Dark Lord, and lied they'd never been asked, as if that meant escape from what they'd done. My family still loved me. My family had leaped at Lucifer, knives out for their god, in my defense.

If we love each other as much as we can, if we try as hard as we can ... surely there's a chance everything will work out.

Nick had lied so much and tried so hard to make up for it. To my mind, that was more than enough.

"He did lie. It does matter. But something else matters more."

My words were bright bubbles, floating away. I watched the last bubble travel down, down, down, and the birds followed it. Making a silver trail of bread crumbs for me.

I dived to the bottom of the coldest and deepest lake. Another demon came for me, a drowned girl with a resemblance to me in her rotting face. I threw fire through the water and watched her face sink in and her ashes float away.

There were no stones or fish in this lake. There was only a gleaming surface, as though at the end of the lake was a black mirror. The light of the silver birds and my golden scepter was reflected there. I saw another gleam, pale and faint. I swam closer, my hand grasping the scepter so tight it hurt, then realized the gleam was only my own face.

Or was it?

I reached out with my free hand. Mirrors weren't the only things that reflected. Perhaps there was another lake under this one, a lake of darkness. The Lady's true lake. The resting place for the true grail.

I plunged my hand into darkness and drew out a golden cup. Then I waited.

I had the grail, the jewel, the sacred bough, and the cloak of feathers. I should find the Lady. But my friends had seen a shadow, a side profile, heard his voice. The veil between earth and hell must lift, for the Morningstar Princess. I wanted to see Nick.

Where are you, Nick? You said we have a connection. I believe you.

If we had a connection, I could make that a path to follow. Through the connection, I could pull him toward me.

Every night I dreamed of seeing and saving him. The boy who sacrificed himself for me. It was all my fault. I had to make this right.

I lifted the golden scepter and struck out at the darkness. A crack appeared along the lake bed, a line in the darkness that flashed pale.

Peering through that break in the dark, I saw a face lifted up to mine. A face I knew and loved to look at. Dark, watchful eyes. Lips parted, eager to speak or smirk. Not usually vulnerable, but—every now and then. For me.

Nick.

Steel gleamed against his skin, weight bowing his back. He was on his knees in chains, and I had to get him out.

I would smash the dark mirror, tear the veil between earth and hell to shreds. I brought the scepter down again and again, in a frenzy of violence and whirling water. I tasted blood and ash in my mouth. Nothing could make me stop.

A hand caught my next swing.

Fingers encircled my wrist, warm and trembling in the cold waters. The touch was light, not demanding, but Harvey held on. I turned to him in horror, barely able to discern his face in the shadowy tumult of the lake. He shouldn't be here. He was only mortal.

I lifted my eyes, to the circle of light above. He belonged up there.

When my gaze returned to him, Harvey was shaking his head, his hair tumbled by the current. I could see he was already struggling against the urge to breathe. His grip on my wrist was going slack.

I slid my arm around him, not letting go of the scepter or the grail, but holding him, fragile and mortal and more precious to me than gold. I felt his heart hammer in his chest and his last breath sigh between us as I pressed my mouth on his and let the enchanted pearl pass from my lips to his.

It wasn't a kiss.

When I drew away, Harvey was breathing, pearl caught in his throat and distant gold reflected in his steady eyes. The spell I'd murmured would save a witch from drowning, for a time. Not long.

He should leave me down here in the dark, but he never would. It must be both of us, or neither.

I had to go, but I didn't want to. I could live as a mortal and a witch. I could save them both.

Except Harvey's arm warm around me reminded me that you had to reach somebody to save them. I couldn't rescue Nick like this, any more than I could kiss a reflection in water. All I could do was stay, and stare, and fail my quest.

A chill ran through me, colder than the icy waters. This was a trap I'd almost fallen into. I'd come so close to failing. I began to swim away, but I couldn't bear to go just yet.

The Lady's warning echoed in my memory. *Demons and death will threaten, but she must not falter, and she can never look back.*

Before I could think again, I turned to catch one last glimpse of Nick. I strained desperately to see him, past the veil between heaven and earth, through the fracture in the dark.

My mouth shaped his name. A silent promise. I wouldn't leave him down there. I would never desert anyone I loved.

Then I struck for the surface. I didn't have the pearl anymore and my spell was failing, the lack of air burning my throat. The wet feathers of the cloak seemed to turn to lead, dragging us down.

When our heads broke the surface of the water, I gasped frantically for breath. My limbs felt even heavier than the cloak. The cliff was high above, the lake stretching around with no shore in sight. We sank down again, my lungs filling with water. I choked and flung up the hand holding the scepter, got my elbow up on the water as though it were solid as ice. I could pull myself up.

The water was only water to Harvey, no handholds or landing possible. I remembered a safety lesson on swimming in Baxter High, and Ms. Wardwell saying that if people held on to each other, they would drown.

I twined my other arm around Harvey, the golden cup pressing into his back. I'd drown rather than let him go. Magic could take both of us, or neither.

When I tried to lift us both, this time it worked. Somehow Harvey was able to scramble up with me. We weren't walking on water, but we knelt on the surface of the lake wrapped in each other's arms.

"Harvey," I gasped against his cheek. "You shouldn't have jumped."

Harvey whispered, "You did."

I curled in close, pressing my face down into the soaked hollow between his neck and shoulder. Then I heard the sound of footsteps, echoing as though the water were marble.

I thrust my body protectively in front of Harvey's. I was on my hands and knees gasping for breath, but I glared defiance up at the Lady.

The Lady of the Lake, Eostre of the springtime, stood before us robed in shadow and light. Once again, sun and moon shared the same sky. Behind one of the Lady's shoulders was darkness. Behind the other was clear day. She wore two feathers where her eyes should have been, one silvery bright and one the color of midnight.

"Daughter of fallen angels and rising mortals, bring my gifts to me!"

"In return, I demand what you promised. I want a way to save the man I..."

The man I love. I still had my arm around Harvey. I could feel his warm breath, going uneven against my cheek.

I did love Nick. I would shout that at the gates of hell or heaven. But it was hard to say it now, in front of Harvey. If hearing it might hurt him.

Harvey cleared his waterlogged throat. "Nick Scratch." He sounded exhausted. "The man I...am prepared to put up with."

"You're sure that's what you want?"

"Yes!" I exclaimed.

"Let me make you a different offer," said the Lady of the Lake. "One shining princess to another. The dark days are coming for you, and a darker quest than this. When a void is created, the power of the void fills it. We minor gods linger on the edges of this world, but there are other gods. Older than worlds, devourers of the universe. The gates of heaven and hell barred them, but no longer. I will not be here when they come. You could go with me."

I hesitated. "Where are you going?"

"Somewhere it is always bright, and never day," replied the Lady. "A place where there is no sorrow, and no joy. You will forget both, and feel neither. It is your only chance of safety."

I looked down at my hands filled with magic, then up at Harvey. I shook my head. "Not even tempted."

"Then bring me my gifts," said the Lady. "If you can." I rose and walked across the shining waters. One last demon descended, and I was lost beneath the shadow of a great dragon.

The short, sharp crack of a rifle rang out. The demon disappeared in a burst of ashes, leaving only a lick of flame upon the air. The fire didn't burn the blue of balefire, but celestial gold.

I twisted around and stared at Harvey. He grinned up at me. "Well done, 'Brina."

Did I do that? I must have.

"Thanks for helping out."

Harvey nodded. "Thought it was worth a shot."

"You four insist on helping one another," said the Lady. "My birds saw everything. Not only the birds. I watched you through so many eyes."

Her image was suddenly disrupted, like a reflection on a pool with a stone thrown into it. She became smoke, wings, a creature with too many eyes, a ghost girl, half a dozen faces I loved.

"Was it all lies?" Harvey faltered. "Everything we went through, was it your illusion?"

The Lady smiled at him. "It never is all lies. There's always truth in illusion. Peace in war. Love in hate. You never get only one thing. Do you understand?"

"I don't," Harvey told her.

She said absently: "A time will come when you do."

"To be *clear*..."

"As you always want to be..." murmured the Lady.

"*Would* you have fed us to demons and turned our souls to birds?"

"Naturally! The gods aren't kind."

"Great," Harvey muttered.

The Lady's focus shifted to me, like light moving on water. "Congratulations on escaping certain doom."

I shrugged. "Try attending two schools and staying top of the class."

The Lady of the Lake laughed, and the waters shivered.

I walked under the light of sun and moon, under the falling ashes, to lay the Lady's gifts at her feet. They spread before her, shining like dreams.

She leaned and took up the cloak of feathers. When she shook the cloak out, the feathers were suddenly dry and shining. She drew the cloak about her slender shoulders and grasped the scepter. Then she reached for the cup. I caught her wrist, as Harvey had caught mine.

"Saving Nick *is* possible."

Light and shadows swayed as the Lady nodded. "Everything is possible, but everything has a price."

"I'll pay."

"Be sure you will," whispered the Lady. "Ask yourself again, later. If it was worth the price. When the Queen of Hell closes a gate, the devil's daughter will open a window. I see the window frame now, looking out upon Pandemonium. Many ways are opening."

The only way I cared about was the way to Nick.

"Soon?" I begged, my voice trembling. "Will the path to Nick open soon?"

The Lady touched my face. Her fingertips were as cool as water.

"Soon," she promised.

"And you'll give me what I need to save him?"

"Will I?" the Lady murmured. "Morningstar Princess. Did you really succeed in your quest? No wavering of faith? No lie before a truth? No betrayal of love? No looking back?"

I recalled the last glimpse I'd stolen of Nick and crossed my fingers behind the golden surface of the grail. "No."

The Lady's laughter sang out like a bird. "You fiendish liar. Princess of Lies. I told you not to help each other, and never to look back."

"Why shouldn't we help and look for each other?" I demanded. "What's the point of a quest without love?"

"The point is to test you." The Lady's voice crashed down on me like a wave. "You told lies, broke rules, hurt people. You loved too many and demanded too much. Can you truly say you are worthy?"

I fought back tears. "I've decided I'm worthy," I said. "Nobody gets to decide that but me."

"And your companions?" asked the Lady. "Are they worthy? All five of you?"

"Five!" I exclaimed.

The Lady laughed. "Of course," she murmured. "Your paramour is being tested too. Is Nick Scratch worth saving?"

"I'm sure he is. I'm sure of them all," I said. "As sure as I am of my own heart."

"Are you sure of your heart? What did you call yourself once?"

"The Dark Lord's sword," I whispered.

"What are you, Sabrina Spellman, Morning Star on the Path of Night?"

A rush of water came sparkling into her hand, like a waterfall in reverse. Clear liquid shaped itself into a sword, diamond bright. The Lady rushed at me.

I shouted: "I am no one's sword but my own!"

She smiled a bright merciless smile and brought the sword down.

A blade shouldn't be afraid of a blade. I refused to be afraid of anything. I accepted the sword, and accepted myself. On my knees with a sword hurtling down toward me, I performed a magic trick. I swallowed the sword. I felt the blade burn its way through me.

"I agree that you are more than worthy," murmured the Lady of the Lake. "Princess Sabrina, I give you all you will need in hell. Your own flawed self."

Swallowing the blade had hurt, but transformation always did. You can't have light without burning. I felt myself become one with the sword, my purpose sure as steel. I knelt on the surface of the lake, and around me the waters shone.

The Lady of the Lake closed her fingers around one handle of the golden cup. She used the grail to scoop water from her lake. In the gold-touched depths I saw both sun and moon reflected. The Lady lifted the grail to her lips and drank deep.

The water seemed to become the sky and the sky the water, the world reversing. The cloak of feathers billowed out for one final flight. The Lady leaped into the white lake of the moon.

A ripple ran through the world, and the goddess was gone. The waters moved beneath us, fragile balance disrupted, and Harvey and I were pitched back into the lake. Over the side of the white cliffs, a rope was hurled.

The rope was made from leaves and vines, a flannel shirt and feathers. Our friends' faces peered from the edge of the cliff.

"Hey, guys!" called Theo. "I asked the birds to help us make a rope. Think it's mostly working on faith, so you'd better get up here quick."

"You first," I told Harvey.

"No, you."

"I'm the leader!"

"I'm gonna drop rocks on both your heads," said Theo.

I sighed, grasped the end of the rope, and climbed up the cliff face slowly. I didn't think I had a drop of magic left.

When I reached the top, Roz took me in her arms, rubbing my chill limbs and my back. Harvey scrambled up onto the ground, then picked up his dry jacket and settled it on my shoulders.

He put his arm around Roz. I drew the jacket tight around me.

The cliff was sinking gradually down into the earth, the lake drying up until it was nothing but a shimmer in the air.

"Quest accomplished?" Theo asked.

"I..." I said. "I think so."

We high-fived.

"Did you see Nick?" Roz asked, with concern.

"I did see him," I said eagerly. "I—I'm sure it was him."

I remembered the Lady's words about illusions. All the demons we'd seen, taking the shapes of our fears and doubts and desires. Seeing Nick was intended to make me stay underwater and fail my quest.

But there was reality in every illusion.

I paused, lost in uncertainty, and my eyes found Harvey's.

Harvey nodded slowly. "I don't know if he was real. But I saw him too."

I said, "I believe."

We made our way through the woods. The trees I'd seen topple were standing again. The sun lit a quiet path for us under the leaves.

"Quick question," said Harvey. "Why was he shirtless? Do they require you to be shirtless in hell?"

I blinked. "I don't know. I didn't really notice. I've seen Nick shirtless a lot, what with the—"

"Cool, we know!" exclaimed Harvey, before I could say "moon festivals and fighting giant squids." Harvey was shaking his head. "When we go to hell," he muttered, "I will keep my shirt on."

Roz slid her arm around his waist. "About hell. Maybe we won't have to go yet. Maybe it will take a while."

I opened my mouth to correct her.

Theo jumped in. "That's true. We can chill."

Harvey flashed Theo a grin. "Start our band."

My friends were flushed with victory, in the light. But Nick was trapped in darkness. I must go to him. The sooner the better, and the Lady had promised the way to hell would open soon.

I closed my mouth. It wouldn't do Nick any harm to let them enjoy this moment of peace.

Roz's eyes were on me, searching, until Harvey said: "Rosalind?"

She swallowed. "Harvey. I've been thinking, I want to see…"

I saw Harvey tense and wasn't sure why.

"Can I," Harvey said, a pleading note in his voice, "try this first?"

Surely Roz couldn't say no to him when he asked like that. It would be impossible.

She waited. Harvey looked desperately around at the trees, and our expectant faces.

"Less scary than demons covered in eyes," he muttered. "Slightly. Rosalind, this one's for you."

He swallowed, setting his shoulders, the way he had when he first walked into the mines where demons lurked with me. Being the bravest.

Then he tipped back his head and started to sing. He kept his eyes on the sky, faltering a few times, but his song grew clearer and more confident. His voice went up through the leaves as the light filtered down, and everything in the springtime started to be gold.

Roz was smiling, her eyes on his face. I sped up, walking ahead, but I could still hear them.

"You're my love song, Roz," Harvey murmured. "I—I'm sure you are. I needed time, to learn how to sing you."

"I want to see you every day," Roz burst out.

Harvey sounded surprised by his own happiness, the way he used to on the phone with me. "Yeah? I think that can be arranged."

They both sounded full of joy, my dearest friends. They made each other so happy. I was glad for them.

Theo fell into step with me, shaking his head. "Serenades. Harv is the greatest sap this world has ever known. Back to an earlier topic!"

I blinked. "Hell?"

"Nick Scratch shirtless," said Theo. "Can this be described in detail? By the way, I'm into guys."

"Cool, I love you! But are you trying to say you think *my boy-friend* is hot?"

Theo blinked. "Well…"

I laughed. "It's okay. My boyfriend *is* hot."

And I was getting him back. Nick and I would be walking together through these woods, soon.

"Just wanted to let you know," said Theo. "Looking out for a hot boyfriend. Of my own, not yours."

"Maybe one of the guys from Riverdale?" I asked. "Word is, Riverdale boys are babes."

Roz and Harvey drew level with us among the trees, Harvey's arm still around Roz's shoulders.

Roz warned, "Riverdale boys are trouble. It's well known."

We discussed the issue of Theo's prospective boyfriend. Then we debated potential names for a band. Theo beat time against several tree trunks, and Harvey twirled Roz over the grass. Together we reached the curve in the road and followed the path to my house.

As soon as we opened the door, Aunt Hilda pounced.

"Did you fall in a river? Did a kelpie try to abduct you as his bride?"

Theo boggled. "Does that happen?"

The Academy students, watching from the stairs as though we were free entertainment, nodded.

"Constantly," Aunt Hilda said. "Oh, you'll catch your deaths!"

I was bundled up in Harvey's dry jacket. Aunt Hilda stripped Harvey's wet shirt off his body, leaving him dazed and shirtless in our hall.

Elspeth sat down with a thump on the steps, whispering: "I want to do the will of heaven."

"Could I get a towel," Harvey said in a small voice. "Melvin?"

"I'll kill you, Melvin." Elspeth didn't take her eyes off Harvey. "I'll kill you while you sleep. I'll kill you tonight."

Harvey shot Roz a frantic glance, but Roz was stifling her laughter. Theo wasn't trying to hide his laughter at all.

Materializing from above, a towel came fluttering down. Harvey snatched at it.

"Thanks, ghost children," Harvey called out. "You guys are the only ones I can rely on."

Quentin and Lavinia shimmered into existence only to look smug. Aunt Zelda emerged from her office to see the hall crowded with ghosts, witch students, and mortals.

She gave a vexed sigh, then noted Harvey was wearing a towel.

"Congratulations, Harvey," said Aunt Zelda, while Harvey made a faint traumatized noise at the back of his throat. "Wouldn't have thought it of you. Not a patch on Nicholas Scratch, of course. Hells below, that young man was strapping. Sorry to remind you of lost glories, Sabrina."

"That's okay," I said.

"I'd like to go home," Harvey murmured, clutching his towel.

"Do so!" said Aunt Zelda. "I'm thinking of throwing every soul in this house out of doors and praying to any dark goddess who will heed that they perish in the woods. That means you too, Hilda and Sabrina!"

Aunt Hilda blew Aunt Zelda a kiss.

Harvey stared at the floor. "Yeah, I'm going."

"Aunt Zelda didn't mean that," I said as we trooped onto the porch away from Aunt Zelda's wrath. "You're always welcome."

"Thanks for saying so, 'Brina," mumbled Harvey. I got the feeling he wouldn't be dropping by my house anytime soon.

Aunt Hilda gave Harvey back his shirt, magically dry and pressed.

"Thanks." Harvey gave her a shy kiss on the cheek. Aunt Hilda beamed.

"Anytime, my love. Sorry about Zelda. We know how she is. I could write a book."

"Lady Blackwood's patience is wearing thinner than a skeleton," observed Quentin. "We ghosts have decided to return to the Academy and await the return of the living."

"Lady Blackwood's going to toss us out soon," Melvin agreed ruefully. "Hope we can get a few more dinners in."

The Academy students looked depressed at the idea of being without Aunt Hilda's cooking. The ghost children seemed sad too.

Harvey's gaze went to Lavinia. Suspicion and doubt crossed his face. I knew he was remembering the Lady indicating she'd used the ghost to spy on him.

I remembered the Lady saying, *It never is all lies.*

Harvey crossed the porch and knelt.

"Bye, my small sweetheart," he murmured.

Lavinia reached out to touch his cheek. "It was nice to be warm for a little while."

Even as she spoke, her hand faded and her voice became a sigh. The dead vanished away and left Harvey kneeling alone.

"She liked the Spellman house a lot, I guess," said Harvey wistfully. "I wish she could've stayed."

I moved forward, but Roz was closer. Harvey took her offered hand with gratitude. They went down my porch steps together.

"Goodbye, beautiful mortal," called Elspeth.

"Super inappropriate to the end, Elspeth," muttered Harvey. Louder, he called: "See you tomorrow, 'Brina!"

Roz looked back and waved. Theo and I fist-bumped over completing our quest, then Theo charged down the steps after them, yelling: "*No romance.* This means you, Harv!"

I stood on the porch of my witches' house, watching my friends walk into the woods. Trailing behind them, distant and sweet, came the sound of Harvey singing a new song.

"Coming inside, my love?" asked Aunt Hilda.

I was exhausted and chilled, but I tried to smile for her. "Just a minute."

A breath of winter lingered in the wind. I shivered and watched a single fleck of silver race to me across the sky. It was the last of the Lady's birds, the one with blue human eyes. The bird flew right into my waiting hands.

"Consider me a gift."

"For my cousin." I kissed the tiny bright bird, opened the cage of my fingers, and let the winged thing go free into the bright new sky.

Just in case. I wanted to make sure everybody I loved was safe. If Nick was the man I believed he was, he would understand.

I only hoped I hadn't ruined anything by turning back to look at Nick.

ON THE ROAD

Some might face their imminent death in a spirit of solemn reflection. Prudence and Ambrose were making fun of everyone they knew.

Prudence leaned across the shadows and broken bones of the pit toward Ambrose, murmuring in a high voice: "'Precious flower, I would reduce Greendale to rubble to make you smile.'"

"'Don't do that, Sabrina, it would be...wrong,'" mumbled Ambrose. "'Let's keep everything low-key and mind-numbing, right up until I snap and start shooting family members.'"

"'Oh, Harvey,'" sighed Prudence. "'I adore your witch-hunter ways. Ruin and devastation are among my top ten turn-ons!'"

"You must remember." Ambrose broke character. "I love

Sabrina, so I don't want to be too mean about her. Everyone else is fair game. Maybe I should be Sabrina from now on."

"Fine. I won't be that mortal, though. I'll be Nick. 'Hey, girl, I'm some sugar from your daddy.'"

Ambrose threw back his head and laughed. "'Hello, Nicholas Scratch, you seem trustworthy. Would you be interested in giving up carnal joys with a variety of hot magical entities in exchange for milkshakes and hand-holding?'"

"'Definitely,'" said Prudence, pitching her voice deep and low. "'Reading has turned my brain to treacle.'"

"'Fascinating, tell me about books but keep your shirt on, because why double our fun when we should always single our fun!'" said Ambrose. "'Would you like to hear me speak about my favorite topic? His name is Harvey.'"

"'I don't know who that is, but I would die for him!'" declared Prudence. "'Because you asked me to, and I have a crush for the first time and it turned me feral.'"

Prudence cackled. Ambrose wondered if she was bravely hiding pain at the thought of Nick preferring another woman.

"Let's do my aunties," he suggested. "You be the bad one; I'll be the good one."

Prudence considered. "I'm not sure I can do Hilda."

"You think *Auntie Hilda* is the bad one?"

"The infidel who conspired to get a helpless baby *baptized*?" said Prudence. "Obviously!"

There was a pause.

"We have a fundamental disagreement on this topic."

Prudence shrugged. "Very well. You be Harvey; I'll be Nick."

"Yes, comedy gold!" Ambrose bit his lip. "Wait. Does it help you? To talk about Nick? Considering your feelings for him."

"My feelings for Nick? Oh, yes."

"You must think about him a lot."

"I think he was better than average in bed," conceded Prudence.

"That's—touching?" said Ambrose.

"I don't really think about people," Prudence told him.

Ambrose hesitated. "Did you ever think about me?"

He heard the bed of bones crack beneath Prudence as she shifted.

"Why would I?"

"I'm sure you didn't, much," said Ambrose. "But when Father Blackwood had me in the dungeon, you told me...that I lived with honor."

"I also said that you would *die with it*. Which you soon will. In a pit full of ancient French skeletons."

"Prudence, you are hilarious and brilliant and beautiful, but you always focus on the negative." Ambrose shook his head. "I hadn't known that you thought about how I lived. Or what honor meant to you."

"Honor's something you have," Prudence snapped. "And I don't."

That took a moment to sink in. Ambrose tried to make out her expression in the gray dimness of the pit.

"We both made mistakes when we let Father Blackwood lead us down his vision of the ideal Path of Night."

"Ambrose, you attended a couple of noxious meetings and spoke sharply to Sabrina. I helped torture you at my father's bidding."

"Don't worry about it."

"I told my father to execute you," burst out Prudence. "I said that was the way to control Sabrina. Because Sabrina loved you, and would fight for you. I used the love between you for my father's evil ends."

The sound of her breathing was erratic, the only disturbance in the dusty air.

Ambrose said: "I thought something like that must have happened. Father Blackwood doesn't understand enough about love to know it would work. But you do."

She lifted her eyes to the circle of paler darkness high above. "I'm a terrible person."

"Yes, probably," admitted Ambrose. "Me too. We worship Satan and ruin lives. What's the big deal?"

"You wouldn't have done what I did."

"I tried to blow up the Vatican to make my father proud," said Ambrose. "Long after he was dead. Your father's still alive, but you already broke away from him and made a path for yourself. You're doing great."

"Does it hurt less," Prudence asked in a distant voice, "once your father is dead?"

Ambrose didn't want to mislead Prudence. "It hurts differently, but you're free. Even if that takes a while to realize."

She was silent. Usually when Prudence disagreed with him, she let him know. Ambrose felt encouraged.

"We're all villains, my magnificently wicked witch. But we're not under orders anymore. We're not bearing the weight of our fathers' expectations. We're free to see what else we can be."

Just then, there was light.

Soft as dawn and strange as love, at the mouth of the pit, in flew a bird. The winged thing shone as though it was plated with silver. Prudence shied back, and Ambrose stood with his hands open in welcome.

The strange silver creature settled in the hollow of his palm. With the bird's light in his hand, Ambrose was able to see an arrow marking carved on a skull.

"From my cousin," said Ambrose, and kissed the bird.

"What's Sabrina been up to," Prudence mused.

Ambrose beamed proudly. "Something terrible, no doubt."

"Here we are in a pit, and light comes to you." Prudence rolled her eyes. "That's you."

Light dawned on Ambrose, somewhat late, but beautiful. He remembered Prudence talking to the seller of dreams.

Someone on the Path of Night, walking in so much light.

"Oh, it's *not* Nick Scratch, is it?"

"Yes, it is!" Prudence snapped. "I—uh—love him!"

"It's me," Ambrose said, softly. "I had no idea."

By the silvery light Ambrose could see Prudence's horror, even as she snarled: "It doesn't matter."

"What if it did?"

"I am on a mission of vengeance. Cease harassing me about absurd emotions."

Prudence punched the skull with the arrow marking. The skull exploded into dust beneath the force of her blow. With a groan of bone on stone, a narrow passageway opened.

Ambrose believed it would've sufficed if Prudence had

gently pushed the skull, but Prudence seemed in no mood for quibbling.

Ambrose almost reeled in the fresh air as they emerged from the empire of the dead. They were free once more, under the purple evening sky of Paris.

"What about Nick?" he asked, as they traveled down the Champs-Élysées.

Prudence made an irritated sound. "Why must you harp on Nick? Are *you* in love with him?"

"Pass," said Ambrose. "But you talked about someone who nobly sacrificed himself."

"Look." Prudence sounded exasperated. "Nicky was bright, aside from ditching me and my sisters. He was a solid eight out of ten in bed, and seven out of ten for looks—"

"I would've said eight for looks," objected Ambrose.

"His hair went wrong sometimes," Prudence explained. "He was the only man at the Academy I would partner in fencing class. I'm … not glad he is in hell."

Ambrose understood. "He was your friend."

Prudence made an embarrassed face. "But he didn't sacrifice himself for the world. He did it to atone for deceiving the girl he wanted. My tolerance for men who betray women is limited. Nick can't be compared with you. Father Blackwood can't be compared with you. Luke Chalmers can't be compared with you."

"Luke Chalfant," Ambrose murmured.

Prudence waved a hand irritably. "Whatever his name was. Nicholas Scratch can't be compared with you. No other warlock compares. We tortured you at the Academy. You escaped, then saw the witch-hunters coming. You had nothing to gain, and everything to lose. You warned us anyway."

"I had to," Ambrose murmured.

He couldn't let witches die like his father and Luke had.

Prudence's lips curved. After a day in the catacombs, her lipstick wasn't perfect, but her mouth was.

"I'd never met an honorable man before. The novelty attracted my attention. So I let you accompany me on my mission, I let you distract me with your antics, and I let myself believe foolish things. None of it matters. What matters is my sister and brother, and my revenge."

"So..." Ambrose said. "You like me?"

The enraged rattle in Prudence's throat caused Ambrose to edge away. Fortunately, Prudence had lost her swords in the catacombs.

"I'm returning to the hotel. Then I go to New Orleans to cut my father's throat. I wish for a bath and vengeance, in that order. There's no need to mention this unimportant issue again."

The Arc de Triomphe was a golden stone monument to victory. City lights fed the stars to make them dazzling. All Paris was a backdrop for the proud line of Prudence's back, retreating from him.

Ambrose hurried after her. "When you say you let me distract you with my antics, you mean you like being with me. You enjoy my company."

"Ambrose!" Prudence hissed. "The mortals can hear you."

A French child gave Ambrose an unimpressed stare. Ambrose grinned.

Prudence's half-hidden smiles when Ambrose made jokes. The way she listened when he talked about poetry. How she'd asked him what he was thinking, her voice halting. In no way used to reaching out, but trying.

Because she *dreamed* of him.

He'd wondered what it would be like, to see Prudence smitten. Apparently he'd seen it.

When they reached the colorful door of their hotel, Prudence swept past the uniformed doorkeeper, who said: "Mademoiselle—"

"Recently buried alive, currently having an emotional conversation, not a good time," whispered Ambrose, then chased after Prudence. He caught her at her door with her hand on a doorknob painted with tiny stars and harps. "Prudence, wait!"

She whipped around. "I would never expect mercy from any man but you. Try to understand how mortifying it is for me, to know you don't—"

He cupped her furious face in his hands and said: "You make me want to write poetry again."

There was a silence more profound than the quiet in the empire of the dead. Prudence's dark gaze fell away from his.

"What?" she whispered.

"I'm slow when it comes to love," said Ambrose. "I turned away from my aunties and got mixed up with a destructive bunch. I had to be trapped in a house so I could grow to love Sabrina. I only admitted I *did* love her a few months ago. All our lives, we're taught that we can't love, that we shouldn't love. All my life, I've been restlessly searching for something that might do instead. Nothing else will do."

Prudence's mouth twisted. "Are you claiming to love me? You don't. You would see me gutted on an altar to save Sabrina, or one of your aunts."

"I might," Ambrose admitted. "I don't love you. And you don't love me. You'd see me gutted on an altar to save one of your sisters."

Prudence smiled, as though catching sight of somebody she recognized. "I might."

"If we got to know each other more," Ambrose murmured. "It might be a more difficult choice. It might be an impossible choice. That's what I was doing, in Italy. As the mortals say, I want to get to know you better. I don't love you. Not yet."

She startled out of his hands, a movement like that of the silver bird that had flown to him.

"So..." Prudence savagely mimicked the question he'd asked in front of the Arc de Triomphe. "You *like* me? I dressed in my best garments. I brought my most seductive friends to your door. I showered you in blasphemous compliments. I was desperately obvious—"

"Genuinely, none of it came off that way to me—"

"—Then I helped my father torture you and your family, dedicated myself to revenge, promised my heart would be stone, and *now* you like me?"

Ambrose shrugged, helpless. "People say I'm contrary."

Prudence pushed open her door, revealing a high, arched window flung wide on the city and a canopy bed with fluttering curtains. Ambrose stayed back. Trapping her was one mistake he refused to make. She could slam the door in his face again, if she wanted.

Prudence didn't, so Ambrose went to her. He reached out and drew her close.

"I'm slow, but I get there. I couldn't tell at a glance, when you came in beauty to my door. I couldn't see all of what you were. I see you now. I've searched across the world. I've never seen anyone I thought more worth loving than you."

He'd always thought if love came, it would be someone who could tame his own wild heart. How much wilder and sweeter, to discover the lioness rather than the fawn.

Prudence let out a shuddering breath. "I have a mission."

"Which I support," said Ambrose. "I like you. I like your ruthless, gorgeous quest for revenge. I'd like to pursue this. But it's up to you. Think it over in the bath."

He sketched a bow, then turned away. He heard Prudence sigh and step through her door.

Ambrose turned back for one last glimpse. The door was swinging closed, but not shut yet. He saw Prudence spinning giddily in the center of her room, her curtains dancing in the wind, her hands clasped to her chest. In that brief unguarded moment, she let herself be simply happy. Simply young.

Ambrose started to smile.

He caught the door before it closed.

"Sorry, I'm being a total Harvey about this situation."

Prudence stopped dead. "How dare you say that name in my bedchamber?"

"Witches aren't used to love," said Ambrose. "So I was trying to do this the mortal way. Except I personally find the mortal way to be absurd. Say the word and I'll go. But in Italy, you asked me to stay. Pursue bloody vengeance, my darling...in the morning."

Prudence toyed with the curtains of her canopy bed. "I will," she said, with dignity.

She glanced up. Ambrose smiled for her. The line of Prudence's mouth relaxed slightly, and Ambrose realized with dawning delight that this was Prudence melting.

"Can I...recite a poem to you?"

"Oh, by the unholy name of Lucrezia Borgia." Prudence sighed. "If you must."

"I must." Ambrose stepped into the veil of her curtain, murmuring poetry in her ear. "*Lion, dear to my heart. Goodly is your beauty, honeysweet. Lion, take me to the bedchamber.*"

Prudence slid her arms around his neck and purred: "Finally."

Ambrose swung her in a dizzy, delirious circle. The curtains whirled around them as they danced, the wind carried the jaunty music of Paris into their chamber, and he was almost sure he caught Prudence laughing. The lights spilling through their window became a ring of brilliance meant only for them.

Prudence leaned in to kiss him. Ambrose whispered: "I will want to cuddle."

"For *five minutes*," Prudence told him sternly.

Ambrose laughed as they kissed and felt her lips curve into an answering smile. He closed his eyes, city lights turning even this dark to silver, and her mouth tasted as sweet as freedom.

HELL

WHERE THE SUN IS MUTE. —DANTE

Nick stayed kneeling, even after the snowy mountain melted away. He looked around the dark enclosed room where he truly was, with its many sloping sides, and at the cage door swinging open. He watched as the Father of Lies stepped out. Lucifer's smile was wolfish.

Nick hung his head.

"It was a good effort, boy," murmured the Dark Lord. "While it lasted. Now move aside."

Boy. He'd called Nick that on earth too. Nick had come when Lucifer called, thinking of Sabrina and the mortals in peril, but imagining too that Satan would praise him. Instead, Nick had been dismissed.

He didn't want to have rebelled against Satan for wounded pride. He wanted to be a rebel for love alone.

"Tricky little mind you have there," Lucifer continued.

"Thanks," muttered Nick.

"It wasn't a compliment."

Nick glanced up and caught a glimmer of wrath in his lord's face. Nick wanted to cower, but he made himself sneer. "Sounded like one to me."

Lucifer ignored Nick, concentrating on his grievance. "Your subconscious built many elaborate scenarios to fence me in and hide yourself. I went through a great deal of trouble, clawing through your pathetic memories and even more pathetic dreams to find something to break you. In the end, I had to lift the veil between the worlds. Was it necessary to be so stubborn? It was always going to end like this."

"I know," Nick whispered.

Lucifer had lifted the veil. The vision of Sabrina turning back in the dark was real. Her dear worried face, framed by pale hair flaring underwater, her mouth shaping a word.

Not a word. A name.

His name.

That didn't make much sense, given the story he'd been presented with. Nick set his mind to this problem.

Each of those mortals, and Sabrina, fighting demons alone. Sabrina, with a golden grail in her hands. Unlike the mortal, Nick could read. He knew a quest narrative when he saw one.

"Boy?" Lucifer said sharply.

"I've seen mortal movies," mused Nick. "I'm starting to think I was shown some *heavily* edited footage."

What the heaven did they think they were doing? What where they questing for?

It was obvious, if he let himself believe, past the fearful hammering of his own heart saying: *It can't be, nobody ever came, you don't deserve it. This can't be for you.*

Nick, Sabrina had said.

They were coming for him. They absolutely shouldn't be. It was a suicide mission. With luck, Zelda would find out and stop the lunacy. But... maybe Sabrina did love him. She hadn't forgotten him. They were all trying to save him. Sabrina, the queen of everything. Lovely Roz. Clear-eyed Theo. And that idiot. Nick smiled, just for himself.

"Yes," Lucifer murmured, voice bored. "You were tricked by the Great Deceiver. What a surprise."

Nick stopped smiling at the ground and glared at Satan.

Basically, Nick didn't like Lucifer. He'd imagined he would. He hadn't expected Lucifer to remind him of Father Blackwood, imposing limits on people for no reason except that despite his great power, he was small-minded.

When Nick beheld the Son of the Morning on his golden throne, the god whose gift had released Nick from the wolves, Nick thought: *This is the kind of man who cages. And I helped him.*

"You're trapped in a prison of the body and mind," Nick told Lucifer softly. "I'm the box now. I'm the riddle. You have to get past me."

Those last glimpses of the mortal world were real, but the rest was Nick's dream. Any love, any kindness, any light or sweetness in hell, was in Nick himself.

He opened his eyes.

"I know I'm lost," said Nicholas Scratch. "But I'm hoping to be found."

Satanic laughter sent cold fire through Nick's bones. "Too late. You surrendered your body and mind, as you signed away your soul. The devil has come to collect."

"*I*," said Nick, "withdraw my consent."

Lucifer's voice struck like a lash. "You can't do that!"

"Can't I? It's my body." Nick had always been a liar. He could pretend he wasn't afraid. "You tore down my barriers, but you haven't gotten past me yet. You keep saying I have no choice. If I didn't, you would have taken control of my body already. You can't, without my permission. And you don't have it."

Nick saw the last of the sinister humor drain from Satan's countenance and knew he was right. This was why those who liked cages banned books, which taught people to think their way free.

"It's to be a fight, then?" asked Lucifer Morningstar, formerly his god.

"Sure. We can wrestle." Nick winked. "Let me clarify. You being the incarnation of evil is cute and all, but lately I go for more substance. I'm your daughter's man."

Even if I cannot see the sun, I know that it exists.

Even if he got out, nothing would be the same between him and Sabrina. Not after the lies. But he could keep her as his talisman of love and light. He'd never found a way for love without cages, but if there was a way, Sabrina might find it. Nick believed in her.

"How much longer can this empty swagger last?" demanded Lucifer.

If we love each other as much as we can, if we try as hard as we can . . . surely there's a chance everything will work out.

Sabrina smiled when the mortal said that, bright as the sun. What a stupid thing to say. But . . . all right. Nick would try.

Nick said: "I can last a little longer."

Get up. It's no good if you don't get up.

With the last of his strength, Nick Scratch rose and faced down his god.

He bared his teeth. Proud as the devil, or trying to be. "You're the one who belongs in a cage. Not her."

"You cannot imagine how much this will hurt, boy," Lucifer murmured, as though remembering a fall. "Surrender and be spared."

The devil set his burning hands against Nick's skin.

Into pain and shame and darkness, Nick snarled: "I said *no*."

"Well, well," murmured Lilith. "Ladies and demons, it seems we have a fighter on our hands!"

She retreated entirely from the warlock's dreams, then made a sweeping gesture toward Nick Scratch, in chains on his knees. The demons, fans of chaos and the wildly unexpected, applauded.

Except Prince Caliban and Lord Beelzebub.

ABOUT THE AUTHOR

Sarah Rees Brennan is the #1 *New York Times* bestselling author of over a dozen books, both solo and cowritten with authors including Kelly Link and Maureen Johnson. She is the Lodestar Award and Mythopoeic Award finalist for her book *In Other Lands.* She was born in Ireland by the sea and lives there now in the shadow of a cathedral. Visit her at sarahreesbrennan.com, or follow her on Twitter at @sarahreesbrenna (they stole her last N, and she may resort to magic to recover it).